soldiers alive

ishikawa
tatsuzō

soldiers alive

translated,
with introduction
and notes, by

zeljko
cipris

university of hawai'i press
honolulu

© 2003 University of Hawai'i Press
All rights reserved
Printed in the United States of America
08 07 06 05 04 03   6 5 4 3 2 1

Library of Congress Cataloging-in-Publication Data
Ishikawa, Tatsuzō.
    [Ikite iru heitai. English]
    Soldiers alive / Ishikawa Tatsuzō ; translated with introduction
and notes by Zeljko Cipris.
        p. cm.
    Includes bibliographical references.
    ISBN 0–8248–2696–5 (cloth : alk. paper) —
ISBN 0–8248–2754–6 (alk. paper)
    1. Sino-Japanese Conflict, 1937–1945—Literature and conflict.
I. Title.
PL830.S55I413 2003
895.6'09358—dc21

                                    2003048401

University of Hawai'i Press books are printed on acid-free
paper and meet the guidelines for permanence and durability
of the Council on Library Resources.

Designed by Diane Gleba Hall
Printed by The Maple-Vail Book Manufacturing Group

To MY SONS, Shane Satori Cipris and Ljubomir Ryu Cipris,

and to the creation of a humane, egalitarian world

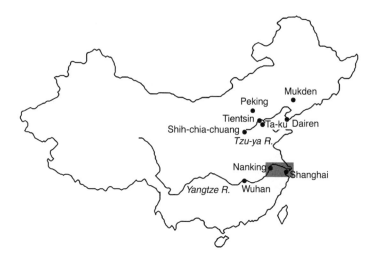

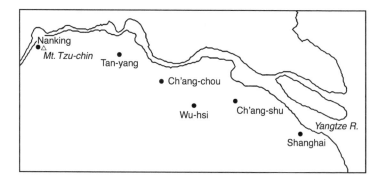

Map of China, showing the major cities traversed by the Nishizawa regiment of Ishikawa's *Soldiers Alive*. The regiment's likely destination as the narrative ends is Wuhan.

Contents

Acknowledgments

My warmest thanks go to more people than I have space to enumerate, so what follows is only a partial list of individuals to whom I feel most grateful indeed: Professor Chiba Sen'ichi, my immensely kind and knowledgeable mentor, who patiently taught me a great deal about war literature and encouraged me to translate Ishikawa's work; Dr. Shoko Hamano, my friend, colleague, coauthor, and all-around bodhisattva, who is doing her tireless best to transform a happy-go-lucky dilettante into a reputable scholar; my old professors at Columbia University: Paul Anderer, Wm. Theodore de Bary, Irene Bloom, Carol Gluck, C. T. Hsia, Donald Keene, Barbara Ruch, Edward W. Said, Edward Seidensticker, Haruo Shirane, Paul Varley, Yasuko Ito Watt, Philip Yampolsky, and Pauline Yu. Ryoko Amamiya, though far from Columbia, made the graduate school years even more delightful. My thanks also go to Professors John Dower, David Goodman, Yoshio Iwamoto, and Moss Roberts (each from a different university), who all gave me greatly appreciated assistance when much of the present book was still taking shape as part of a fledgling, sprawling, unrefined dissertation manuscript. A generous dissertation fellowship from the Japan Foundation enabled me to do the basic research in Japan and to enjoy the open spaces and hospitality of Hokkaido — especially the town of Obihiro — together with my family for a full fourteen months. For kind and encouraging words about the finished product, I thank Robert

Eno, George M. Wilson, Gregory Kasza, Sumie Jones, Gloria Bien, and J. Thomas Rimer.

A more recent debt of gratitude is due to Pamela Kelley, my extremely helpful and encouraging editor at the University of Hawai'i Press, and to the two anonymous reviewers for the Press who made useful and constructive suggestions for improving the manuscript, while enthusiastically recommending its publication. To the family of Ishikawa Tatsuzō, the author of *Soldiers Alive,* I owe profound thanks for their openhearted support. Ishikawa Yoshiko readily granted her permission to publish the translation of her late husband's work, while Dr. Ishikawa Sakae, the author's daughter, efficiently mediated the authorization process and has been a pleasure to correspond with.

Last, but by no means least, I would like to thank my parents, Dr. Divna Popovic-Cipris and Dr. Marijan Cipris; my loving and magnanimous wife, Etsuko; and my sons, Shane and Ryu, to whom the book is dedicated. The responsibility for any errors of omission or commission rests squarely on the narrow shoulders of our family's diminutive and charmingly noisy canine companion, Piccolo.

IN TRANSLITERATING Chinese names, terms, and places into English, I have used the Wade-Giles system, which was prevalent in the 1930s. For Japanese names and terms I have relied on the commonly utilized Hepburn system. Except for authors of Western language publications, Chinese and Japanese names are written in the East Asian sequence—family name first and personal name second. The macrons encountered in some Japanese words (e.g., Kondō) indicate that the marked vowel is doubled in length. In a few cases, such as the names of well-known Japanese cities like Tokyo or Osaka (properly pronounced Tōkyō, Ōsaka) macrons have been omitted.

Introduction

The First War on China

One of the most influential events conditioning Japanese popular attitudes toward their nation's worth and place in the world was the Sino-Japanese War of 1894–1895. The country's first major overseas war since its start of industrialization earlier in the century, this initial clash with China was the culmination of a struggle for control over Japan's continental neighbor, Korea. Expansionist in nature, the war was an early manifestation of modern Japan's imperialism.[1] It fostered a high degree of national pride and confidence among large sectors of the Japanese population and a concomitantly sharp decline in China's long-standing prestige.[2] This perceptual framework was to persist and even be reinforced during the ensuing half-century of Japan's economic and military involvement on the Asian continent. To an extent, the triumphalist outlook engendered in the 1890s may still affect Japan's prevailing views of itself, its erstwhile antagonist, and the international status and potential of each.

Japanese cultural atmosphere attending the 1894–1895 conflict was for the most part enthusiastically supportive of the war effort.[3] Newspapers published a profusion of pro-war articles, and sponsored war-song contests. Artists produced a great many colored woodblock prints illustrating stirring war scenes. Numerous war plays were written and staged; books with war themes sold extremely well.[4] The great majority of intellectuals—including such liberals as Fukuzawa Yukichi and Tokutomi Sohō—strongly championed the war.[5] Fukuzawa, convinced the war was essential to the spread of "enlightenment," called it a "battle for the sake of world culture."[6] Other leading thinkers, including the nonsectarian Christian (and future pacifist) Uchimura Kanzō, viewed the war as a just and humanitarian mission carried out to liberate Korea from Chinese oppression.[7] The larger cause was that of progress and freedom. "Japan's victory," Uchimura wrote, "shall mean free government, free religion, free education, and free commerce for 600,000 souls who live on this side of the globe."[8]

Most Japanese literary figures did not treat the war in their writings; those who did almost invariably backed it.[9] The latter group includes the novelists Kunikida Doppo and Mori Ōgai and poets Toyama Masakazu, Yosano Tekkan, and Masaoka Shiki. Doppo, who traveled to China as a newspaper correspondent, wrote of the war in lyrical, fervently patriotic terms.[10] Ōgai's wartime diary, by contrast, is crisply matter-of-fact, in keeping with his role as a professional army officer.[11] The war poetry of Toyama and Tekkan tends to be belligerent and shallow and does not attain the quality of Masaoka Shiki's. Shiki visited the front during the last days of the fighting and, while not questioning the value of the war itself, compellingly recorded the shock and sadness evoked by witnessing its aftermath.[12] Seeing the bodies of Chinese soldiers killed at Chin-chou, Shiki wrote:

nakihito no	Hide from sight
mukuro o kakuse	the corpses of the dead,
haru no kusa	grasses of spring.[13]

Despite a considerable measure of freedom of expression that existed at the time, there was virtually no literary opposition to the war.[14] It has in fact been argued that the freedom of expression remained in effect precisely because no dissenting voices arose to challenge the war.[15] At any rate, the government did not at any point appear to pressure the writers into supporting the war effort.[16]

Japan's victory, concluding after more than eight months of hostilities, was fairly rapid and decisive. Won largely because of the superior equipment, organization, and leadership of the Japanese military, the war's outcome surprised outside observers more than it did the Japanese. The political, economic, and cultural impact of the victory was immense. For China, it entailed loss of territory and additional deterioration of its national sovereignty. Among the concessions extracted from China by Japan were the acquisition of Taiwan and the Pescadores Islands, the right to manufacture goods on Chinese soil, and the payment of a large indemnity that greatly stimulated Japan's continuing industrialization. Even worse, by dramatically exposing China's vulnerability, its defeat opened the way for further encroachments by Japan and other powers.[17]

Japan, on the other hand, heretofore considered a marginal player in global politics, suddenly acquired the stature of a regional power, as the hegemonic center of gravity in Asia shifted for the first time ever from China to Japan.[18] Success in the war boosted further military expansion, strengthened Japan's position in the international economy, and for the first time made Japan into a colonial power.[19] Launching itself along an imperialistic trajectory, the nation henceforth systematically emulated the practices of Western imperialism.[20]

The triumphalism inspired by a spectacular demonstration of armed might carried over into the cultural sphere, giving rise to grave doubts or outright denials of China's cultural supremacy. Long accustomed to looking up to China as Japan's mentor in the arts of civilization, many Japanese began to feel that they had finally surpassed it. The denigration of China's greatness was accompanied by a jubilant acclaim of Japan's own.[21] On the popular level, there arose a sense of ethnic superiority—"a race feeling"—as Lafcadio Hearn called it.[22] Among the Japanese scholars, the long and complicated love/hate attitude toward China likewise intensified in the wake of the war. The conviction grew—nurtured by jingoistic wartime portrayals of the Chinese as backward, cowardly, and contemptible[23]—that the Chinese had proven themselves unworthy of inheriting their own cultural tradition. Japanese scholars, better acquainted with China's classical art and literature than the Chinese themselves, were the only ones properly qualified to study and appreciate it. The field of Chinese studies, insisted the philosopher Inoue Tetsujirō, must become a Japanese province.[24] The art historian Okakura Kakuzō concurred, asserting that Japan, not China, was the true heir of ancient Chinese glories.[25] China thus seemed about to be stripped not only of its physical wealth but of its cultural identity as well. In the meantime, European powers, impressed by Japan's military prowess into recognizing it as a civilized nation,[26] joined Japan in looking down on China and continued to exploit it.

Within the drastically altered political landscape of East Asia, Japan came to regard itself (and be regarded by others, including some Chinese) as both a military and cultural leader. Culture and imperialism converged in pursuit of a radiant enterprise, as envisioned by the sinologist Naitō Konan:

> Japan's mission is to promote Japanese culture with the taste unique to Japan and to brighten the universe. Since Japan is located in the East and since China is its largest neighbor in the East, Japan must begin its task in China.[27]

The feeling of national righteousness and self-assurance, enunciated here and widely shared, constituted a helpful ideological rationale for a government engaged in expanding and consolidating Japan's continental influence. Ten years after defeating

China, Japan won a war against imperial Russia and became a world power. Some two and a half decades later, it found itself once more at war with China.

THE SECOND Sino-Japanese War, fought from 1931 to 1945, was in a sense a continuation of the first, yet differed from it in significant ways. Although as before, Japan prosecuted the war from a position of military strength and popular support, its opponent was no longer a weak imperial China but a much more vigorous and nationalistic republic. The war lasted much longer, was broader in scale, and was more murderous. The level of Japanese nationalism was as high as earlier, but there was markedly less freedom and no toleration of open dissent. The government this time did make an organized attempt to recruit writers into promoting the war, thereby contributing to a much greater output of war literature.[28]

Although the style and substance of the new wave of war writings were affected by a diversity of factors, the first war continued to exert both direct and indirect influence. The work of Kunikida Doppo and other writers about the earlier war provided literary models that the later writers might choose to emulate or proceed beyond. Also, the psychological environment of intense patriotism and relative arrogance toward the Chinese, which gained strength in the 1890s, remained operative during the 1930s.[29] Almost every author writing about the second Sino-Japanese War was born after the first and thus grew up in an atmosphere of heightened nationalism that viewed Japanese people and their accomplishments as superior to the Chinese. All Japanese were exposed to this chauvinistic ethos, and a great many accepted its premises. The propensity of many Japanese war writers of the 1930s and early 1940s toward depicting the Chinese they encountered with supercilious detachment or condescending sympathy had very much to do with the highly nationalistic ambience of their own upbringing and everyday cultural milieu.[30] Chauvinism tended to result in dehumanization.

Following the first war with China, the writer Shimamura Hōgetsu posed the question, "Will not the future Japanese literature come to be based, directly and indirectly, on the feelings of the Japanese people aroused by the conquest of China?"[31] Whatever the answer, those feelings remained alive, and most writers of the new generation seemed proudly convinced that the conquest was continuing.

Clash of Imperialisms

In 1901, with impressive accuracy of foresight and appraisal, the Japanese anarchist Kōtoku Shūsui designated imperialism the monster of the twentieth century.[32] A decade later Shūsui and eleven of his comrades were killed by the state (for allegedly having plotted to assassinate the emperor), while the chief practitioners of imperialism at the century's outset—the European powers, the United States, and Japan—went on to fulfill his prophecy.

China, a huge, resource-rich nation badly weakened by internal turmoil and foreign interference, presented a major and highly inviting target for economic aggression.[33] Relentlessly assaulted by the West since at least the 1840s—when the British, in the name of free trade, coerced it into legally importing opium —China was for the most part not directly colonized by the powers but was kept instead in semicolonial subordination for the benefit of them all.[34] China's attractions were immense: a wealth of natural resources such as raw cotton, coal, and iron ore; a vast supply of inexpensive labor power, and mouthwatering market potential. Consistently professing the highest regard for China's sovereignty and territorial integrity, the imperialist powers vigorously proceeded to violate both in their pursuit of profit. In the nineteenth century they set up international settlements and treaty ports, instituted extraterritoriality, and stationed troops to ensure that their "rights and interests" enjoyed optimum advantage. The principle guiding their actions was enunciated in the Open Door Policy, which endorsed freedom of competition with regard to the exploitation of China. Long practiced, the Open Door was officially reaffirmed by the 1922 Nine-Power Treaty signed in Washington.[35]

For the century's first three decades, Japan was a relatively cooperative participant in this enterprise of orderly and systematic plunder, but then it rather abruptly abandoned its policy of "peaceful" expansionism in favor of an explicitly violent independent approach. Japan's change of course may be attributed to its leaders' growing conviction that the primary national objectives were no longer attainable by compromising with other imperialist powers but required new, more forcible measures. Several developments contributed to this view. In the wake of the Great Depression, Western powers erected prohibitive tariffs and quotas severely restricting the influx of Japanese exports into their metropoles and colonies. At the same time, they sought to curtail the growth of Japanese armaments relative to their own, as at the 1930 London Naval Conference. China's nationalists and communists were in the meantime intensifying their efforts at national unification and resistance to foreign supremacy, thus endangering Japan's freedom of action on the continent. The Soviet Union's strengthening of its armed power in eastern Siberia constituted yet another perceived menace.[36]

In the light of such events, Japan's governing elite came to consider it imperative for Japan to gain clear hegemony over East Asia in order to maintain the nation's economic and military security and its status as a great power. The international order, formulated mainly for the benefit of England and the United States, had become an obstacle to Japan's expansion and had to be shunted aside or, if necessary, overthrown.

In late 1931 Japan made its first resolute move against an undesirable status quo by occupying China's northeastern region of Manchuria and turning it the following year into the pseudo-independent state of Manchukuo. It thus gained unimpeded access to all of Manchuria's resources and extended its formal, tightly controlled empire just when the more loosely dominated informal empire it shared with the other powers was threatening to disintegrate.[37] Undaunted by Western anger over this bold seizure of more than its share of the loot, Japan shortly severed its remaining links to the Washington system of collaborative pillage and went on to operate in "splendid isolation."[38] Such decisive action was greeted domestically with a great deal of popular enthusiasm and a surge of nationalistic pride. Powerful Western nations had long since established control over vast stretches of the globe. Many Japanese now seemed to feel that it was their nation's manifest destiny to expand into continental Asia.

Emulating the 1823 United States proclamation of guardianship over the American continent, Japan in 1934 issued its own Asian Monroe Doctrine declaring that Japan would henceforth be the sole peacekeeper in Asia. The announcement met with a storm of Western indignation. United States Secretary of State Cordell Hull retorted that while the original Monroe Doctrine was defensive in nature, its Japanese counterpart was nothing but aggressive.[39] Undeterred, Japan persisted in its self-proclaimed role as the continental policeman and continued to make armed and diplomatic inroads into northern and central China. A seemingly unpremeditated clash with a Chinese unit near Peking in the summer of 1937 rapidly escalated into full-scale undeclared warfare that was to last eight years, engulf a large portion of China, and ultimately end in Japan's defeat.

The war started out badly for China in 1937 as Japan's troops—better armed, better trained, better led, and better fed

—swept over the nation's northern, eastern, and central regions, annihilating armed opposition and massacring huge numbers of civilians and fleeing or captive soldiers in the capital, Nanking, and elsewhere. Made confident by the ease of this and the earlier Manchurian campaign and the purported lack of fighting spirit among the Chinese, the Japanese anticipated a decisive victory, and for the first year and a half of the war their expectations seemed justified. By 1939, however, the lightning war had turned into a war of attrition, and although the Japanese controlled the major cities and railways—points and lines *(ten to sen)*—they were unable to subdue the rest of the country and suffered from intensifying attacks by the communist and nationalist soldiers and guerrillas.[40] Moreover, Japan's war against China had come to arouse widespread international condemnation, not only by the imperialists alarmed at the prospect of losing their markets, but by genuine anti-imperialists worldwide, including a few in Japan.

The bulk of the Japanese populace, nonetheless, remained supportive of the nation's troops and convinced that the war they were waging was not only winnable but just. For the most part they seemed to lend credence to the patriotic messages relayed by the press, radio, cinema, records, and lectures; eagerly followed news from the front (often with the aid of large maps on which they pinned and shifted small flags as the military situation warranted); and took part in the daytime flag processions and evening lantern parades celebrating the numerous victories. Schoolchildren and adults from all over the nation sent letters and packages to the front as tokens of gratitude for the soldiers' sacrifices, while idolized athletes and actresses traveled overseas to entertain the warriors, and hundreds of journalists, photographers, and cameramen recorded the troops' brave deeds in ostensibly defending peace and justice.[41]

The euphoric home-front atmosphere—to which the profusion of flags and uniforms had imparted the colors of red, white, and khaki—was not significantly dampened even by the protracted fighting or the war-induced shortages. The government responded to the latter by instituting rationing and promoting sumptuary slogans such as "Luxury is the enemy" and "We shall ask for nothing until we win."[42] Overall, the people's ardor—or docility—held, thus reducing the likelihood of effective resistance to the government and helping to make the crimes of the military possible.

War as Loving-Kindness

"Down with Japanese imperialism!"

The ubiquitous slogan, its eight characters reading *Datō Nippon teikokushugi!* in Japanese, greeted Japan's troops and civilians wherever they moved in China. Although this slogan and others like it, painted on countless walls, clearly and loudly expressed Chinese outrage and protest, Japanese correspondents and other writers reported them freely, seldom adding any comment because none was needed. The charge of imperialism struck most Japanese as absurd, merely demonstrating how ignorant and misled the Chinese were concerning Japanese actions and motivations. The charge contradicted the official narrative, that of Japan's benevolence, and could thus be silently dismissed.

Although the horrendous war unleashed by Japan against China seemed to be a clear-cut manifestation of imperialism at its most vicious, Japanese statesmen, soldiers, and sundry commentators did not appear to see it that way at all. Japan's mission, they publicly insisted, was not a quest for wealth or power, but rather a moral crusade for freedom, peace, and justice. Goodness was at work, not greed. As a Japanese editorial of the late 1930s phrased it, "Our responsibility is not the conquest of the world; it is the emancipation of the world."[43]

While some of Japan's propaganda regarding the national

objectives was directed at the outside world, most of it was intended for domestic consumption. Persuasion was an important instrument in unifying the popular opinion in support of official policies because the Japanese government did not rule by coercion alone. Far from comprising a solid totalitarian monolith capable of imposing its will through sheer force, Japanese rulers of the 1930s formed an uneasy coalition of elites—key military officers, high civil bureaucrats, leaders of big business, party politicians—that relied on active mythmaking no less than on active suppression of dissent to obtain the desired degree of patriotic conformity.[44]

Frequent discord within and among the elite groups certainly did not preclude a strong use of repression, as is evident from the enactment of harsh legal measures exemplified by the notorious Peace Preservation Law of 1925, the existence of a stringent and increasingly restrictive censorship system, periodic mass arrests, numerous cases of torture, and several extrajudicial executions of activists such as the proletarian writer Kobayashi Takiji (1903–1933) and the Marxist theoretician Noro Eitarō (1900–1934).[45] Nonetheless, the authorities generally preferred converting their opponents to crushing them, and the hundreds of political prisoners who broke away from Marxism—many of them genuinely—testify to the efficacy of this approach.[46] The population at large was likewise more often subjected to efforts to convince than to bludgeon.

The vital task of manufacturing popular consent to actions decided upon by the state devolved to a large and cooperative body of journalists and academics who provided prolific and plausible justifications for predetermined policies through numerous articles printed in the mass-circulation daily newspapers and monthly magazines and in the widely distributed government publications. In addition to being disseminated by the print and broadcast media, versions of their views were also propagated by

schools, reservists' associations, and other ideological state appa-
ratuses, with the intended effect of mobilizing public opinion to
favor authoritarianism and war.[47]

Bolstered by wartime patriotism, the combined usage of
compulsion and indoctrination yielded remarkable results inso-
far as it thwarted the development of a radical mass movement,
coopted or quelled worker and peasant activism, and stifled
nearly all publicly voiced criticism. Public obedience was largely
secured and any major challenge to the extant politico-economic
arrangement and its undertakings successfully kept in check.
Most of those who might have been expected to exhibit a mod-
icum of defiance—like the reformists in the national assembly—
vacillated and then threw in their lot with the war.[48]

The myth elaborated by the apologists for the warring state
helped to shape both the popular perceptions of the armed conflict and those espoused by the majority of Japan's writers. The
essential tenets were simple. Japan's objective was to establish
peace, freedom, and stability in East Asia. The obstacles standing in its way were "red" and Western imperialists, native war-
lords, communists, terrorists, bandits, and xenophobes. The
means employed to eliminate them were, for the most part,
regrettably violent but indispensable to the achievement of a just
and worthy goal: the creation of a free and peaceful China within
a cooperative East Asian bloc.[49]

The myth made it clear that while China's leaders were
mostly so wicked, stubborn, and misguided as to deserve destruction, the Chinese people themselves were not the enemy and
were being scrupulously protected from harm by the imperial
Japanese forces. This was only natural, for the war was fought
largely on their behalf, elevating Japan to the stature of China's
"champion" and "benefactor."[50] A fleeting period of bloodshed
was not allowed to obscure the underlying truth that the guid-

ing principles of Sino-Japanese relations were "love, benevolence, and mutual aid."[51]

Despite an occasional brusque call to "chastise China," most
of the arguments upholding the war tended to be moderate and
peaceable in language and tone, stressing Japan's eagerness for
sharing and reciprocity while abjuring any self-serving intent. In
the words of one publicist:

> The objective of Japanese expansion is neither the attain-
> ment of capitalistic supremacy nor the acquisition of
> colonies, but the realization of harmony and concord
> among the nations of East Asia and the promotion of
> their common happiness and prosperity.[52]

Lest any skeptic suspect that such reassuring language served
merely as a smoke screen concealing old-fashioned aggression,
exploitation, and mass murder, the narrative's producers took
care to emphasize the unprecedented nature of the current ven-
ture. Outworn conceptual frameworks were utterly inapplicable
to what was taking place, which was nothing less than the creation by Japan of new thought, a new culture, a new life, a new
Asia, and ultimately a new world order *(sekai shin-chitsujo).*[53]
The specifics of each were seldom explicitly spelled out, but the
alleged novelty of the events helped the war's advocates to trans-
mute what only appeared to be devastation and subjugation
into construction and harmony.

In addition to employing the notion of newness, the propa-
gandists often imbued their nation's exploits with brightness,
presenting Japan as a light from the East—*"lux ex oriente"*—
coming to the aid of a beleaguered continent and a troubled
planet.[54] What made Japan admirably suited for such a role were
its unique national character and its brilliant cultural tradition

permeated by a transcendent—ancient but ever new—spirit of goodness and beauty. Japan was termed "shining," its virtue "enlightening," its history "ever brighter," and its way "enlightened."[55] Blessed by such attributes, Japan was virtually incapable of doing evil and gravitated almost inevitably toward benevolence and perfection. While other heavily militarized nations showed a propensity toward terrorizing the globe, Japan constituted an altruistic—indeed a miraculous—exception. As "The Principles of Our National Polity," a widely studied nationalistic text published in early 1937, explained:

> Our martial spirit does not have for its objective the killing of men, but the giving of life to men. . . . War in this sense is not by any means intended for the destruction, overpowering, or subjugation of others; and it should be a thing for the bringing about of great harmony, that is, peace. . . .[56]

The mystical rhetoric concerning the harmony that was to be Japan's gift to the world was based on the assumption that the Japanese people were by their very nature harmonious, as was evident from the cordial class, race, and gender relations. Class struggle was a phenomenon fundamentally alien to Japan, racial discord was equally absent, and women worked cheerfully in their subordinate social roles. Such ideal harmony was made possible by the inborn virtues of loyalty and filial reverence that enabled all Japanese to cooperate with one another, each accepting his or her proper place within the hierarchy of a nationwide family headed by the emperor. This superior ethical nature was said to arise from a matchless purity frequently represented as radiance.[57]

Reinforcing the fiction of Japan's exemplary morality was a repertory of religious values that the Japanese were deemed to have absorbed and come to live by. Japanese interaction with

China was thus supposedly marked by Shinto purity and simplicity, Confucian humaneness and decorum, and Buddhist compassion and wisdom. Japan's most prominent religious institutions did little to dispute such claims or to oppose the war against China, generally choosing instead to give tacit or overt assent to the ongoing bloodbath.[58] Japanese Confucianists of the 1930s, for instance, asserted that Japan was unique in having preserved moral virtues and therefore had a mission of extending moral influence to the rest of the world.[59]

The glowing myth summarized above was contradicted by a less illustrious, though temporarily obscured, actuality. Japan's superficial unity masked great inequalities in the distribution of wealth and power, severe social tensions, and class conflict.[60] The war functioned as a distraction from a multitude of political, social, and economic ills—the last of these being particularly serious, having been aggravated by the worldwide depression. Despite a recovery in certain sectors of the economy stimulated by yen devaluation, deficit financing, and armaments production, material deprivation continued to afflict millions. Sexual oppression was widespread and resented, although the war granted women the dubious liberty of aiding the imperialist endeavor through participating in patriotic organizations, laboring in munitions and other war-related factories, and serving at the front as war correspondents, nurses, or, for those of the lowest strata, prostitutes.

Racism likewise continued to flourish both domestically and overseas, hardly reflecting the government's professed policy of fostering racial harmony. Koreans, whether living in their colonized country or laboring in Japan, suffered relentless discrimination. China and its people—once held in the highest esteem for their immense contribution to Japan's culture and civilization—were viewed largely with contempt, one commentator describing the Chinese as having "deteriorated in racial quality and stamina."[61] The primary reasons for this shift from respect to scorn involved China's slow pace of modernization, the complacency and corruption of Chinese leadership, the country's defeat in the earlier—and ostensibly in the present—war with Japan, its political fragmentation, and its people's seeming fondness for drugs.[62] Thus, with many Japanese despising the very people the war purported to be liberating, racism performed its traditional task of facilitating expansionism by removing ethical objections to even the most brutal forms of domination. Japan's harsh colonial rule of the territories it had already taken over— Korea and Taiwan—demonstrated concretely the glaring discrepancy between the rhetoric of love and harmony and the actual practice.[63] Such discrepancy, of course, is not rare in the conduct of international affairs.

Imperial Yarnspinners

Much as the practice of cooperation with foreign powers that characterized Japan's diplomacy in the 1920s seemed reflected in the atmosphere of cosmopolitanism then prevalent among the nation's intellectuals, so the 1930s diplomatic shift toward defiant isolation and assertion of Japanese hegemony in Asia found its intellectual counterpart in a new mood of Japanism and an eager quest to identify those cultural traits that entitled Japan to continental leadership. The process was aided by a sense of resentment many Japanese intellectuals harbored against the cultural arrogance of the West, which they tended to view as no less objectionable than its high-handedness in the economic and military spheres.[64] A government that proposed to liberate Asia from the West could thus count on enthusiastic support by a significant number of intellectuals. A question they were largely inclined to overlook, however, was whether the replacement of Western supremacy by the Japanese could genuinely be said to constitute Asian liberation.

The instances of active opposition to war and quasi fascism were relatively few and isolated but were sufficient to ensure constant government vigilance. Some antiwar intellectuals were imprisoned or put under surveillance, others chose to go into exile, and a small number—including the scholar Yanaihara Tadao, who persisted in writing and sending out an antiwar newsletter—managed to keep up a solitary struggle against the war throughout its duration.[65] The existence of opposition, scattered and unorganized though it was, suggests that dissent—although hazardous and arduous—was neither impossible nor inevitably suicidal and could perhaps have grown much stronger than it did before encountering more stringent efforts at repression.

As part of combating dissent nonviolently through constructing a patriotic consensus, the government in the 1930s welcomed and encouraged artists as well as thinkers to cooperate and assist in carrying out the national agenda. Numerous filmmakers, songwriters, composers, painters, and sculptors responded positively by producing works expressive in various ways of the beauty of the national character and justice of the official policy.[66] Motivated like the other artists by conviction, convenience, or financial concerns, a sizable sector of literary critics and authors did the same.

Much Japanese literature of the 1930s, like the mainstream national culture, showed a tendency toward introversion as many of its practitioners seemed to secede from literary internationalism (Japan PEN Club withdrew from the International PEN in 1938[67]) and turn to eulogizing and seeking to recreate the nation's literary classics. Writers Hori Tatsuo and Tanizaki Jun'ichirō produced retellings and translations of millennium-old masterpieces such as *The Gossamer Years* and *The Tale of Genji,* while nationalistic groups—the Japanese Romantic School prominent among them—energetically propagated a "return" to

Japan and a reinvigorated appreciation of the Japanese aesthetic genius.[68] The Romantics' belief in a transhistorical, timeless essence of Japan was shared by other cultural conservatives of the period, as was their conviction that the nation's literary classics were manifestations of the superlative Japanese spirit.

Assisted by exaltation of the native tradition and antipathy toward foreign ideology, intensified censorship and police activity effected a temporary dissolution of the proletarian literary movement ascendant since the previous decade and represented by such authors as Tokunaga Sunao, Hayama Yoshiki, Miyamoto Yuriko, Sata Ineko, and numerous others. Efforts to create a literature of liberation from poverty and oppression faltered as writers began to disengage from progressive political activism and in some cases even to identify with ultranationalistic goals. The 1930s vogue of *tenkō* (recantation) literature, written by leftists pressured into renouncing their beliefs and generally marked by guilt, self-pity, and anguished search for new ideals, tended to add yet another regressive element to the literary climate.[69] Such developments suggest that Japanese writers were unlikely to offer much resistance to the war against China. Indeed, most did not.

Instead, a great many poets, essayists, novelists, and playwrights were impelled by patriotism or ambition to take part in the officially sponsored literary conferences, publicity campaigns, and patriotic organizations whose aim was both to keep the writers under control and to recruit them into promoting national unanimity. In a striking example of literature voluntarily enlisting in the service of aggressive war, dozens of writers eagerly accepted the government's invitation, extended in August 1938 by the Cabinet Information Division, to travel to China and write about the ongoing armed offensive.[70] The Pen Corps *(Pen Butai)*, formed following a cordial meeting between government officials and major literary figures, received so many applicants that some had to be turned away. No overt or covert pressure appears to have been exerted to obtain the writers' compliance, and no measures were taken against the two or three people who declined to participate. The authorities, hoping for hortatory narratives from the front that would enhance support for the war and inspire civilians to emulate the soldiers' spirit of cheerful self-sacrifice, promptly organized the corps and flew it overseas.[71]

Whether or not they formally belonged to the Pen Corps, the writers who supported the war generally perceived things in a similar way. They seldom questioned either the meaning or conduct of the war, assuming it to be a high-minded affair undertaken for the benefit of both China and Japan. None of the writers took a harsh view of the Chinese, treating them usually with sympathy, mild contempt, or indifference. The Chinese were viewed as touchingly similar to, if fundamentally different from, the Japanese. The points of resemblance lay in their physical appearance and sporadic capacity for courage and nobility, but— a few exceptions aside—their dirt, stench, moral unpredictability, and alien language set them unmistakably apart. In contrast to China's largely undistinguished citizens, Japanese servicemen in China were accorded unalloyed admiration. They were warm, dependable, loving, and lovable men thoroughly dedicated to their country and to each other. The war, which seemed to possess purifying powers, stripped them free of extraneous intellectual and moral complexities and gave them heroic stature. The field of battle across which they irresistibly surged became a realm of heightened existence where the fiery spectacle of combat, the soldiers' indomitable spirit, and even the bittersweet sadness of their deaths gave strength to the conviction that war is beautiful.[72]

In beautifying the war, authors tended to write lyrically and to make ample use of the traditional aesthetic preferences for evanescence and simplicity. They showed the soldiers as attractively simple in character and motivation and the common brevity of their lives as imbued with a poignant loveliness. Although the writers employed a wide range of literary genres, such time-honored forms as the diary, travelogue, and discursive essay seemed to enjoy special favor.[73] The textual language ranged from the realistic mode embellished with lyrical touches to the documentary that often veered toward poetic diction. Because they represented eloquent, stirring articulations of officially sanctioned attitudes, the works circulated abundantly and freely, both thriving on and nourishing the prevailing war fever. The paper rationing in effect after 1940 favored the creation of pro-war narratives over most other kinds of writing.[74] The authors who produced them rendered valuable service to the warring state by supplying a multitude of accessible, open-ended narratives, capable of mobilizing and enlisting readers as homefront or battlefront protagonists in the momentous unfolding events.

Numerous as they were, the literary artists who openly embraced the war were a minority. The great majority of Japanese writers continued writing "as usual," without making any literary or extraliterary statements for or against the war in China. Even though their posture has sometimes been granted the status of "passive resistance,"[75] it might be more accurate—since silence signifies acquiescence more than it does opposition—to call it passive complicity or simply indifference. The lengthy roster of authors evidently indifferent to the war includes the most highly acclaimed and well-established literary figures of the period, whose works still evoke great and justified interest: Shiga Naoya, Tanizaki Jun'ichirō, and Kawabata Yasunari.

Shiga Naoya (1883–1971), whose major work concentrated to an almost claustrophobic extent on the emotional life of a single individual who ultimately rises both figuratively and literally above the anguished realm of human relations, rarely seemed to take much notice of the wider workings of society or politics.[76] The completion of his novel *A Dark Night's Passing* in 1937 appears to have enabled Shiga to attain a state of Olympian serenity, which the war's agony was powerless to disturb. Shiga's narrow social focus was a trait largely shared with the otherwise much more playful writer Tanizaki Jun'ichirō (1886–1965), who is considered by many the best Japanese novelist of the twentieth century. Tanizaki, conceding a basic lack of interest in politics, preferred to promote and take delight in the sensuous beauty of the indigenous cultural tradition.[77] Even so, Tanizaki was willing to voice his approval of the prevailing current of events. In "A Preface to *The Tale of Genji*," published in the January 1939 issue of the highly prestigious intellectual journal *Chūō kōron* (Central review), he had the following to say apropos his "translation" of the celebrated classic into modern Japanese:

> In the four calendar years since I took up the pen, social conditions have conspicuously changed, until at present the high and low of our country are working together, advancing boldly in the task of rebuilding East Asia. Perhaps it is an act of fate that in such an age a product of our classical literature should appear in its modern incarnation, a work we believe we may positively take pride in before the world.[78]

Other writers, not usually regarded as collaborationist, were even more amenable to compromise with the authorities. Kawabata Yasunari (1899–1972), the future Nobel prizewinner, who produced one of his most admired novels—the icily beautiful *Snow Country*—during the 1930s, spoke and wrote on behalf of the war effort, defended censorship, joined patriotic literary organizations, and used the money he accepted from the military-dominated government to buy a house in the resort town of Karuizawa.[79] Kawabata twice traveled to occupied China, where he was impressed at witnessing the creation of a colonial-ist utopia. As late as August of 1941 he was able to write:

> The greatest joy of my most recent journey came from being
> able to meet intimately many of the good Japanese carrying
> out magnificent work in Manchuria and China.[80]

The contemporary work of many writers, regardless of whether they backed or ignored the war, manifests traces of the dominant temper of the era. The officially encouraged emphasis on self-denial and power of the spirit is reflected in the literary output of writers like Dazai Osamu (1909–1948), Nakagawa Yoichi (1897–1994), Yoshikawa Eiji (1892–1962), and others. Dazai's delightful short story "A Promise Fulfilled," written in August 1938 and centered on a young woman whose years of self-sacrificing abstinence are rewarded at last with ecstasy, owes much to the relative lightheartedness of that moment in the author's life, but its exaltation of present self-restraint as a path to future bliss also strikingly parallels governmental sumptuary exhortations to postpone desire until victory.[81] Renunciation plays an even greater part in Nakagawa's widely read novella *Heavenly Moonflower*, likewise published in 1938 at the height of the war with China, whose two lovers—convinced that "the power to be achieved beyond all other powers is the power of self-control"—willingly defer sexual gratification forever.[82] While the spiritual endeavors adumbrated by these and other authors tend to assume outwardly nonviolent forms, the quest could take a more explicitly martial turn, as it does in Yoshikawa's immensely popular historical novel *Miyamoto Musashi*, serial-ized between 1935 and 1939 and named after its warrior hero who, trusting in "the sword of the spirit," fights and kills in the pursuit of spiritual excellence.[83] By conveying the impression of having embraced officially countenanced values, many writers thus wittingly or unwittingly contributed to the war effort.

The reasons why unequivocal rejection of the war by literary figures was rare are not altogether elusive. Indoctrination effected by mass education and mass media had convinced most of them that the war was just and thus worthy of their vocal or tacit approval. Censorship rendered all active opposition difficult, dangerous, and (to say the least) economically unprofitable. The relative public prominence of many writers made their activities easier to scrutinize, and the suppression of oppositional mass movements to which they might have belonged and drawn strength from further increased the isolation and vulnerability of those prone to resist. In addition, the Japanese literary tradition itself, with its propensity toward introspection and comparative scarcity of social criticism, may have contributed toward decreasing the likelihood of literary opposition to the war, but here the case is less clear-cut and deserves brief elaboration.

Traditional Japanese literature chooses to depict the delicate anguish of love, the beauties of nature and its seasons, the passage of time, and the pleasures or melancholy of travel far more frequently than it treats, say, the pain and cruelty stemming from unjust social arrangements or from violent pursuit of elite ambitions. Even when subjects such as war are dealt with, literary decorum tends to obscure their most disagreeable aspects in the interests of maintaining refinement and elegance. The impulse toward excluding the unattractive is evident in the following admonition by the venerated poet Matsuo Bashō (1644–1694), contained in his travel diary of 1687:

> The artist sees nothing that is not a flower, thinks of nothing
> that is not the moon. If he sees other than the flowers, he is
> no better than a barbarian. If he thinks of other than the

flowers *[sic]*, he is not different from a beast. Leave the
barbarians and part from the beasts: follow nature and
be at one with nature.[84]

The very fact that Bashō felt impelled to offer his advice,
however, suggests that all Japanese writers did not always abide
by it. Lyrical aestheticism may form the mainstream of traditional
Japanese literature, but contrary tendencies also constitute a
forceful presence. There are the passionately indignant verses of
the great *Man'yōshū* poet Yamanoue Okura (660–733), employing potently harsh imagery to address the miseries of poverty.[85]
Compelling lines denouncing injustice and hypocrisy are found
in the *Essays in Idleness* of Yoshida Kenkō (1283–1350).[86]

As the nation encounters modernity, the critical spirit grows
much stronger, first evidenced perhaps by the enthusiastic lib-
eralism of the 1880s political novels. By the early twentieth century, the poet and journalist Ishikawa Takuboku (1885–1912) is
calling for the development of systematic thought to counter the
intensifying power of the state and insisting that "the attitude of
a writer toward life must not be that of a spectator; a writer must
be a critic."[87] The criticism called for by Ishikawa reaches its
apogee with the proletarian literary movement of the 1920s,
whose writers aim at no less than a revolutionary reconstitution
of society. The existence of these and similar oppositional strands
within the national literary tradition indicates that far from making inevitable the disregard or the uncritically lyrical celebration
of the war, it provided both the language and the precedent for
protest.

Censorship certainly presented a formidable obstacle to the
articulation of protest or radical aspirations, but its power—
given sufficient courage and ingenuity—was not insurmount-
able. Literature is easier to produce and circulate than, say,
motion pictures. There is consequently a variety of ways in which

manuscripts objectionable to the authorities could have been manufactured and distributed to a limited audience. These range from reproduction by mimeograph to copying by hand—a strenuous but time-honored practice in Japan as elsewhere. The texts could have been disseminated manually, smuggled through the mail, or even—emulating Shelley—cast adrift in bottles or aloft in balloons. Moreover, when possessing adequate allegorical camouflage, they invited the possibility of open publication.

That these and other options were seldom fully explored and utilized points to a lack of conviction in the importance of opposing the war, which in turn attests to the efficacy of the indoctrination system and the susceptibility to it of the majority of Japan's writers. In a sense, their often unquestioning affirmation of government policy made little difference, for even had they all energetically resisted, they could not by themselves have terminated the war. They could, however, have created an indelibly inspiring example of that struggle against injustice which is a universal responsibility and privilege. Instead, most engaged in complicity or inaction while their nation lost over half a million of its own people and killed more than ten million Chinese men, women, and children.[88]

Radiance and Beyond

Reading the novels, poems, essays, and reports by Japanese writers concerning the war against China, one is likely to get the impression that the war possessed a certain shining quality, that it was a radiant enterprise. Many of the writings show Japanese officers, soldiers, and the battlefields across which they advance as sporadically illuminated by, or emanating, an attractive brightness.

The imagery of brightness tends to be manifested in a variety of forms. Prominent among the objects touched by the radiance are members of the Japanese military personnel carrying out the imperial will on the continent. The highly acclaimed author Hayashi Fumiko (1903–1951), who visited the Chinese front several times and supported the war with infectious enthusiasm, writes in her 1938 travelogue *The Battlefront* that each of the Japanese soldiers running against the backdrop of a burning Chinese village seems to her to be enveloped by a nimbus of sacred light.[89] Authors like Hino Ashihei, Satomura Kinzō, and Ishikawa Tatsuzō portray intrepid commanding officers—whose status and noble conduct make them implicit surrogates of the emperor—as radiant, dazzling, or glowing with valor.[90]

Sometimes the radiance is psychological, intimating that a state of spiritual or emotional brightness could be attained by those with the proper attitude toward the war. The renowned literary critic Kobayashi Hideo (1902–1983), in his 1937 essay "On War" urging vacillating intellectuals to give their resolute support to the war, speaks of "a radiance which visits only the men unflinchingly resolved to deal with the present."[91] An angst-ridden young officer in Ishikawa Tatsuzō's 1938 novella *Soldiers Alive*, translated here, begins to feel a liberating sense of brightness the moment he grows indifferent to his own death, thus becoming an ideal soldier.[92] This newly found luminescence also enables the officer to condone without protest an atrocity committed by his subordinates: the deliberate killing of a young Chinese woman. Displaying a similar lack of concern over civilian deaths, the writer Hayashi Fumiko celebrates a Japanese victory—the capture of the city of Wuhan, at which she was personally present—with tears of joy and a feeling of radiance.[93]

Territory conquered by Japanese troops also has a propensity to acquire luster. The cheerful and pointedly symbolic conclusion of Ozaki Shirō's 1937 lyrical essay "A Thousand Miles of Plaintive Winds" shows the rising sun shining down on the old imperial palace at Peking, where "dreaming of tradition while bathed in sunlight, the palace tiles are radiantly glowing."[94] The best-selling war writer Hino Ashihei (1907–1960) concludes his 1939 autobiographical novel *Flowers and Soldiers* with a scene of blissfully drunk Japanese soldiers sailing across the brilliantly sunlit waters of China's West Lake. "Is this a battlefield??!!" he asks rhetorically.[95] The critic Kobayashi Hideo, visiting the same location, proclaims the white magnolia blossoming alongside the lake "radiant as if ablaze."[96] Disinclined merely to extol the existing conquests, the distinguished poet Saitō Mokichi predicts a splendid future for the entire continent: "Enemy forces utterly destroyed: a great dawn's brightness to Asia comes."[97]

The actual business of killing and destruction, being deemed indispensable to the creation of a new and peaceful Asia, could also be depicted in a bright light. It was thus natural for Hayashi Fumiko to utilize the flames of blazing Chinese houses in endowing Japanese soldiers responsible for the conflagration with an aura of holiness. Hino Ashihei, in his 1939 book *March into Canton,* describes an attack on this major city in glowing terms:

> Heralded by an exhilarating roar, a formation of airplanes flies over us. Glittering silver in a dazzlingly blue firmament, the planes lightly circle the distant sky, dropping into dives then suddenly nosing up again. The thunder of bombardment reverberates in our ears. White shells seem to be fluttering over a deep blue carpet.
>
> "That's Canton down there," we tell each other. A wind has risen. At the foot of a mountain thickly wooded with pines, pampas grass growing tall along rice fields is swaying with a beautiful shine.[98]

The aftermath of a military assault could afford a comparable measure of sunny aesthetic satisfaction. Kobayashi Hideo, in a 1938 sightseeing report entitled "From Hangchow to Nanking," takes in the view from atop one of the Nanking city gates:

The trenches, dug at six-yard intervals, were strewn with hats, leather belts, birdcages, and other objects that had escaped the flames. The unburied bones of Chinese soldiers stood like sticks stuck in the soil. Sleek, brown thighbones shone beautifully transparent in the sunlight. Vertebrae moistly glistened, as if tarred. Flies swarmed and the luminous air stank.[99]

The bright and peaceful scene Kobayashi Hideo describes may call to mind the fact that the era of the then-reigning emperor was named Shōwa, meaning "bright peace." Wittingly or unwittingly, many of Japan's literary pilgrims touring the continent torn by the sacred war seemed to find the auspicious era name concretely manifested and confirmed by what they saw. The imperial war, as it were, was a bright path to peace.

The small number of Japanese writers who opposed the war against China refused to be dazzled by the blood-drenched radiance. They did not as a rule go to the front and were less likely to use the imagery of light in their work. Those who did resort to it did so with an ironic twist. Kaneko Mitsuharu (1895–1975), who published several antiwar poems thanks to the censors' inability to understand them, even dared to mock the imperial radiance itself. Kaneko's 1935 poem "The Lighthouse" opens with a sneering look at the highest reaches of the Japanese society:

It is forbidden to peer into the depths of the sky.
The depths of the sky
Are swarming with gods.

They drift about in syrupy ether.
Angels' armpit hair.
Hawks' molted feathers.

The fearsome smell of godly skin, like burning bronze.

It is forbidden to gaze into the depths of the sky.
Eyes that do will be burned out by the light.
Descending from heavenly depths is the everlasting power.

It punishes those who defy heaven.

A single white candle
Stands erect in the middle of the sky
To which only the faithful souls ascend
—The lighthouse.[100]

In 1938 the novelist Ishikawa Jun (1899–1987) managed to publish a beautifully written short story called "The Song of Mars," only to have it banned for "fomenting antimilitary and antiwar thought."[101] The story's protagonist is a refractory intellectual doggedly clinging to reason when relinquishing it in favor of patriotic frenzy seems mandatory. At one point, seeking some rest in the darkness of a movie theater, he is confronted instead with a news film showing his country's military in action:

> I blinked up at the screen where a gigantic warship was
> thrusting its long gun barrels over the sunlit water: the guns
> seeming just to have fired, their smug muzzles coolly trailed
> soft wisps of whitest smoke which slenderly rose and dissi-
> pated. For an instant, the smoke impressed me as very tran-
> quil, like puffs from the pipe of an old man basking in the
> sunshine, but I realized with a start it was precisely in such
> feigned innocence the bombardment's ghastliness resided.[102]

The newsreel's brightly peaceful presentation of the war is as typical of the pro-war perspective as it is attractive and persuasive, and even the skeptical protagonist is momentarily taken in by it. The author, however, by having his character see through the illusion, demystifies it for the reader as well.

In Ishikawa Jun's story, brightness seems complicit with the derangement of interminably sung war songs and mindless, compulsive discussions of war. Even during a train ride, his hapless, harried hero can find no respite from the rampant hysteria:

> In the season prevailing within this carriage, joining voices to the Song of Mars was definitely a badge of sanity. Was my own sanity madness, then? The sunlight streaming in through the windows became suddenly intense, setting sprays of saliva to sparkle against particles of dust. The khaki shimmered. Someone's gaiters dropped from the overhead baggage net. Across from me, a child was unsheathing his midget military sword.[103]

The wit and humor characteristic of Ishikawa Jun's writing are also found in abundance in the work of the antiwar poet Oguma Hideo (1901–1940), while Ishikawa's anger against stupidity and injustice is shared by the antiwar novelist Kuroshima Denji (1898–1943).[104] Neither of these two talented and courageous writers chose to make much literary use of radiance, a fact which of course in no way diminishes the quality and value of their work. Radiance, it appears, was largely a province of the hawks.

The resistance writers who opposed the war on political, intellectual, aesthetic, or moral grounds tended to be influenced by Marxist or anarchist thought. They regarded the war as sheer butchery, bringing no advantage to anyone except the elites that coerce and manipulate ordinary people into waging it. Anchored in grassroots internationalism, their works expose the indignities and atrocities inflicted upon the Chinese under the guise of lofty rhetoric, reveal the connections between overseas terror and domestic repression, and deride both thoughtless belligerence and timid submission to authority. Diverse in style and form, and making ample use of contradiction, irony, and humor, the anti-war works tend to favor the jarring modernist imagery (in eclipse during the nativist thirties) as well as the more traditional idiom. The texts' quality, integrity, and clear-sightedness set them apart from the bulk of those produced by their contemporaries. Although few in number and—undermined further by censorship and limited distribution—making little impact on the public opinion of the time, the antiwar writings of Kaneko Mitsuharu, Ishikawa Jun, Oguma Hideo, and Kuroshima Denji deserve lasting recognition as imposing and heartening examples of art's continuing struggle against malevolent power.[105]

Ishikawa Tatsuzō and the War

One of the most explicit accounts of the Sino-Japanese War's impact on the individual Japanese soldiers and Chinese civilians whom it embroiled was supplied by the novelist Ishikawa Tatsuzō (1905–1985). An admirer of Emile Zola and Anatole France, Ishikawa early made his mark as an acute observer of human reactions to conditions of extreme stress. His travel to China as the acclaimed liberal magazine *Chūō kōron*'s special correspondent in late December 1937 was his second trip abroad. At age twenty-five he had spent about two months in Brazil, and the experience had served as a basis for a novella about impoverished Japanese immigrants to that country, which won him the first Akutagawa Prize in 1935.[106]

Enthusiastically taking up his present assignment, Ishikawa worked with unrelenting speed. He arrived at the Chinese capital on January 4 or 5, 1938, just over three weeks after its capture.[107] Still burning and littered with corpses, Nanking struck him as "a city of death."[108] For eight days Ishikawa interviewed the occupying soldiers—though not the officers, talking mostly with men belonging to the Thirty-third Infantry Regiment of the Sixteenth Division of the Shanghai Expeditionary Force.[109] Ishikawa then took a train back to Shanghai to collect more information, returned to Japan on January 28, began to write on February 1, and completed the manuscript at dawn of the Empire Day, February 11.[110]

The work produced at such white heat was the novella *Ikite iru heitai* (Soldiers Alive), scheduled for publication in the March 1938 issue of *Chūō kōron*. The narrative centers on an infantry unit transferred from northern China to take part in the offensive against Nanking. The story is told in a straightforward, dispassionate manner, using conventional prose that sometimes approaches the matter-of-factness of a military bulletin. Making no attempt to create suspense, the author invariably states the outcome of an incident before relating its particulars. The detached mode of presentation, well suited to delivering glimpses of war in the raw, appears indebted to Neue Sachlichkeit (New Objectivity), a German literary trend of the Weimar Republic years, whose stress on concrete realities rather than abstract conceptions influenced a number of Japanese writers in the 1930s.[111]

The soldiers are "alive" not only because they have not yet been killed, but also because they are creatures of flesh and blood rather than idealized models of chivalrous virtue. Their search for sex, forced or purchased, is one factor setting *Soldiers Alive* apart from most other war literature of the period. In addition to copulating—the details of which are tactfully omitted—the soldiers also plunder, burn, and indiscriminately kill. They are nonetheless not shown as monsters but as men brutalized by a merciless environment who yet remain capable of great love for each other, including even their dead comrades whose bones they faithfully carry along.

Interested in the psychological processes activated to deal

with unremitting exposure to intense violence and imminent death, the author singles out several individuals from an embattled platoon to observe their responses to the deadly surroundings. Private Kondō strives to stave off the horror by maintaining an attitude of clinical detachment from reality. Private Hirao filters the gruesome events through a sentimental sensibility to transform them into a succession of hyperbolic narratives. Unable to diminish the force of actuality by such stratagems, Lieutenant Kurata suffers from acute existential dread. The least inconvenienced appears to be Corporal Kasahara, who takes killing and danger cheerfully in stride.

Unlike Kondō, Hirao, and Kurata, Kasahara is an uneducated rural youth, the second son of a peasant. Contrasted with the harsh life of a tenant farmer he would likely be leading were he not a noncommissioned officer, the author seems to be suggesting, the hardships of army life and even war appear negligible. Accustomed to killing, dependable, and free of excessive psychological complexity associated with education and urban living, Kasahara constitutes the ideal soldier:

> To Corporal Kasahara, killing enemy soldiers was no different than killing carp. The carnage he perpetrated did not affect his emotions in the least. The one emotion that did move him mightily was a virtually instinctive love for his comrades. He was truly a splendid soldier, the very epitome of a soldier. . . . The magnificent steadiness of his mind persisted unshaken amid severest combat and the most bestial slaughter. In short, he was unburdened by either oversensitivity or the intellectual's habit of self-criticism, neither of any use on the battlefield. It was precisely his type of courageous, loyal fighting man that the army wanted. . . . Corporal Kasahara, before ever coming to the front, had been a youth cut out for war.[112]

Though clearly a personification of unreflecting simplicity, much prized at the time, Kasahara is neither an automaton nor a mere stereotype. The author deftly presents him as a lovable rogue who kills with hardly a twinge of conscience but retains his loyal, boyish demeanor in the face of everything except a comrade's death. In doing so he creates one of the most vivid literary characters to emerge from the war.

The ready affirmation of war, which Kasahara achieves spontaneously, is the inevitable spiritual destination of all soldiers, though few attain it with such ease. For Kurata it requires a traumatic event to trigger the liberating brightness:

> He was feeling a vast change within himself. His grating anxiety seemed already abated along with his confused urge to die. In a sense, what had until now been fueling his unease, impatience, and courage was the instinctive terror of a life in peril. But having seen the company commander die before his eyes, that terror had passed into a separate dimension. His emotions soared—or plunged. Perhaps this was a sort of numbing of the sensibility, instinctively activated to avert a disintegration of the self. He grew lighthearted and began to sense a brightness inherent in this life. A feeling did remain that if he probed deeply into that brightness he would uncover a darkness at its nadir, but he was no longer in the least inclined to inflict such probing on himself. He began to feel a great breadth of spirit, a sensation of freedom surpassing all morals. He was already starting to cultivate a character that would enable him to participate calmly in the most gruesome slaughter. That is to say, he was catching up with Corporal Kasahara.[113]

The newly gained serenity of his enlightenment will enable the kindly Lieutenant Kurata to condone without protest the atrocities committed by his subordinates.

The author of course is aware of the murderous consequences for the Chinese of such amoral affirmation and describes
them in some detail. But although he sympathizes with the Chinese and disapproves of plunder and murder, he appears to
regard the troops' conduct as largely unavoidable. On the one
hand, as he often asserts, human life on the battlefield is univer-
sally scorned, while on the other the soldiers are intoxicated with
the volatile arrogance of victors:

> They felt themselves the mightiest creatures alive. Needless
> to say, in the face of such conviction, all morality, law,
> reflection, and humanity were powerless.[114]

Moreover, dangerously incensing the soldiers is the frequent par-
ticipation of civilians in the unexpectedly intense resistance confronting them. Somewhat apologetically, Ishikawa writes,

> Tragic incidents were difficult to avoid when combatants
> could not be clearly distinguished from noncombatants.[115]

In a sense the narrative of *Soldiers Alive* drives toward a violent
culmination that does not entirely take place. Ishikawa was
optimistic enough to hope that most of his text would get past
the censors but realized it was out of the question to write about
what came to be known as the rape of Nanking. Reporting that
event was expressly forbidden.[116] Much of what he does record,
however, leads almost inexorably to Nanking, and foreshadows
the enormity of the worst single massacre in the war against
China.

The unflinching realism characterizing much of Ishikawa's
description of men at war is brutally honest and refreshingly
iconoclastic. Nevertheless, his work is not entirely free of hack-
neyed conventions found in the more run-of-the-mill literary
products of the war. Telling, for instance, of a field commander's

reaction to a dying soldier's insistence on fighting till the end, Ishikawa declares,

> Never until that moment had the colonel so intensely felt the august virtue of His Majesty the Emperor and the sterling worth of the soldiers.[117]

The commander himself, Colonel Nishizawa, is portrayed as an apotheosis of "exalted military spirit."[118] An emboldening presence to the soldiers who worship him boundlessly, he bears himself with such dignity that his very skin seems to radiate valor. "An instinctively peace-loving man," Nishizawa kills with pain in his heart, aware that the nation demands sacrifices that individuals have no right to question:

> War was the undertaking of a nation and the spiritual contentment of a single man held no claim to consideration. Of course he knew that. But while Colonel Nishizawa felt a parental love toward his own subordinates, love for the enemy was not unfamiliar to him either. Though he would not hesitate to kill untold thousands of captives, yet the deed filled him with a certain sad emptiness.[119]

Unlike Corporal Kasahara, who does not feel the sorrow of war, or the soldiers who cease to feel it once they become like him, Colonel Nishizawa's greatness of character allows him to feel the sorrow to the full and still go on. As the highest-ranking officer described in detail, Nishizawa is a surrogate of the emperor himself, whose tacit approval of massive killing goes a long way toward sanctioning and sanctifying the vicious excesses of the soldiers.

There is little in Ishikawa's text to indicate that the author in any way disagrees with Colonel Nishizawa and much to suggest that, like his men, he greatly admires him. Conceding the savagery of the war Nishizawa is helping to wage does not induce the author to intimate that the officer is doing anything other than fulfilling his patriotic duty stoically and well. Condemnation of the military is as absent from the work as condemnation of the war. Realistic but loyal, Ishikawa aims to deglamorize the war against China, not denounce it. Much like his fictional colonel, he accepts that the war is essential to the nation while remaining willing to contemplate concretely the agony that the war causes to individuals.

Ugly and regrettable as it is, the horrendous devastation Ishikawa chronicles does not detract from the war's validity but simply points up the high price of defeat. As one of the characters observes, "Those who lose a war suffer real misery, and there's no help for that."[120] Such criticisms as Ishikawa does make are tactical, being directed not against the war but against the profiteering Japanese civilians, poor conditions at field hospitals, and inefficiency in the delivery of military mail. He refrains from detailed speculation on the war's eventual outcome, except to imply that it promises to benefit both Japan and China. A sight of magpies serves to recall the Japanese warlord Hideyoshi's sixteenth-century invasions of the continent (known to Koreans as Imjin Wars) and impels the author to muse:

> When the China Incident ended and the Japanese army
> returned home, these birds would surely follow the troops
> once more and spread out all across Japan. At least some of
> the Chinese culture would make way to Japan along with
> the returning units. The war was certain to bring about a
> sort of merging of the two countries.[121]

Soldiers Alive concludes somewhat ambiguously, as perhaps befits the depiction of a war in progress. A soldier arrested for committing an act of violence against a Japanese civilian is permitted to return to his unit, which has already departed for a new front. Rather like a lonely lemming, the pathetically isolated soldier manages at last to rejoin the unit, happy to have done so, neither knowing nor caring where its march will take him. The scene may constitute a silent criticism of military tolerance for lawlessness, or it may be an expression of the joy of belonging and a willingness to share without protest whatever is to befall one's compatriots. At any rate, it is clear that despite the capture of the Chinese capital, the war against China is far from over.

Although Ishikawa's *Soldiers Alive* can be read as a damning document of imperialist aggression, it was not intended as such nor is this what the Japanese authorities construed it to be. Nonetheless, Ishikawa's acceptance of the war on its own terms failed to meet with governmental approval. Despite editorial cuts of the most objectionable passages, on February 18, 1938, the Home Ministry blocked the sale of *Chūō kōron*. About a week later, early in the morning, two detectives of the Special Higher Police appeared at Ishikawa's house in Tokyo and took him to the metropolitan headquarters for questioning.[122]

Ishikawa and his editor were indicted for violating two articles of the Press Law, a piece of repressive legislation enacted in 1909 to stamp out socialist and anarchist publications.[123] At the trial, which opened in late spring, Ishikawa explained to the judge what had prompted him to strip some of the gilding from the war:

> Writing about expedient matters, as even our press does, and not reporting the truth, results in a popular complacency which troubled me. People think of soldiers at the front as gods, and believe that, with even the Chinese cooperating, a paradise is built overnight in the territories occupied by our troops. But war is not such an agreeable affair. I was con-

vinced that telling people the truth about war was indispensable in making them aware of the crisis and impelling them to take a determined attitude toward the present situation.[124]

Asked by a judge whether his writing would not damage the people's trust in the Japanese soldiers, Ishikawa replied his intention had been to shatter their trust in godlike creatures and replace it with a trust in human beings. The government, however, appeared unwilling to risk the consequences of showing its soldiers as too fallibly human. Ishikawa was convicted of "disturbing peace and order by describing massacres of noncombatants by Imperial Army soldiers, instances of plunder, and conditions of lax military discipline."[125] He was sentenced to four months in prison with a three-year reprieve. The trial's outcome, widely publicized, served as a clear warning to Japanese writers that overly truthful accounts of the war would not be tolerated.[126]

Significantly, Ishikawa was not accused of antimilitarism or antiwar agitation. Had he been, the following turn of events would have been virtually inconceivable. In September 1938, within days of each other, Ishikawa was sentenced, granted permission to visit China again, and sent there, once more as special correspondent of *Chūō kōron*.[127] Someone in authority appeared shrewd enough to perceive that a clear demonstration of endorsing the war would be all the more valuable coming from a boldly independent-minded popular writer like Ishikawa. With his difference of opinion with the government limited largely to the choice of means in securing public support for the war, Ishikawa did not seem beyond redemption, and so the authorities acceded to the request of the *Chūō kōron* editors that he be given another chance.

Ishikawa's second visit to the continent, from September to November 1938, coincided with that of the Pen Corps members and resulted in a quasi novel called *Bukan sakusen* (The Wuhan

Campaign), published in the January 1939 issue of *Chūō kōron*. In a note appended to the text, after apologizing to the readers for the "inconvenience" caused by *Soldiers Alive* (whose appearance many had looked forward to), Ishikawa explains that this time he hopes to communicate the breadth, depth, and complexity of war through a work that is neither a novel nor a full-fledged military chronicle but a war story striving to be faithful to facts. Abandoning the earlier concentration on individuals in battle, he has now been trying to view the overall activities and suggests that the story's interest will be enhanced if read alongside a detailed map.

The interest does need enhancing, for the work resembles a lengthy press release penned by an eloquent officer. It reads much as *Soldiers Alive* might read if most of its characters, major and minor, were eliminated. *The Wuhan Campaign* contains correspondingly little dialogue, and what there is of it often consists of exclamatory orders or ostensibly overheard snatches of conversation like the following, by soldiers grumbling about a lull in the advance:

> "We didn't come to China to fish!"
> "Nor to dig for potatoes!"
> "We didn't come to sit around in the sun!"
> "Can't they let us go to Wuhan?" [128]

Comprising chapter titles like "The Important Task of Transport" and "The Sugiura Unit Is Surrounded!," *The Wuhan Campaign* is a piece of sanitized reportage adorned with sporadic literary touches. No atrocities are committed in what is now unequivocally termed a "holy war," [129] and no soldier is tormented by thoughts of death. Even the suffering of the wounded is minimized: On the night before the attack against Lu Shan, the field hospital staff is busy polishing scalpels and needles "so that the treatment of the wounded should not hurt in the slightest." [130]

The author seems to be observing events in the war zone from a height that renders individual actions invisible, swooping down occasionally only to record some heroic act. When, for example, a cholera epidemic breaks out in the city of Chiuchiang, seven unnamed doctors from a Japanese hospital in Nanking rush to the rescue:

Their faces were pale with tension, their pupils glistening with a sacred light.[131]

Within two weeks, the mission is accomplished:

A victory for Japanese medicine was also a victory for the Japanese army. The labor of seven doctors had saved Chiuchiang.[132]

Selflessness and heroics form a prominent theme in the narrative, with five anonymous Japanese soldiers beating back an attack by fifty Chinese foes, and Japanese prostitutes on their way to the front to comfort the troops praised for their selfless "life of service."[133]

Although Ishikawa had insisted at his trial that a paradise in occupied territories cannot be created overnight, that is now exactly what seems to be happening. Relations with the local people are cordial. Beginning to live happy lives in the wake of the Japanese advance, Chinese refugees exchange cheerful greetings with pacification unit soldiers. Under Japan's benevolent guidance, a new China is being built.

There is a considerable amount of angry criticism in *The Wuhan Campaign*, but it tends to be directed against safe targets. Foreigners—especially British, French, and North Americans—are denounced for nibbling away at Chinese territory, aiding Japan's enemies, and treating Japan as an international outcast. Chiang Kai-shek is blamed for making his compatriots suffer by prolonging the war. Japanese merchants flocking to China—some of whom even try to sell arms and salt to enemy troops—are bitterly attacked for selling the soldiers atrocious food at high prices:

> These merchants were ticks feeding off the Imperial Army.[134]

Japanese party politicians and diplomats come in for severe berating through the persona of an air corps commander who excoriates them for having in the past (i.e., the 1920s) kept the military budget low and contributed to the armed services' loss of prestige, and for having failed to stem anti-Japanese thought by demonstrating that Japan possesses the stature to be the leader of East Asia:

> It's thanks to the deep-rooted evil of party politics that we're
> forced to be fighting today's big war. . . . The military is
> wiping up the mess left behind by the politicians. What a
> nuisance. . . . With the diplomacy eternally dragging its
> heels, the military has to take the lead.[135]

The military itself remains beyond reproach and consistently victorious:

> For Japan possesses a wonderful army which unfailingly
> takes any objective it attacks.[136]

Its present campaign is clearly blessed, with the gods themselves seeming to favor the drive up the Yangtze. A rare easterly facilitating upriver sailing is surmised to be a divine wind; blown by it, even the reeds and grasses along the riverbanks are bending toward Wuhan.

A few somber notes merge with the triumphant motif as the army surges ahead. Coming upon starving refugees, soldiers feel afresh the misery of a defeated people. Yet neither this nor their knowledge that the Wuhan tri-cities and Canton are being daily bombed is allowed to detract from nationalistic glory:

> To Wuhan, to Wuhan! Along four routes the great army is closing in tide-like on Wuhan. The island empire Japan is thrusting forth into the depth of the continent.[137]

The exultant crescendo builds to a climax with the troops poised before the goal:

> To have assembled the greatest army in its three thousand years of history, and spread the flames of war across an unprecedentedly vast area penetrating so far into the interior of a continent, spoke of the bounding progress of the Oriental nation of Japan.[138]

The jubilation surrounding the fall of Wuhan is tempered only by the awareness of Japanese losses. Worried lest his compatriots quickly forget the soldiers' sacrifices, the author emphasizes the need to welcome the disabled veterans and postpone rejoicing until they have regained peace and happiness. As for China, the forecast is bright. Its cities have already begun to recover and will continue to do so.

> The Yangtze River will forever flow under the Rising Sun flag; the continent will be cultivated basking in the glory of the new Empire.[139]

With the publication of *The Wuhan Campaign,* Ishikawa Tatsuzō's formerly heterodox support for the war became firmly orthodox, and such it mostly remained. In July 1939 he published yet another war novel, and in 1940 he traveled throughout Japan lecturing with the Literary Home-Front Drive, a speechmaking troop organized by writer and publisher Kikuchi Kan to promote patriotism and support for the war.[140] In one of his regularly delivered talks, entitled "Atarashiki jiyū" (The new freedom), Ishikawa asserts that discomforts caused by material scarcity and censorship represent a loss of small, trivial freedoms. True freedom permits expression of individuality not through self-indulgence but through self-sacrifice. Ishikawa cites the example of his own patriotic uncle, who found his freedom through working as a volunteer spy during the 1894–1895 Sino-Japanese War until being captured and shot at the age of twenty-seven. In the current difficult situation, it is such people who are to be emulated:

> The present China Incident may also be viewed as a fight by Japan for its own freedom. Japan may be thought of as having flung away an unstable peace and resolved upon a great national sacrifice, demanding great sacrifices from its people in the fight for greater peace and freedom fifty or a hundred years hence.[141]

Selflessly following the national policy, Ishikawa declares in closing, will enable everyone to attain the new and greater freedom. The applause greeting his speeches only accentuated the fact that Ishikawa had long since learned to articulate officially approved ideas.

Ishikawa Tatsuzō's reversion to conformity, however, could not negate the fact that he had produced one powerful narrative for which he will continue to be justly remembered. The unexpurgated version of Soldiers Alive was published in 1945. It remains an invaluable testimony of some of the horror inflicted by the Japanese power structure upon China and a salutary reminder that imperialist enterprises are inherently inseparable from the commission of horrendous crimes against humanity.

Notes

1. Noriko Mizuta Lippit, "War Literature," in *Kodansha Encyclopedia of Japan* (Tokyo: Kodansha, 1983), 8:225.
2. For a comprehensive account of this process, see Donald Keene, "The Sino-Japanese War of 1894–95 and Japanese Culture," in *Appreciations of Japanese Culture* (Tokyo: Kodansha International, 1981).
3. Mikiso Hane, *Modern Japan: A Historical Survey* (Boulder: Westview, 1992), 160.
4. Keene, "Sino-Japanese War and Culture," 265–270, 282–289.
5. Hane, *Modern Japan,* 160.
6. Keene, "Sino-Japanese War and Culture," 263.
7. Hane, *Modern Japan,* 160.
8. Keene, "Sino-Japanese War and Culture," 264.
9. Ibid., 289.
10. Ibid., 264; Lippit, "War Literature," 225.
11. Keene, "Sino-Japanese War and Culture," 264.
12. Ibid., 264–265; also, Donald Keene, *Dawn to the West,* vol. 2, *Poetry, Drama, Criticism* (New York: Holt, Rinehart and Winston, 1984), 101.
13. Donald Keene, "The Sino-Japanese War of 1894–95 and its Cultural Effects in Japan," in Donald H. Shively, ed., *Tradition and Modernization in Japanese Culture* (Princeton: Princeton University Press, 1971), 129.
14. Keene, "Sino-Japanese War and Culture," 289.
15. Richard H. Mitchell, *Censorship in Imperial Japan* (Princeton: Princeton University Press, 1983), 124.
16. Keene, "Sino-Japanese War and Culture," 289.
17. Janet E. Hunter, *Concise Dictionary of Modern Japanese History* (Berkeley: University of California Press, 1984), 206–207; Martin C. Collcutt, "China and Japan," in *Kodansha Encyclopedia of Japan,* vol. 1, 286.
18. Collcutt, "China and Japan," 286.
19. Janet E. Hunter, *The Emergence of Modern Japan* (London: Longman, 1991), 271.
20. Ibid., 45.
21. Keene, "Sino-Japanese War and Culture," 280–281.
22. Ibid., 280.
23. Ibid., 273.
24. Ibid., 293.
25. Ibid., 274.

26. Ibid., 294–295.

27. Marius B. Jansen, *Japan and Its World: Two Centuries of Change* (Princeton: Princeton University Press, 1980), 72.

28. Yasuda Takeshi and Ariyama Daigo, eds., *Kindai sensō bungaku* (Tokyo: Kokusho Kankōkai, 1981), 329–353.

29. John W. Dower, *War without Mercy: Race and Power in the Pacific War* (New York: Pantheon, 1986), 285–286.

30. As Ienaga Saburō has observed, ordinary Japanese citizens of the time "were made to believe that Japan was a superior nation whose mission was to lead the world." Haruko Taya Cook and Theodore F. Cook, *Japan at War: An Oral History* (New York: New Press, 1992), 442. The Chinese, by contrast, were regularly presented "as an obtuse people because they failed to recognize that their own interests coincided exactly with those of Japan." Harry Wray, "China in Japanese Textbooks," in Alvin D. Coox and Hilary Conroy, eds., *China and Japan: Search for Balance Since World War I* (Santa Barbara: Clio Books, 1978), 128.

31. Keene, "The Sino-Japanese War and Culture," 295.

32. Shuichi Kato, *A History of Japanese Literature* (Tokyo: Kodansha International, 1983), 3:170.

33. Peter Duus, "Japan's Informal Empire in China, 1895–1937," in Peter Duus, Ramon H. Myers, and Mark R. Peattie, eds., *The Japanese Informal Empire in China, 1895–1937* (Princeton: Princeton University Press, 1989), xi–xxix.

34. This is true for China as a whole, but not for some of its parts. Taiwan, for example, was directly taken over by the Japanese, as was Hong Kong by the British.

35. Ikuhiko Hata, "Continental Expansion, 1905–1941," in Peter Duus, ed., *The Cambridge History of Japan*, vol. 6, *The Twentieth Century* (Cambridge: Cambridge University Press, 1988), 283; Gabriel Kolko, *Main Currents in Modern American History* (New York: Pantheon, 1984), 215.

36. Noam Chomsky, *American Power and the New Mandarins* (New York: Pantheon, 1967), 174–175.

37. Duus, "Japan's Informal Empire," xxix.

38. Hata, "Continental Expansion," 298–299.

39. Chomsky, *American Power,* 205.

40. Hata, "Continental Expansion," 307.

41. Conversations with Japanese eyewitnesses, including Professor Chiba Sen'ichi (formerly of Obihiro National University, currently at Hokkai

Gakuen University). For a revealing account of Japan's wartime atmosphere, see Cook and Cook, *Japan at War.*

42. Conversations with witnesses; also Dower, *War without Mercy,* 230; Cook and Cook, *Japan at War,* 169. The two slogans—and there were many others—are, respectively, *Zeitaku wa teki da* and *Hoshigarimasen katsu made wa.*

43. Yonezo Hirayama, *Japan Forges Ahead* (New York: Japan Institute, 1940), 26.

44. On elite pluralism, see George O. Totten III, "Japan's Political Parties in Democracy, Fascism and War," in Harry Wray and Hilary Conroy, eds., *Japan Examined* (Honolulu: University of Hawai'i Press, 1983), 258; also, Gordon M. Berger, "Politics and Mobilization in Japan, 1931–1945," in Duus, ed., *Cambridge History of Japan,* 6:97, 104–105, 133, 148, 152. For some of the rationales put forward regarding the war, see Hugh Borton, *Japan since 1931* (New York: Institute of Pacific Relations, 1940), 116–117.

45. Kato, *History of Japanese Literature,* 3:230–232; Hane, *Modern Japan,* 217–218; Mitchell, *Censorship in Imperial Japan,* 254–336.

46. Tsurumi Shunsuke, *Senjiki Nihon no seishinshi, 1931–1945* (Tokyo: Iwanami Shoten, 1982); Richard H. Mitchell, *Thought Control in Prewar Japan* (Ithaca: Cornell University Press, 1976).

47. W. G. Beasley, *The Rise of Modern Japan* (New York: St. Martin's Press, 1990), 185; W. G. Beasley, *The Modern History of Japan* (Tokyo: Tuttle, 1982), 254–255.

48. Totten, "Japan's Political Parties," 264. Anyone inclined to criticize the political status quo or its policies risked being stigmatized as "un-Japanese" *(hikokumin)*—a technique effectively contributing toward silencing opposition. See Junichiro Kisaka, "Detour through a Dark Valley," in Wray and Conroy, eds., *Japan Examined,* 247.

49. For vigorously presented arguments of this sort, see among others The Foreign Affairs Association of Japan, *The Sino-Japanese Conflict: A Short Survey* (Tokyo: Kenkyusha, 1937) and Kiyoshi Karl Kawakami, *Japan in China: Her Motives and Aims* (London: John Murray, 1938).

50. Tatsuo Kawai, *The Goal of Japanese Expansion,* (1938; reprint, Westport: Greenwood Press, 1973), 66–67; Hirayama, *Japan Forges Ahead,* 7.

51. Kawai, *Goal of Japanese Expansion,* 93.

52. Ibid., 67.

53. Dower, *War without Mercy,* 256, 356n. 37.

54. Kawai, *Goal of Japanese Expansion,* 114.

55. Hirayama, *Japan Forges Ahead*, 24–26.
56. Ryusaku Tsunoda, Wm. Theodore de Bary, and Donald Keene, eds., *Sources of Japanese Tradition* (New York: Columbia University Press, 1964), 2:283.
57. Dower, *War without Mercy*, 205, 210–213, 279–280.
58. On the cooperation of Japanese religious institutions with government policy, see H. Byron Earhart, *Japanese Religion: Unity and Diversity* (Belmont, Ca: Wadsworth, 1982), 158. This cooperative attitude manifests itself in literary texts, too. Belligerent Buddhist priests in uniform appear in the wartime writings of Niwa Fumio, Hino Ashihei, and Ishikawa Tatsuzō, among others. Ishikawa's priest in *Soldiers Alive* hates the Chinese so much he bashes out their brains with a shovel. It deserves to be noted that there was at least one religious group who refused to support the war and preferred imprisonment to conscription: the Jehovah's Witnesses.
59. Joseph M. Kitagawa, *Religion in Japanese History* (New York: Columbia University Press, 1966), 259. Ironically, the heart of Confucius' teaching is reciprocity: do not impose on others what you yourself do not desire.
60. Dower, *War without Mercy*, 281.
61. Kawai, *Goal of Japanese Expansion*, 61, 425.
62. Alfred W. McCoy, *The Politics of Heroin* (New York: Lawrence Hill Books, 1991), 266–268.
63. Yanaihara Tadao pointed out in 1941 that the rough and exploitative rule of Japan's existing colonies "contradicted the declarations of racial harmony toward Manchuria and China." Saburo Ienaga, *The Pacific War: 1931–1945* (New York: Pantheon, 1978), 155–156.
64. Tetsuo Najita and H. D. Harootunian, "Japanese Revolt Against the West: Political and Cultural Criticism in the Twentieth Century," in Duus, ed., *The Cambridge History of Japan*, 6:818; Norma Field, "Beyond Pearl Harbor," in *The Nation*, 23 December 1991.
65. Ienaga, *Pacific War*, 120–121, 209–210.
66. Among the films which directly or indirectly endorsed the war were Tasaka Tomotaka's *Five Scouts* (*Gonin no sekkōhei*, 1938), *Earth and Soldiers* (*Tsuchi to heitai*, 1939), and *Airplane Drone* (*Bakuon*, 1939); Yoshimura Kōzaburō's *The Story of Tank Commander Nishizumi* (*Nishizumi senshachōden*, 1940); and Ozu Yasujirō's *The Brothers and Sisters of the Toda Family* (*Todake no kyōdai*, 1941). For a collection of contemporary war songs, some of them winners of contests sponsored by the government and by newspaper companies, see Nakada Masayoshi, ed., *Kōgun shū* (Osaka: Bunkadō, 1939).

67. Tsuzuki Hisayoshi, "Senjika no bungaku," in Ōkubo Norio et al., eds., *Gendai Nihon bungakushi* (Tokyo: Kasama Shoin, 1988), 305.
68. Najita and Harootunian, *Japanese Revolt*, 755–758; Kato, 237.
69. Donald Keene, *Dawn to the West: Fiction*, 846–898; George T. Shea, *Leftwing Literature in Japan* (Tokyo: Hōsei University Press, 1964), 356–357. Some *tenkō* works, notably those of Nakano Shigeharu, are far more discerning and noncompliant than most.
70. Yoshio Iwamoto, "The Relationship Between Literature and Politics in Japan, 1931–1945," (Ph.D. diss., University of Michigan, 1964), 270–271; Keene, *Dawn to the West: Fiction*, 927.
71. The following writers were sent toward Wuhan in September 1938 as members of the Pen Corps:

Asano Akira	Nakatani Takao
Fukada Kyūya	Niwa Fumio
Hamamoto Hiroshi	Ozaki Shirō
Hayashi Fumiko	Satō Haruo
Kataoka Teppei	Satō Sonosuke
Kawaguchi Matsutarō	Shirai Kyōji
Kikuchi Kan	Sugiyama Heisuke
Kishida Kunio	Takii Kōsaku
Kitamura Komatsu	Tomizawa Uio
Kojima Masajirō	Yoshikawa Eiji
Kume Masao	Yoshiya Nobuko

Sent toward Canton in November 1938 were:

Haji Seiji	Koyama Kanji
Hasegawa Shin	Minato Kunizō
Hōjō Hideji	Nakamura Murao
Kikuta Kazuo	Sekiguchi Jirō
Koga Saburō	

See Miyoshi Yukio, ed., *Nihon bungaku zenshi* (Tokyo: Gakutosha, 1978), 6:259.
72. The beauty and sadness of war are vividly expressed in the works of Ozaki Shirō, Hino Ashihei, Hayashi Fumiko, and others. These and other pro-war writers are discussed in Iwamoto, "Relationship between Literature and Politics," 267–305; Takasaki Ryūji, *Sensō to sensō bungaku to* (Tokyo: Nihon Tosho Sentā, 1986), 123–139; Yasuda Takeshi, *Sensō bungakuron* (Tokyo: Daisan Bunmeisha, 1977).

73. This applies to the wartime writings of such authors as Hino Ashihei, Hayashi Fumiko, Shimaki Kensaku, Yoshiya Nobuko, and Ozaki Shirō. The predilection for traditional literary forms was part of the larger cultural trend of the 1930s, exemplified by the nativist interests of a writer like Hori Tatsuo, for one. See Keene, *Dawn to the West: Fiction,* 705–707.

74. Iwamoto, "Relationship between Literature and Politics," 273; Mitchell, *Censorship in Imperial Japan,* 305–307.

75. Kato, *History of Japanese Literature,* 3:197; Ienaga, *Pacific War,* 204–208.

76. On Shiga's neglect of social issues and disdain for things "unpleasant" *(fukai),* see Keene, *Dawn to the West: Fiction,* 445, 469.

77. In 1934 Tanizaki wrote, "I am basically uninterested in politics, so I have concerned myself exclusively with the ways people live, eat and dress, the standards of feminine beauty, and the progress of recreational facilities." See Keene, *Appreciations of Japanese Culture,* 184–185.

78. *Chūō kōron* (January 1939): 334. The essay's title is "Genji monogatari jo."

79. Keene, *Dawn to the West: Fiction,* 803, 819; Kon Hidemi, ed., *Bungei Jūgo Undō kōen shū* (Tokyo: Bungeika Kyōkai, 1941), 146. Kawabata's lecture, delivered under the auspices of the Literary Home-Front Drive, was entitled "Writing of the Incident" *(Jihen tsuzurikata).*

80. Kawabata Yasunari, *Kawabata Yasunari zenshū* (Tokyo: Shinchōsha, 1982), 27:300.

81. Dazai Osamu, "Mangan," in *Dazai Osamu zenshū* (Tokyo: Chikuma Shobō, 1975), 2:95–97.

82. Nakagawa Yoichi, *Nakagawa's Ten no Yūgao,* trans. Jeremy Ingalls (Boston: Twayne, 1975), 129.

83. Yoshikawa Eiji, *Musashi,* trans. Charles S. Terry (New York: Harper & Row/Kodansha International, 1981), 970.

84. Nihon Koten Bungaku Taikei, *Bashō bunshū* (Tokyo: Iwanami Shoten, 1985), 52.

85. Hiroaki Sato and Burton Watson, trans. and eds., *From the Country of Eight Islands* (New York: Columbia University Press, 1986), 44–45.

86. Donald Keene, trans., *Essays in Idleness: Tsurezuregusa of Kenkō* (Tokyo: Tuttle, 1981), 128–129.

87. Kato, *History of Japanese Literature,* 3:193. Takuboku Ishikawa, *Romaji Diary and Sad Toys,* trans. Sanford Goldstein and Seishi Shinoda (Tokyo: Tuttle, 1985), 69–70.

88. John H. Boyle, "Sino-Japanese War of 1937–1945," in *Kodansha Encyclopedia of Japan* (Tokyo: Kodansha, 1983), 7:199. Many estimates of the total number of Chinese people killed run much higher. At the top end of the spectrum is the Beijing government's claim of up to thirty million Chinese deaths. Mark Selden of Cornell University estimates that between fifteen million and thirty million people died, the vast majority of them civilians. James Hsiung maintains that some four million Chinese soldiers and eighteen million Chinese civilians were killed in the war. See James C. Hsiung and Steven I. Levine, eds., *China's Bitter Victory: The War with Japan, 1937–1945* (Armonk, NY: M. E. Sharpe, 1992), 295–296. See also a thought-provoking analysis by Mark Selden entitled "Terrorism before and after 9–11," in Bombay's *Economic and Political Weekly,* 31 August 2002; reprint, ZNet (zmag.org).

89. Hayashi Fumiko, *Sensen* (Tokyo: Asahi Shimbunsha, 1938), 130.

90. Hino Ashihei, "Mugi to heitai" (1938; reprint, Hirano Ken et al., eds., *Sensō bungaku zenshū,* Tokyo: Mainichi Shimbunsha, 1972), 2:150; Satomura Kinzō, *Daini no jinsei* (Tokyo: Kawade Shobō, 1940), 1:180; Ishikawa Tatsuzō, *Ikite iru heitai* (1938; reprint, Tokyo: Kawade Shobō, 1945), 60.

91. Kobayashi Hideo, "Sensō ni tsuite," *Kaizō* (November 1937): 222.

92. Ishikawa Tatsuzō, *Ikite iru heitai,* 67.

93. Hayashi, *Sensen,* 157.

94. Ozaki Shirō, "Hifū senri," *Chūō kōron* (October 1937): 436.

95. Hino Ashihei, *Hana to heitai* (Tokyo: Kaizōsha, 1939), 268.

96. Kobayashi Hideo, "Kōshū" 1938; reprint, in *Gendai bungaku taikei 42 Kobayashi Hideo shū* (Tokyo: Chikuma Shobō, 1965), 435.

97. Saitō Mokichi, in Hirano et al., eds., *Sensō bungaku zenshū,* 7:185.

98. Hino Ashihei, *Kanton shingunshō* (Tokyo: Shinchōsha, 1939), 166.

99. Kobayashi Hideo, "Kōshū yori Nankin" (1938; reprint, in *Gendai bungaku taikei 42 Kobayashi Hideo shū*), 452. Within three consecutive months of 1938 (May, June, and July) Kobayashi Hideo published no fewer than six essays based on his travels through war-torn China. One critic calls them Kobayashi's "sightseeing reports" *(kenbutsuki).* See Tsuzuki Hisayoshi, *Senjika no bungaku* (Osaka: Izumi Sensho, 1985), 20.

100. Kaneko Mitsuharu, "Tōdai," *Chūō kōron,* December 1935, 360–361.

101. Odagiri Hideo, *Watakushi no mita Shōwa no shisō to bungaku no gojū nen* (Tokyo: Shueisha, 1988), 1:132.

102. Ishikawa Jun, "Marusu no uta" (1938; reprint, in Ishikawa Jun, *Fugen, Yakeato no Iesu,* Tokyo: Horupu, 1985), 202.

103. Ibid., 235. For a complete translation of "The Song of Mars," see Zeljko Cipris, "Radiant Carnage: Japanese Writers on the War against China" (Ph.D. diss., Columbia University, 1994), 193–223. For a translation of the same story by William J. Tyler, see "Mars' Song" in Ishikawa Jun, *The Legend of Gold and Other Stories* (Honolulu: University of Hawai'i Press, 1998), 3–37.

104. Oguma Hideo, "Pulambago chūtai," (1934; reprint, in *Oguma Hideo zenshishū,* Tokyo: Shichōsha, 1971), 117–126; Kuroshima Denji, *Busō seru shigai* (1930; reprint, in *Kuroshima Denji zenshū,* vol. 3, Tokyo: Chikuma Shobō, 1970).

105. For discussions of literary resistance to the war, see for example Odagiri Hideo, *Watakushi no mita,* 1:122, 132–136; Hirano Ken, *Shōwa bungakushi* (Tokyo: Chikuma Shobō, 1963), 236; Kobayashi Shigeo, *Puroretaria bungaku no sakkatachi* (Tokyo: Shin Nihon Shuppansha, 1988), 87, 98–100. Also of interest may be a forthcoming collection of translations by the present writer entitled *A Flock of Swirling Crows: Proletarian Writings of Kuroshima Denji.*

106. Kubota Masafumi, "Ishikawa Tatsuzō nenpu," in *Nihon kindai bungaku zenshū* (Tokyo: Kōdansha, 1961), 86:473.

107. Hamano Kenzaburō, *Hyōden Ishikawa Tatsuzō no sekai* (Tokyo: Bungei Shunjū, 1976), 116.

108. Ishikawa Tatsuzō, "Ano toki no ikisatsu," in *Hon to techō,* 46 (August 1965), 577.

109. Kajimoto Masato, *The Nanking Atrocities,* Online Documentary, 2000.

110. Hamano, *Hyōden Ishikawa,* 117. Empire Day commemorates the founding of Japan's imperial line, which—according to myth—took place in 660 B.C.

111. Professor Chiba Sen'ichi, lecture of 28 December 1987.

112. Ishikawa Tatsuzō, *Ikite iru heitai* (Tokyo: Kawade Shobō, 1945), 60–61.

113. Ibid., 67.

114. Ibid., 83.

115. Ibid., 100.

116. Shimada Akio, "Ishikawa Tatsuzō, 'Ikite iru heitai,'" in *Kaishaku to kanshō,* August 1973, 105. See also Takasaki Ryūji, *Sensō to sensō bungaku to,* 78, 81. Takasaki strongly argues that no soldier is likely to have told Ishikawa about the Nanking massacre, and that Ishikawa

would not have written the kind of work he wrote had he known of the massacre. The strictness with which *Soldiers Alive* was suppressed, maintains Takasaki, was due to its timing.

117. Ishikawa, *Ikite iru heitai,* 117.
118. Ibid., 60.
119. Ibid., 55–56.
120. Ibid., 131.
121. Ibid., 151.
122. Ishikawa, "Ano toki no ikisatsu," 578.
123. Mitchell, *Censorship in Imperial Japan,* 141. For a detailed examination of multiple layers of censorship affecting Ishikawa's narrative, see Haruko Taya Cook, "The Many Lives of *Living Soldiers:* Ishikawa Tatsuzō and Japan's War in Asia," in Marlene J. Mayo, J. Thomas Rimer, H. Eleanor Kerkham, eds., *War, Occupation, and Creativity: Japan and East Asia 1920–1960* (Honolulu: University of Hawai'i Press, 2001), 149–175.
124. Hamano, Hyōden Ishikawa, 115.
125. Ibid., 122.
126. Odagiri Hideo, *Watakushi no mita,* 1:148.
127. Kubota, "Ishikawa Tatsuzō," 474.
128. *Chūō kōron* (January 1939): 124.
129. Ibid., 145.
130. Ibid., 66.
131. Ibid., 51.
132. Ibid., 52.
133. Ibid., 134. Japanese prostitutes served mostly officers. Ordinary soldiers were served largely by local women driven to prostitution by force, deception, or poverty.
134. Ibid., 84.
135. Ibid., 114–115.
136. Ibid., 146.
137. Ibid., 136.
138. Ibid., 146.
139. Ibid., 148.
140. As of 1940, the following fifty-four writers were active in the Literary Home-Front Drive (Bungei Jūgo Undō):

Abe Tomoji	Kume Masao
Fujimori Seikichi	Muramatsu Shōfū
Funahashi Seiichi	Nakamura Murao

Hamamoto Hiroshi
Hasegawa Shigure
Hasegawa Shin
Hayashi Fumiko
Hayashi Fusao
Hibino Shirō
Hino Ashihei
Hirotsu Kazuo
Ishikawa Tatsuzō
Joshi Kotsurugi
Kataoka Teppei
Katō Takeo
Kawabata Yasunari
Kawaguchi Matsutarō
Kawakami Tetsutarō
Kigi Takatarō
Kikuchi Kan
Kimura Tsuyoshi
Kishida Kunio
Kitamura Komatsu
Kobayashi Hideo
Koga Saburō
Kojima Masajirō
Kon Hidemi

Nakano Minoru
Nakayama Yoshihide
Niwa Fumio
Okada Saburō
Osaragi Jirō
Ozaki Shirō
Sasaki Kuni
Satomi Ton
Serizawa Kōjirō
Shikiba Ryūzaburō
Shimaki Kensaku
Shimomura Kainan
Shimozawa Kan
Shirai Kyōji
Takada Tamotsu
Takami Jun
Tatsuno Kyūshi
Tokugawa Musei
Tomizawa Uio
Toyoshima Yoshio
Ueda Hiroshi
Yokomitsu Riichi
Yoshikawa Eiji
Yoshiya Nobuko

The above roster is found in Kon, ed., *Bungei Jūgo*, 145–146. The book offers a selection of inspirational speeches by the most prominent of the participating writers. Hayashi Fumiko, for instance, urges Japanese women to help their warring nation by being frugal, working beautifully and spiritedly, marrying, and raising happy children. See her *Jūgo fujin no mondai* (The issue of home-front women), in Ibid., 110–115.

141. Ibid., 80.

soldiers alive

1

The main force of the Takashima Division disembarked at Ta-ku directly after the fall of Peking, just when the late summer heat struck the continent. The sweating, dust-covered soldiers marched, accompanied by countless swarms of circling flies.

For two months the troops advanced southward, pursuing the enemy along the banks of Tzu-ya River. By the time they heard that Shih-chia-chuang had fallen to their comrades, it was already deep autumn and frost lay white on the sentries' shoulders.

Takashima Division's main force marshaled the rest of its units in the village of Ning-hsin and rested for ten days while awaiting its next orders. During that time, each company conducted a memorial service for its war dead. Two company commanders had been killed in the fighting, and the infantry had lost one-tenth of its numerical strength, but there was no talk of coming replacement units.

FLAMES SUDDENLY shot up just to the rear of the private house assigned to the regimental headquarters. Reflections of the thick smoke raced furiously across windows shining in the evening sun.

The first to run up, Corporal Kasahara and two of his men seized a Chinese loitering at the scene—a shabbily dressed youth of twenty-two or so, his neck, hands, and feet streaked with dirt.

"*Nii!*" bellowed Corporal Kasahara, addressing him brusquely as "you." But he did not know enough Chinese to be able to interrogate him. With a vigorous sniff of his runny nose, he told a subordinate, "Go call the headquarters interpreter."

As the soldier ran off, Kasahara sat on a cauldron that had been thrown out into the street and turned his attention to the fire. Flames snaked along the walls to the second-story ceiling and reached the ridge of the roof. Gaps between the tiles began to glow white with heat; blazing whirlpools streamed within the windows.

"Oh, how it burns! This is hot!" Holding out his arms as if over a charcoal brazier, the other soldier scrutinized the face of the Chinese. "By the look of that mug, I'd say he did it."

Solitary, like a dead tree, the youth stood beside the two men, his face expressionless, thin, vaguely stupid. Seven or eight more soldiers rushed up and surrounded him. Hands in pockets, legs gaitered, interpreter Nakahashi arrived, a holstered pistol slung over his rocking shoulders.

"Did this one do it?"

"Looks that way. Just ask him a few questions. Trying to torch the headquarters, the son of a bitch."

The interpreter spat out a match he had been chewing and directed two or three sharp words at the youth, but the latter only glanced at him and remained silent. Shoving his shoulder, the interpreter asked again. In a quiet voice, the youth briefly replied. The interpreter suddenly struck him across the face. The youth staggered. In the midst of the raging flames a mass of tiles broke away from the ridge and crashed to the ground.

"What did he say?" asked the watching soldiers.

"Bastard says setting fire to his own house is his own business!"

Corporal Kasahara, who had been sitting on the cauldron and warming himself by the fire, jumped to his feet, grabbed the youth by the arm, and started off.

"This way. On the double."

The youth obediently began to walk, and the two soldiers followed. After some ten paces, Kasahara turned and threw interpreter Nakahashi a meaningful grin.

At the village outskirts a hundred yards off, a willow-lined creek with rice fields stretching away from both banks formed a silent evening landscape into which the four emerged. The sun had set, dyeing the sky red. Red clouds reflected mutely in the waters of the stream. The autumn was tranquil, unruffled by wind. Farmhouses stood here and there but lacked any sign of human life. After jumping over several dead Chinese soldiers, the men stood at the creek's edge. The last of the wild chrysanthemums blossomed in clusters by the water's surface; new circular pools had appeared throughout the fields in the wake of an artillery attack.

Kasahara turned around. The youth had bowed his head and was gazing at the creek's barely moving water. The rounded rump of a well-fed horse protruded above the surface. Floating weeds clung to the Chinese saddle; the horse's head was invisible.

"Look away!" barked Kasahara and waited. "Doesn't understand, does he. The man's a nuisance."

Out of necessity he stepped behind the youth and drew the Japanese sword, rasping, from the scabbard. Catching sight of it, the scrawny, crowlike youth dropped to his knees in the mud, began to shout a stream of incomprehensible words, raised his clasped hands, and pleaded. But Kasahara was used to such pleas. Even so, he did not enjoy them.

"*Ei!*"

The youth's screams instantly ceased, and the fields reverted to the hushed silence of a twilight landscape. The head did not fall, but the cut was sufficiently deep. His body still upright, a geyser of blood overflowed the shoulders. The body tilted to the right, toppled into the wild chrysanthemums on the bank, and rolled over once. There was a dull splash as the torso plunged in alongside the horse's rump. The muddy soles of his bare feet turned up toward the sky.

The three wordlessly retraced their steps. At several places in the village, Rising Sun flags were still visible in the failing light. The smoke from the burning house began to mirror the redness of the flames. It was just about dinnertime.

By NIGHTFALL the fire subsided of its own accord. In the rear garden of the regimental headquarters, four or five soldiers surrounding the bonfire were, as always, roasting sweet potatoes. Smashed up chairs blazed, twisting in the bonfire. Army priest Katayama Genchō, choking on the dense smoke, rolled a potato over with the tip of his shoe and muttered hoarsely, "It seems the front is shifting."

"Where to, I wonder." With soiled thick fingers, Corporal Kasahara extracted and lit a rationed Golden Bat.

"Back to Tientsin, it seems. His Excellency the Division Commander hinted as much."

"You spoke with the division commander?"

"Yes, about the bones. If the unit were to stay here for a while, I had planned to accompany the bones as far as Tientsin or Dairen, but His Excellency told me not to bother. Most likely we are all going to Tientsin anyway, he says."

"Tientsin!" cried out Corporal Kasahara, slapping his knees. "All right! If it's Tientsin, we'll just live it up to the hilt! Hey, hey!"

A soldier solemnly chimed in: "Call the geishas, buy the whores, swill the *sake*."

"Ah, hahaha!" guffawed Kasahara. Tapped on the shoulder, he turned to see interpreter Nakahashi come to warm himself by the bonfire.

"Did you do in that *nii?*"

"That I did, the son of a bitch," Kasahara replied, as though still indignant over the arson. But in fact he had forgotten all about it until asked. It was not a rare incident for him. "There's a dead horse in the creek. Just about now he's probably getting a hug from the horse."

A soldier sprang to his feet and saluted, alerting everyone to the fact that the regimental commander, Colonel Nishizawa, was strolling toward the bonfire, a cigarette in his mouth. The colonel returned everyone's salute, stretched his arms toward the fire, and asked about the delicious aroma. Drawing up a chair, the men readily replied that they were roasting potatoes.

"Would you treat me to one?"

The soldiers laughed happily. Regimental Commander Nishizawa was a superior they worshipped boundlessly. Lean and tall, he appeared sickly, but bore himself with such dignity that his very skin seemed to radiate valor. Clothing and hands both soiled with mud and grime, he was as filthy as the soldiers. He sat in the chair and began to stroke his unkempt beard.

"You've grown quite a splendid beard, Unit Commander, sir," said the interpreter.

"Not as splendid as the army priest."

Once more the soldiers laughed with delight. They felt immensely grateful that he had chosen to warm himself by the fire with them. Peering into the flames, Corporal Kasahara used a piece of wood to retrieve a potato roasted to just the right degree, then with the help of a piece of paper he had drawn from his pocket, he gingerly picked it up. But he hesitated to present it to the commander.

"Aren't you going to offer it to him?" asked the army priest hoarsely. The commander silently stretched out his arm. Bending forward, Kasahara reverently held out the potato. All intently watched the commander prepare to eat it.

"There's been talk the unit is moving out. Where do you fellows think we're going?"

"To Tientsin, it seems," Katayama Genchō replied.

"Why do you think so?"

"His Excellency the Division Commander seemed to be saying so."

Colonel Nishizawa peeled the potato and tossed a steaming fragment into his mouth. The soldiers gulped.

"Where are we actually going, sir?" asked interpreter Nakahashi.

"I don't know myself. In any case, the front is changing; that much is certain."

"I see."

"Have you gotten your field rations?"

"We have, sir."

As the conversation paused, everyone suddenly thought of the fighting they had been through since leaving Tientsin. They tried to foresee the battles that lay ahead. With the commander so close they grew exhilarated and bold; fighting a war appeared a surprisingly peaceful, effortless undertaking.

A soldier on duty walked up, brought his heels together with a click, and saluted.

"The adjutant asks that you come, sir. A message has arrived from the headquarters."

"Right." Colonel Nishizawa rose from his chair. All the soldiers around the bonfire stood to attention and saluted.

When he had gone, they relaxed, started to chat, and fought to be the first to get the potatoes out of the fire.

Corporal Kasahara took off his right shoe and sock. His large, splay foot, black with encrusted dirt, emitted vapor. His leg was surprisingly white and tender.

"And so within a day or two we finally leave."

He gazed at the sole of his foot by the light of the bonfire. The drone of an airplane became audible. It was impossible to know whether the plane was hostile or friendly. Even so, no one took any notice of it. They were used to such uncertainties and not inclined to worry about them.

His right leg resting on his left thigh, Kasahara again drew the sword, rasping, out of the sheath.

"What are you doing?"

"Well, you see, the skin of this valuable limb that's been made to walk too much gets hard and aches, so the foot can foot it no more. Hurts worse than if a bullet hit it."

He bent his face over the sole and, sniffling, commenced to pare the hardened skin with the sword. The blade was chipped in several places; it had not been sufficiently wiped and showed a reddish tinge. Fat stains had made it lose its luster and acquire the color of lead.

NEXT MORNING at early dawn the order to depart was handed down. The march destination was Shih-chia-chuang, nearly forty miles away. Ruts left by gun carriages and supply vehicles had so ravaged the road that the line of march was frequently thrown into disarray. Transport units and the Third Infantry Battalion of the Nishizawa Regiment remained behind to set out on the following day. By that time a unit was expected to arrive in Ning-hsin to take up garrison duty.

The marching troops consumed their noon and evening meals in the space of a twenty-minute rest. Freezing water from their canteens pierced the men's insides as they drank.

The otherwise uninterrupted march brought them to Shih-chia-chuang late in the night, with the moon risen high. The units headed straight for the train station, entered its grounds—pitch-black, for all the lights had been extinguished—and were billeted for the night in the waiting freight cars. The soldiers took empty oil cans aboard and kindled fires in them to keep warm. Then they curled up to sleep on the straw-littered floor where horses appeared to have lain just a few days earlier. Utterly exhausted, each man drew up his gaitered legs, rested his head on the thigh of a comrade, and slept, immobile as a corpse. At intervals the door was rudely shoved open and a voice shouted in.

"Is First Class Private Noda here? First Class Private Noda!"

The soldier in question groaned a response, his voice unbearably weary. But when the man outside shouted, "Night watch!" for the second time, the replying voice suddenly turned distinct as the soldier hurriedly rose. Even in his sleep he understood the importance of night watch. It was a pitiful spectacle of a man submitting to duty with the virtual precision of a machine. Cradling a rifle in his arms, he crept out from among his sleeping comrades, jumped down onto the darkened rails, drew his bayonet, and fixed it to the rifle with a metallic click. The frozen ground under his shoes was solid as a paved road. He turned up the collar of his coat and walked to the guard room. This was located in the ticket office, behind the sales window, where a dozen relief soldiers were warming themselves around a fire.

The next morning as the eastern sky began to brighten, the freight train, fully loaded with soldiers, started to move. Rising Sun flags fluttering here and there, Shih-chia-chuang was awakening at last from an uneasy slumber. Already dozens of army civilian employees in suits and overcoats, pacification unit armbands on their sleeves, bustled about its streets carrying out their postwar tasks: to build a cheerful North China, to make its inhabitants understand the justice of Japan's cause, to grant them a sanctuary for the pursuit of peaceful lives. The inhabitants, their soiled black clothing like crows' plumage, their bulging, cotton-padded sleeves all twisted, sported Rising Sun armbands and were sure to break into smiles and salute whenever they encountered soldiers. This was merely an expression of their wretched lot. A people accustomed to war's havoc, they had made it a habit since ancestral times to act subservient toward armies of occupation. Despite receiving their salutes, the soldiers did not trust them.

The suburbs of Shih-chia-chuang were littered with the rubble of devastated dwellings. The houses had collapsed into desiccated heaps of roof tiles and bricks; only the thick walls remained standing in rows amidst an eerie stillness. Alongside the railroad tracks, villagers worked under Japanese direction to dispose of the corpses of Chinese soldiers. They had dug a ditch and were burying them. Flung in by the dozen one atop another, gaping like fish, heads limply hanging, the soldiers were covered with earth as they lay. A tomb of the unknown warriors was being built in the middle of a millet field.

Loaded with bored soldiery, the freight train ran north along the Peking-Wuhan railway. It passed through Cheng-ting, Ting-chou, and Pao-ting before stopping for the night at Cho-chou station. This was so far to the rear that even the faces of the local garrison troops appeared tranquil. In a guardhouse some of them went so far as to share the *sake* from their canteens with the arrivals.

The following morning the train set out again, reaching Peking before noon. It merely passed through Peking, however, and started south. Destination Tientsin as expected, thought the soldiers.

A man in the corner of the swaying, dimly-lit carriage broke the silence. "Platoon Commander, sir, what are we going to do in Tientsin?" It was the brave First Class Private Hirao who, whenever drunk, sang "Manchurian Bandits" drumming on his thighs.

Second Lieutenant Kurata turned his mild, bespectacled gaze

toward him and softly smiled. He was clearly at a loss for an answer.

"If the front is changing, then we should be going northwest of Peking, toward Chang-chia-k'ou," grumbled Hirao. "Tientsin is not the front."

"Tientsin is garrison duty," said another soldier.

"I've no idea myself," Lieutenant Kurata replied quietly with a resigned smile and looked out through the carriage door left open a crack to let in light. Framed by the doorway, a plain of withered millet rushed past in an ever receding streak. Farmers were working the fields illumined by slanting rays of the sun. Here peace had already arrived.

That night they pulled into Tientsin. Soldiers worn out by two days and nights on the train sprang to life at last, stooped to pick up their knapsacks, rose hugging them, and jumped down onto the railway tracks. Just then the orderly from the battalion headquarters came running, shouting, "You're not getting off! Get back on! Get back on! Train leaves in a minute!"

In confusion the soldiers scrambled back up into the same freight cars, wondering aloud where in the world they were being taken. The long military train carrying the battalion to its unknown destination began to move once more. The compasses strapped to the men's wrists indicated east. They seemed to be heading for Ta-ku, where they had disembarked two months earlier. After that, perhaps, a triumphant return awaited them.

During the night, however, the train rushed through T'ang-ku and turned northeast.

The Soviet-Manchurian border! The chilling rumor flashed through the train. No doubt they would be fighting the Soviets. A new tension silenced them and put them on edge. Russia was the next enemy. They knew the fearsome strength of the Russian army and had often heard of the heavily armed pillboxes guarding the Soviet border. If such were their orders, they had to be obeyed, and they felt no hesitation whatsoever about carrying them out; but their thoughts suddenly turned homeward, and they recalled once more their native mountains and rivers. It was unlikely they would see them again. They bit their lips hard. Not surprisingly, many soldiers did not sleep that night.

Second Lieutenant Kurata sat cross-legged leaning against the iron door and took out a notebook from his inside breast pocket. Shaking with the train's motion, he began to write the day's diary. Since the start of the campaign, even during the fiercest fighting, he had not missed a single day's entry; he was a methodical man. The brief account jotted down, he next took from his knapsack a postcard printed red, signifying military mail.

"Are you well?" it began. "Your teacher, luckily, is also well and carrying out his military duty. Please grow up quickly and work for the sake of the country." It was that sort of a letter. In his hometown he had been an elementary school teacher. (What a peaceful life that had been!) If the unit were headed for the Soviet-Manchurian border, he wished to send a heartfelt letter of farewell to the children who had been his pupils. But the directions of all military movements were to be kept secret. Hesitant about the impact it might make on the children's minds, he wrote that he would probably be prevented from meeting them again.

The words affected him even before they could affect the children. Startled, he looked around the carriage. Even the awake soldiers were drowsily nodding. What terribly innocent, docile youths they were! He imagined now that he was surrounded by his pupils. Lance Corporal Mita was not among them, nor First Class Private Mizuno, nor First Class Private Taga. He shut his eyes and thought of the battle in the outskirts of Hsien-hsien: I survived! He could not help but be amazed: I am still alive! There was something disturbing, unsettling about it. Perhaps this irritation was a form of unease that would persist until he died. Suddenly he yearned for a furious fight. When next he found himself at the front, he would charge like mad, he thought, and felt his face flush, his heart pound violently.

Yet again they greeted the dawn from inside the freight train. First Class Private Hirao had slept curled up in the very corner and was bathing his face in the morning sun's rays shining in through the door. He rose, yawned hugely, and shouted, "Aah! I want to wash my face! How great I'd feel if I could only wash my face with cold water!"

The forty men in the carriage laughed, all sharing his wish. They could not recall having washed their faces in the past four or five days.

"I'd like to take a leisurely shit," said First Class Private Kondō, a university graduate. Ever since leaving Ning-hsin there had not even been time to go to the toilet. The freight train lacked such facilities and the station stops were too short, and so the soldiers' bowels suffered. But that afternoon the train arrived at Ch'in-huang-tao and remained a full two hours in the station. This was time enough for First Class Private Kondō to satisfy his need.

The troops received another three days' worth of field rations.

AND THEN the train went on, still running northeast. Chin-chou, Kou-pang-tzu, Hsin-min-tun. . . . By the time it reached Mukden, tedium and lack of exercise had made the soldiers profoundly depressed. They had lost their vigor, moved listlessly, and felt irritable.

Commanding officer Nishizawa rode with his adjutant in an armor-plated car at the front of the train. Even he got off at this station to move his arms and legs about and massage the joints stiffened by the long journey. The soldiers quickly sat down on the platform and crossed their legs. Standing produced an unbearable pain in the entire body.

After an hour's rest they boarded a different train. This was not a freight but a passenger train, equipped with toilets and washbasins. It left Mukden and proceeded south.

"Going home!" Within seconds the voice spread along the length of the train. "Hurray, we're going home!" So greatly did they long to return. The joy of the men who had not expected to see their flesh and blood again welled up irrepressibly.

They spent the night on the train before arriving at Dairen and being billeted in the homes of its citizens. Everyone assumed that just as soon as the rear guard joined them they would board the ships together and sail home in triumph. That night they strutted throughout Dairen, drank *sake,* sang war songs, and bought homecoming presents.

The following morning when they were all assembled for the company roll calls, the commanding officer made an announcement.

"We are not going home yet. Stop buying souvenirs."

They then marched to the coast on the city outskirts, where they boarded dozens of waiting boats and conducted repeated amphibious assault drills. For the first time, the soldiers realized they were bound for a new front.

Where that front was, no one knew—neither the company commanders nor the battalion commanders, not even the regimental commanders, and possibly not Division Commander Takashima himself. It was all a strictly guarded operational secret; even the letters the soldiers had mailed were detained at the post office and not forwarded until the right time had come.

Finally on the third day the Nishizawa Regiment embarked. The steamships, numbers painted on each side, flew flags atop the masts identifying them as troopships. Assigned to guard duty in the regimental commander's cabin, First Class Private Kondō noticed a securely sealed packet of documents. Written in red on the outside were the words "Seal to be broken three hours after leaving port." The packet contained classified military maps of the region where they were to go ashore. Minutely detailed charts of the Yangtze River valley from Shanghai to the environs of Nanking, they showed a web of interlacing tributaries and recorded such information as their width, depth, mud depth, fords, width of roads, and places that became mired after rain. This was the battlefield that awaited them.

Without a single siren blast, the three ships followed each other out of the Dairen harbor. The soldiers opened the porthole windows and wordlessly watched the city of Dairen with its outlying islands recede in the distance. They tossed into the waves the gifts they had bought, threw themselves onto the iron-frame bunks, and went mutely to sleep.

2

On the eleventh of November, having overrun Ta-ch'ang-chen and Su-chou to encircle Shanghai, the northern units joined up near Ssu-ching-hsien with the southern units, which had landed at Hang-chou Bay, crossed Huang-P'u River, and marched north. Shanghai was totally surrounded. It was at this juncture that the main force of the Takashima Division sailing out of Dairen entered the Yangtze River delta.

The ships steamed upriver, cleaving the turbid water. Soldiers were warned to stay in their berths; coming out onto the decks was dangerous. Standing on the deck, buffeted by the river wind, Commander Nishizawa and his adjutant closely watched the riverbanks through the binoculars. The land rose a mere two or three yards above the water surface and was flat as a board, so they could see nothing but a long horizontal line of grass and willows along the banks. Above this line dozens of airplanes flew furiously about. The mopping up of the enemy remnants in P'u-tung was on this day being carried out with the utmost ferocity. Black smoke rose to the sky from countless fires; at intervals the dull roar of big naval guns reverberated in the wind.

At length some twenty ships anchored upstream came into view. They were all Japanese troopships, flying the Rising Sun flags, numbers painted on the sides. The newly arrived ships merged with this flotilla and lowered their anchors. The men were now in the vicinity of the Wu-sung fort; what looked like gutted pillboxes were visible through binoculars. The sensation of having reached the front was powerful. Men's nerves, relaxed ever since sailing out of Dairen, grew tense once more.

A three days' supply of field rations was distributed. The ships remained at anchor for the night.

"Each of you'd better write a letter home. We'll have the captain collect them. It might be the last letter you write. The enemy this time are the crack troops of the Chinese army."

Second Lieutenant Kurata took off his jacket to get ready for bed. His voice was extremely gentle as he spoke to his men. A bold platoon leader who fought flushed with rage, muttering "Damn you!" over and over, he nevertheless addressed his own troops with the calm affection of an elementary school teacher, an affection that seemed uppermost in the heart of the thirty-one-year-old unmarried officer.

First Class Private Hirao lay on a tiered, iron-frame bunk with his head pillowed on his arm. Suddenly he began to sing in a quiet voice.

"We warriors face
Death with open eyes.
Crickets in the grass,
Hush your trilling cries."

In the stillness of the berth, interrupted only by the sound of the river waves, the voice rose and fell with a strange emotional power. When the song had ended, he turned his face away and cried. His was not the sadness of a man going into battle or fearing violent death. It was, rather, the unendurable sadness brought on by the spectacle of 180 men around him silently waiting to be killed in tomorrow's battles. This spiritual oneness, which kept even a single soldier from muttering against the imminent doom, struck him as worthy of tears. Hirao was a romantic young man who had worked as a proofreader for a city newspaper. His highly receptive, delicate nerves, out of keeping with his large body, could not but helplessly shatter in the harsh world of the battlefield. Coming to animate him instead was a kind of desperate belligerence. After arriving at the front he had suddenly learned to boast. With the skill of a professional storyteller, he delivered vivid accounts of cutting down the foe. This was his romanticism in its new form. During the war's quieter moments, however, his delicate feelings revived and threw him into utter confusion.

"Hirao, aren't you going to write any letters?" asked First Class Private Kondō, who lay nearby writing yet another in a growing heap.

"I'm not!" snapped Hirao.

"Why not?"

Hirao said nothing for a while. At last, pulling a blanket over his head, he declared conclusively, "Those people at home have no idea how I feel."

Kondō lifted his pen from the paper and gazed at his friend's reclining form. He thought he fully understood Hirao's feelings, but he did not share them. "So what if they don't? Write anyway! When you've finished you'll feel so refreshed, dying won't bother you."

"Heh, heh, he talks as though he knows!" guffawed Corporal Kasahara, who had been licking his pencil and writing postcards. The second son of a farming family, he possessed no learning whatsoever but had an unshakeable heart all the more unquestioningly steady in his present circumstances.

Footsteps of the guards patrolling the deck—now approaching, now receding—rang overhead throughout the night. Visible through the portholes, the sky over P'u-tung blazed a festering red.

Early the following morning Lieutenant General Takashima, who had been sailing on a different ship, boarded a launch accompanied by the divisional staff and adjutants and set off up the Huang-P'u River. They were going to the headquarters, the soldiers rumored. In the afternoon the officers returned to their ship.

That evening perhaps a hundred smaller vessels swarmed around the troopships. Where they had come from was a mystery. They ranged in size from twenty to sixty tons. The sun was beginning to set. The soldiers shouldered their knapsacks, loaded their rifles, and transshipped one by one, groping for footing in the deepening darkness. Two destroyers had somehow materialized alongside the ships.

Just then a brilliantly illuminated passenger ship of about a hundred tons came steaming up the river as if meaning to cut through the throng of smaller craft. "Wu-Ch'ang, Great Britain" proclaimed the great white letters beneath the Union Jack. It was almost as though the ship had appeared in order to observe the units going ashore.

Men of the Kurata Platoon packed themselves tightly into a vessel named *Nagayama-maru,* which resembled a river steamer. They could not budge once they had sat and embraced their rifles and knees. The river night wind moaned in their ears, bringing with it the early winter's chill.

One hour past midnight they received orders to proceed upriver. One of the destroyers led the way; the other, on full alert, patrolled ceaselessly up and down the line of boats. Neither stars nor moon shone on this cloudy night, nor a single light on land or water. Only the sky over P'u-tung to the rear burned as red as the night before. The voyage was extremely slow. The soldiers spoke in whispers and shivered with the cold; half of them had not yet been issued their winter coats.

The only man asleep was Corporal Kasahara, who snored, hugging his sword. "Admirable," muttered Lieutenant Kurata and chuckled. Though all knew this was the time they ought to sleep, no one could.

At early dawn the procession of ships arrived at the confluence of the Pai-mao and Yangtze Rivers. Nearly thirty small warships had lined up there, guns trained on the right bank; just as the day broke, they opened up with a volley of fire. It was a spectacular attack. The riverbank was instantly lost in clouds of dust and sand that obliterated daylight. The enemy fought back mostly with machine guns. The bullets pinged and ricocheted off the ships' sides. Soon a smoke screen began to spread near the bank. Stirred by the morning breeze, dense billows of pale yellow smoke settled heavily over the water.

Bows side by side, the first and second landing parties entered the smoke screen; the Kurata Platoon was part of the third. Lieutenant Kurata, one knee pressed against the prow, his sword planted in front of the other, kept his eyes fixed on the boat bearing the company commander, Kitajima. The company commander was a captain in the reserves, a man past forty; from early morning on, even during severe fighting, he drank the cold *sake* kept in his canteen and gleefully smiled. Big and slow-moving, he ran a small trucking business in the countryside. Instead of shouting his order, he had merely said, still beaming his habitual smile, "Well, shall we go?"

As his boat began to advance, machine gunners crouched by the gunwale, cheeks tight against the cold stock of their weapons. The other boats, too, swung into a line and advanced.

Finally entering the cloud of smoke, Lieutenant Kurata was suddenly assailed by fear. He could see nothing in front. What if he emerged from the smoke only to collide with a large enemy troop? His unit was in the worst possible position.

Enemy bullets flew past with a sharp twang. He had not heard that sound in a while, and each shot echoed in his heart. Yet he wanted to be killed, and he chafed with impatience for the end. Prepared for death at any moment, he wished to die quickly and be done with it, rather than fight on. With his right hand shielding his eyes from the thick smoke, he tried to peer ahead.

The enemy bank suddenly appeared directly in front, and the boat struck against it. Jumping into the water up to their calves, the soldiers rapidly fanned out and lay flat in the riverbank grass. They met no attack. A rather sharp fight seemed to be starting to their right, but the shore facing them had already been secured several hundred yards ahead.

The expected battle never materialized, so Kitajima Company began to advance south. That evening they heard that a number of divisional staff officers on the right flank had been wounded.

While cooking rice in his mess tin over a fire on the floor of an occupied house, Second Lieutenant Kurata conscientiously

recorded the day's events in his diary. First Lieutenant Furuya
of the same company laughed, nibbling on a cracker. "You do
like to write, don't you! Think you'll have a chance to read it
over?"

In fact, keeping a diary was meaningless even to Lieutenant
Kurata. He did not think he would leaf through its pages again;
for that reason he wanted to write it all the more. Perhaps it was
a womanish sentiment, but being unable to tell another about
his final days struck him as much too lonely. The feeling was natural and one he could not discard to attain spiritual freedom.
Consequently he was tormented by a fretful anxiety and numbly
came to long for a quick death.

NEAR SUNDOWN, interpreter Nakahashi was wandering around
a village looking for a horse some artillerymen had asked him to
requisition. There were no more than five or six hundred houses
in the village and, it became clear after twenty minutes of walking, not a single horse. The horse that had been pulling the cannon had fallen into a creek and broken its leg, creating a difficulty
for tomorrow's advance. The artillerymen gave up on finding a
horse and instead suggested getting an ox.

"If it's an ox you want, I see no problem. A water buffalo!
You don't mind, do you? Off the horse and onto the buffalo!"
said Nakahashi, laughing. Still only nineteen, he had volun-
teered to be an interpreter as soon as the war had started but was
rejected as too young. He quickly filed a petition and was allowed
to accompany the army. Although high-spirited, he did not yet
seem physically strong.

A water buffalo stood tethered in a shed by a farmhouse at

the edge of the village. Deciding to take it and go, the interpreter looked in at the rear of the house. A wrinkled old woman was silently bending in front of the oven, kindling the fire.

"Hello, granny," called Nakahashi from the doorway. "We're Japanese soldiers and we need your ox. Terribly sorry, but we'll just take it and go."

The old woman shrieked in violent opposition. "Don't talk rubbish!" she screamed. "We finally bought that ox just last month, and how are we to farm without it?!" Furiously waving her arms, she rushed out of the earth-floored house only to see that three soldiers had already pulled the ox out of the stable and were discussing its uncertain merits, concluding it might be of use. In a breathtaking display of hysterical rage, the crone shoved the man holding the rein and sent him staggering, then planted herself in front of the ox and screeched at the top of her voice.

Hesitant to intervene, the soldiers looked on with wry smiles at the vehement exchange between Nakahashi and the old woman.

Suddenly interpreter Nakahashi erupted with peals of laughter.

"This granny is outrageous! The ox is out of the question, she says. She's got two sons and she doesn't mind if we take them and put them to work, but not the ox!"

Standing around the placid water buffalo and the woman, whose temples throbbed with indignation, the soldiers burst into loud laughter.

"Maybe we should get her sons to crawl on all fours and haul the cannon!"

But by now the sun had begun to set. The area was still dangerous after dark. The men resolved to take the animal.

"Move!" A soldier thrust the old woman aside and took hold of the rein. "Keep still or you're dead!"

Wailing and screaming, spittle flying, the woman resisted all the more tenaciously. "The bitch!" Clicking his tongue, the interpreter grabbed her from behind by the nape and knocked her down with all his might. The woman tumbled backward and collapsed into a rice field by the side of the road. A shower of mud washed over the soldiers.

Nakahashi laughed and started to walk off.

"You may keep your life but not the ox. We'll send him back to you when the war is over."

The ox began to plod along the crumbling, dusty road. The soldiers felt elated. This continent teemed with boundless riches; one merely had to take them. A vista was opening up before them in which the inhabitants' rights of ownership and private property were like wild fruits for the soldiers to pick as they chose.

The water buffalo exacted its revenge, however. At departure time the next morning when all preparations had been completed and the order to start was being awaited, the ox lumbered off straight into a rice paddy, dragging the gun carriage with it. Forced to heave the cannon out by themselves, the soldiers became coated with muck from head to foot.

ON THE FOURTEENTH of November the Nishizawa Regiment met stubborn enemy resistance at a village on the approach to Chih-t'ang-chen. Stark, leafless willows lined the banks of a stream traversing the desolate landscape where the fight was taking place. Cotton grew over the expanse of the endlessly flat fields, white down shining in spots amid dry, rusty-red stalks.

Setting up a disagreeable howl, incoming trench mortar shells tore open fresh holes in the soil.

First Class Private Hirao lay in one of the holes with his rifle at the ready but feeling somehow devoid of fighting spirit. With the midday sun overhead the battlefield was bright and warm. Whenever the sound of machine-gun fire briefly ceased, a foolish sense of tranquility permeated him. Heads were visible moving along the enemy trench less than sixty yards away. He aimed carefully and fired at each one.

Crawling through cotton stalks, First Class Private Fukuyama drew near and rolled into the crater. Taciturn and stolid, the man had been a factory worker.

"Give me a cigarette, will you?"

Hirao handed him one. Neither man had a match. Cigarette in his mouth, Fukuyama clicked his tongue.

"Well, guess I'll go get a light," he muttered to himself and cautiously raised his head for a look. In the field some five yards ahead, four soldiers clustered by a ridge, firing.

Hirao plucked a white strand of cotton, stretched it out, and twirling it between his fingers began to make cotton thread. Suddenly Fukuyama jumped out of the crater and sprinted forward. But before reaching the ridge he dropped flat, tried to rise by propping himself on his arms, then fell again. This time he remained still.

Watching from the rim of the crater, First Class Private Hirao quietly continued twining the thread. It seemed as though countless thoughts were rushing through his brain, or possibly none at all. He appeared serene as much as gripped by violent turmoil.

All of a sudden rapid-fire cannons commenced to bang away

furiously from the rear, throwing the enemy trench into a plainly visible chaos. With that signal came the order to charge.

Hirao sprang up, rifle and bayonet at the ready, and bolted forward ahead of everyone. Some hundred yards to the right, old Kitajima, the company commander, was running along a ridge, brandishing his long sword. The immaculate whiteness of the rabbit fur wrapped around the commander's neck impressed itself for an instant in the corner of Hirao's eye. The enemy trench was less than two feet wide and a full four feet deep. Chinese soldiers in blue cotton-padded uniforms scurried like moles along this narrow ditch in their haste to escape. Hirao jumped into the trench, lay limply on the ground, and gasped for breath. "I'm alive, still alive!" he murmured. Suddenly he was seized with unbearable pity for Fukuyama. They had never been particularly close, but the placid nature of the man who had gone to get a light for a cigarette struck him now as irresistibly sad.

Covered with dirt, he clambered out of the trench, picked up the rifle, which had suddenly grown heavy, and retraced his steps to search for Fukuyama.

Fukuyama lay prone in the field, the cigarette still in his mouth. Hirao rested his rifle next to Fukuyama's head and looked down at him. A wave of blinding anger surged up within him.

He glanced around. A number of dead Chinese soldiers lay strewn about in ditches, behind a small grave mound, and throughout the field. With the stock of his gun Hirao turned the bodies over onto their backs and searched through the pockets; the fourth had matches. Hirao returned to where Fukuyama lay, sat cross-legged beside his head, and lit the cigarette in the dead man's mouth. He could not rest content until he had done so.

The cigarette feebly smoldered between the lips of the man now powerless to inhale. "Fukuyama!" whispered Hirao in a choked voice as he joined his hands and closed his eyes.

The unit was swiftly receding in the distance, relentlessly attacking the fleeing enemy. He stood up and gazed at the rust-red solitary sweep of vast, dead cotton fields. The dust of battle had settled, leaving not a creature in the vicinity. Far to the rear reserves could be seen advancing. Perhaps it was the medical corps.

He lifted Fukuyama's heavy body onto his back. Holding the rifle and knapsack with one hand he started after his comrades along an elevated footpath.

BEFORE SUNDOWN the Nishizawa Regiment had disposed of the enemy remnants and completely occupied the town of Chih-t'ang-chen. Kitajima Company had suffered eight soldiers killed and twenty-three wounded. The dead were reverently cremated the same night. The soldiers dug a large hole for them and lay the corpses side by side with heads to the north.* First the company commander used scissors to clip a few strands of hair from above the ear of each dead soldier; then the platoon and squad commanders did the same, wrapping the clippings in white paper.† Brushwood was piled atop the corpses, and while the entire company stood at present arms, Company Commander Kitajima lit

---

* Bodies of the dead have traditionally been laid out with their heads to the north, the reason most Japanese avoid sleeping that way.
† The strands of hair will be given to the soldiers' families as mementos of their lost sons, brothers, or fathers.

the brushwood. Next to the flames, army priest Katayama Gen-chō, still wearing a khaki uniform, rattled the beads and chanted a sutra.

That night, horses remained saddled in preparation for an enemy attack, and the men, covering themselves with straw, slept by the side of the road with their rifles.

First Class Private Hirao sat cross-legged with about ten other soldiers near the flames and smoked all night, feeding wood to the fire and waiting for it to burn down. The night sky over the darkened city glowed red in four or five places with the chilling blaze of cremation fires.

As he sat staring into the flames, resting his cheeks in his hands, Hirao's sensitive nerves started once again to rush out of control. He felt gravely imperiled, enveloped with the horrible sensation of going insane. The unleashed nerves would scatter and smash up, he thought, leaving his brain certain to grow deranged. He must summon up his entire energy to grapple with this madness. An unspeakably painful, anxious struggle ensued.

"I was the first in my platoon today to jump into the enemy trench!" he abruptly shouted, unsure at whom. He had the hollow feeling the words were directed not so much at the soldiers seated by the fire as at those who continued to burn inside the hole. And yet he knew he could not bear to cut short the bragging.

"The enemy were tossing hand grenades all over. I dodged through and leaped into that slit of a trench. They came at me, but I stuck the gun right up against their noses and shot them. First, second, third—I blew a hole through each one. The one in front dropped dead, spouting blood out of the side of his nose . . . Fukuyama got hit. He's lying down there now, the fourth man over. 'Give me a cigarette,' he says, so I give him. 'Got a match? No. Too bad . . . Well, guess I'll go get a light.' He says it so damned casually, and just when he bolts ahead . . . I'd plucked some cotton and was making thread inside the hole. I worked it very carefully and got about five inches of even thickness. I kept twining it and watching . . . He still had the unlit cigarette in his mouth, the son of a bitch."

Hirao suddenly rose and moved away from the cremation fire into the roadside darkness. The sky's expanse shone white with the light of innumerable stars. He stood with his legs apart and urinated while tears trickled down his face. As the threat of nervous disintegration abated, his emotions seemed gradually to grow calmer. Utterly worn out, he paced aimlessly about.

3

After the morning roll call and breakfast, the off-duty soldiers left the camp with grins on their faces. Asked by others where they were going, they replied, "To get vegetables" or "To forage for meat." With the army advancing rapidly into the country's interior, the transport corps could not keep up, and the expense of supplying the troops grew formidably high; thus, many front line units came to live off the land. In North China the smallest requisitioned object had to be paid for in the interest of the postwar pacification efforts, but on the southern front there was no choice but to rely on unrestrained foraging. Soldiers assigned to kitchen duty prowled the fields, piling carts high with vegetables, or fastened ropes around pigs' necks and kicking their rumps returned to base.

Before long, foraging became a pretext for going out. It next came to be used as a code word. "Foraging for meat" meant looking for *ku-niang*—girls. The soldiers hungered to find young women. Anything connected with young feminine beauty was treasured: a glimpse of a face, a view from the rear, a photograph, a painting. Those who chanced upon a woman's handkerchief or a pair of embroidered silk slippers brought them back and flaunted their prized acquisitions.

But in the villages they took from the enemy there were seldom any young women, only old people and children. The young men had been forcibly conscripted as soldiers or laborers and the young women taken somewhere by the retreating army or fled to a place of refuge on their own. Having experienced frequent civil wars, they well knew that young women were made a bloody mess of in villages turned battlefields. This is why though the soldiers who went in search of *ku-niang* were many, those who came across any were few.

This morning, too, groups of three or four men, cigarette in mouth, set out in quest of *ku-niang*. The burned-out streets of Chih-t'ang-chen swarmed with strolling soldiers.

First Class Private Kondō was quick to spot a young woman inside a crumbling farmhouse at the edge of town. "There she is, there she is!" he exclaimed, nudging the soldier walking next to him.

The woman was steadily watching them from the inside of a dark room. One could see even from a distance that she was not much over twenty. Kondō and his three comrades sauntered across a narrow field and brazenly halted under the farmhouse eaves.

The woman stood motionless behind small latticed shutters. The room was extremely dark and narrow. A plow, hoes, and other farming tools leaned against the walls; the earth floor was piled with humble furniture and a washbasin containing wilted cabbage and potatoes.

"Hey, *ku-niang!*" a soldier called out, beaming with delight. The woman's face was grave and tense; her eyes shone blackly with fear. She was beautiful, but her clothes were terribly dirty and her hair was stained gray.

"She's good-looking but filthy," said one of the soldiers with regret.

"Let's go in anyway," First Class Private Kondō said, pushing at the door made of boards. It seemed to be locked. He gave a shout and lunged against it with his shoulder. The door crashed into the room, the wooden jamb splintered, and a fragment came off together with the lock.

Slowly he stepped inside. The woman suddenly took a step backward, aimed the revolver in her right hand and pressed the trigger. There was a click as it misfired.

Kondō crouched and flung himself like a ball against her breast, knocked her to the dirt floor in a flash, wrested away the gun, and rose.

"Bitch!" he panted. "Who the hell is this woman!?"

Surrounded by the three soldiers who had entered behind Kondō, the woman lay sideways on the dirt floor without stirring. Only the violent heaving of her chest and abdomen marking her every breath registered vividly in the four men's eyes.

They were suddenly seized with a furious desire and a savage urge to inflict maximum torment upon this woman who had resisted.

"Let's strip her and find out!" proposed Kondō. Somewhat embarrassed lest his words be interpreted as an expression of lust, he added in a small voice, "She might be a spy. Maybe she's got something on her."

The woman was unspeakably dirty. Her hands and bare legs were black with mud and grime. Grimacing, a soldier laid hands on her clothing and ripped it open. Soiled gray underwear came into view. In a cloth purse that fell from a pocket of her jacket they discovered a piece of paper covered with incomprehensible marks resembling shorthand.

"See! She's a spy," said Kondō caressing the captured revolver. "She might have something else."

Another soldier tore off her underclothes. The woman's entire body, white and naked, lay abruptly exposed before their eyes. It dazzled them so much they almost could not bear to look at it straight. Firm breasts rose round and full from a finely fleshed torso. The hips' rich curve glimmered white above the dingy earth floor. Without knowing why, Kondō squeezed the trigger. The gun missed fire as earlier.

"Damn her, I almost got killed."

"She's a spy, for sure. No farming woman would own a gun," said the soldier who had stripped her.

Transferring the revolver to his left hand, First Class Private Kondō drew a knife from his belt and slowly straddled the nude woman. She had closed her eyes. He looked down at her for a while and as he did so a furious passion boiled up within him again. Whether rage or lust he could not tell; he could only feel the pit of his stomach grow hot.

Without a word he drove the knife into the woman just below her breasts. The white flesh flew up in a terrific convulsion. The woman clutched at the knife with both hands and groaned in agony. Like a pinned mantis, she writhed, soon ceased stirring, and died. Dark blood spread in a wet stain under the shoes of the watching soldiers.

There was a clatter of footsteps outside the door, and three or four soldiers peered in through the latticed window.

"What've you done?" asked Corporal Kasahara.

Wiping the blood from the blade, First Class Private Kondō briefly explained, unfolding the scrap of paper to show the marks written on it. "I was sure she's a spy, so I killed her."

Kasahara surveyed the naked woman, sniffled through his runny nose, and laughed. "You sure wasted a good lay!"

Dangling a cigarette from his lips, he traversed the ridges of the plowed field, and returned to the road.

To BUILD a campfire the soldiers had laid stones side by side in the shape of a horseshoe, set up a metal bar over the flames, and suspended six mess tins from it. Six men sat cross-legged around the fire, waiting for their lunch to cook. The noon was windless and the sunny spot behind a house was warm enough to make them drowsy. A rumor was spreading that fellow units had sallied forth from Shanghai to seize Lo-tien-chen and Chia-ting and had yesterday occupied the walled town of T'ai-ts'ang. Less than ten paces from the seated soldiers, a pile of refuse rose by the corner of a wall. Red bones and intestines had been tossed on it, and a pig's head lay showing its teeth. These appeared to be the remains of a previous night's meal.

First Class Private Kondō stretched out his legs and exposed the back of his neck to the warm sunshine while toying with the newly confiscated revolver. Never having handled this model, he was investigating how it worked. The gun was an old-fashioned six-shooter.

He took out the bullet that had failed to fire and, rolling it in his palm, thought about the woman. For him, a medical college graduate who had worked in a research laboratory, dissecting a female corpse was no novel experience, but he had never before stabbed a living woman.

He did not think what he had done was particularly brutal; it was standard procedure for dealing with a spy. It made no difference whether she was killed with a pistol shot or a blade through the heart. What preoccupied him was the ease with which life yielded to death. That was a problem he had thought of countless times since coming to the battlefield, and he felt it all the more keenly now that he had killed a woman.

It was the nature of medicine to investigate all the life phenomena pertaining to the human body. Medical students like himself were thoroughly serious about this and ready to devote their entire lives to such research. And then this phenomenon of human life that constituted the object of their study proved to be so fragile, so easily, effortlessly extinguished. How scorned life was on the field of battle, how utterly ignored.

Why ever was this so, wondered bachelor of medicine Kondō. If the lives of friend and foe were held equally in contempt, it meant the science of medicine itself was held in contempt. Though he was a medical man himself, he had insulted that very science.

Having thought it out this far, he tumbled into a labyrinth and began to feel confused. What about my own life? Supposing the enemy troops consider my life worthless, what happens to the medical science superimposed upon it? No doubt it is even more worthless.

Come to think of it, since coming to the front he had not once been treated as a bachelor of medicine, nor put his knowledge to practical use. His intelligence had been asleep ever since the campaign started. That was it, he thought: Intellect was superfluous in battle. Whether or not this definitively solved his problem he did not know, but he felt that becoming lost in such speculation was in any case badly out of place in his present circumstances. With this he put the question out of his mind and, removing the lid from the mess tin, whose contents were by now fully cooked, smiled and addressed a soldier beside him.

"The *ku-niang* I killed just now was a true beauty. Hmm. Maybe I should have let her live."

COMPANY COMMANDER KITAJIMA planted a chair in the earth floor of a house allotted to the company headquarters, stretched his hands over a pan piled with burning embers, and began to drink cold *sake* from his canteen. First Lieutenant Furuya, Second Lieutenant Kurata, and Warrant Officer Nanbu were with him.

"Judging by his uniform, I'd say Lieutenant Kurata has done some gallant fighting." Apparently a little drunk, Captain Kitajima narrowed his eyes and laughingly pointed to the uniform.

"Yes, it is dirty," conceded Lieutenant Kurata looking over the bloodstains on his right arm and hip. "I had the men wash it, but it would not come off."

"How many did you cut down?"

"I don't know. It was a mess inside the trench." The gentle, fair face behind the horn-rimmed spectacles glowed with a healthy complexion. He thrust out his chest proudly but spoke in a modest, quiet voice. "It felt good to fight after such a long time. Being in war, it's depressing not to be at the front."

"Mm, that's right," said the company commander, tilting

the canteen once more. "Return home safe and triumphant, get the Order of the Golden Kite,* and you're sure to find a good bride."

"No, I don't expect to go home alive," said Lieutenant Kurata with uncompromising gravity.

"That's a good attitude," put in Lieutenant Furuya. "It's a mistake to think of going home alive."

"I'm telling you the truth. There are five men in my village who have the Order of the Golden Kite and every one of their wives is *schön*.† Without that Golden Kite—nothing. Mark my words, Lieutenant Kurata."

A soldier on kitchen duty pushed his way past the door, his hands filled with plates and dishes.

"Dinner is ready. *Nii* cooked it up, so I don't know if it's good or not."

"So *nii* cooked it, eh? Didn't put in poison, I hope."

The company commander put away his canteen and reached for the chopsticks. "Chinese cooking, is it?"

"Yes, sir, it's a kind of hodgepodge. We don't have the ingredients to make it right."

Captain Kitajima picked up a bowl of soup, hunched his back, and sipped.

"Mm, this is delicious, soldier!"

"Really, sir? There's more, if you like it."

"Mm. *Nii* did a pretty good job. Even the Chinese have their use; don't you think so, Lieutenant Furuya?"

"Indeed," replied Furuya noncommittally.

---

* A Japanese military award for bravery or leadership (no longer given).
† Beautiful (in German).

Seven or eight more or less forcibly recruited Chinese laborers with impassive faces worked diligently in the kitchen. They silently followed the gesticulated directions of three kitchen-duty soldiers and were so loyal in their work that the soldiers shook their heads with wonder. Feeling suddenly apologetic about having killed many of their brethren, the soldiers would nudge their shoulders and offer each a cigarette.

"*Hsieh-hsieh, hsieh-hsieh!*" With the guileless joy of chickens given their feed, they accepted the cigarettes and smoked.

Japan-China friendship is a simple affair, thought the soldiers. Indeed it was simple for men placed in such an extraordinary situation to establish individual friendships. With the lives of each side endangered by the other, not because the individuals willed it but because their nations did, they drew closer together and sympathized with each other as fellow sufferers from the same sickness. Both the soldiers and the Chinese yearned for human company.

That evening, Lieutenant Kurata again opened his notebook and picked up a pencil but closed his eyes to observe the waves of emotion swelling within him. Directly after a vicious fight he invariably felt tranquil. Perhaps stupefied was the right word. All the same, it was a feeling he could take some pride in before the people at home.

But the fight had ended dozens of hours ago. As the breathlessness of battle wore off, a new anxiety began to plague him. What was it? He had felt it on the train coming from North China, and at Pai-mao River before landing against the enemy fire. It seemed to be the anxiety of being alive.

There was talk the unit would be facing its next battle within a day or two. He looked forward to it. He wanted to start fighting soon and fight without cease. Soldiers were at the front to fight, not reflect.

Unable to bear the tangled emotions any longer, Lieutenant Kurata put a stop to the rush of thought by opening his eyes, taking up the pencil, and making an extremely brief diary entry: "Chih-t'ang-chen, November 15. Third Battalion attacks Pao-mai-hsin-shih to the west. Same town returns to calm."

4

On the morning of the seventeenth of November, Kitajima Company set forth from Chih-t'ang-chen and spent the next night in the recently taken town of Pao-mai-hsin-hsih. Since starting to advance up the Yangtze River, the company had received a mere three days' worth of field rations. Because the supply ships had not yet landed, the soldiers were compelled to search for rice, meat, and vegetables wherever they went.

When Chinese harvested rice they did not polish it but stored it unhulled; consequently every house contained bags of rice in the husk. The soldiers had to find a mortar and hull it before they could eat it; but the rice itself was of good quality, tastier than that of North China.

The following day, the company resumed the march and reached the front. On to Ch'ang-shu! The population of Ch'ang-shu was only five thousand, but the city, situated in a fertile plain and ringed with walls, was a wealthy trading center of rice, cotton, and raw silk. For the Chinese army, which had lost Shanghai and was constructing a second line of defense of the capital, Ch'ang-shu was also a northern link in a lengthy protective chain stretching from Chia-hsing in the south and including Su-chou. The friendly forces had already occupied K'u-shan and in pursuing the enemy had reached Wei-t'ing-chen and Lake Yang-ch'eng. Su-chou would fall in a day or two. To the south, Chia-hsing was under siege. On to Ch'ang-shu, on to Ch'ang-shu! The Nishizawa Regiment speeded up its march, advancing straight across vast rice paddies and cotton fields.

On the nineteenth, in the vicinity of Ku-li village, they collided with the flank of a large enemy unit fleeing from K'u-shan. Devoid of fighting spirit, the enemy abandoned the village after a three-hour gun battle and fell back in the direction of Ch'ang-shu. The Nishizawa Regiment cleared the village of enemy remnants and set up camp for the night.

That evening, interpreter Nakahashi was boiling his rice over an open fire with army priest Katayama and some signal corpsmen.

"I don't know what can be done about our regimental commander," said the interpreter. "He has a habit of taking casual walks just when the bullets are flying thick and fast. It's dangerous as hell. Actually, it's only the regimental commander and the adjutant who don't even duck when a bullet zips by. I was with them once and I said, 'Regimental Commander, sir, it's dangerous.' 'You stay back and get down,' he says and takes a calm stroll at the very top of the bank. It's a real problem."

"That's something one can't imitate," said the army priest hoarsely. "But he's been losing weight. Almost ten pounds, I hear."

"It's the adjutant who's been losing weight," said a signal corpsman. "When we got off the ship at Ta-ku he had a fine, heavy frame, and look at him now: He's all wrinkled. A lot more than ten pounds."

"It makes the horses happy," observed a soldier. "They love skinny riders."

"You did some killing today, Mr. Katayama, didn't you?" asked the interpreter.

"Sure I did, same as you."

"How many did you kill?"

"I wasn't keeping count but probably five or six," replied the priest nonchalantly.

It had happened only three hours earlier. Katayama Genchō, rosary beads wrapped around his left wrist, right hand gripping an engineer's spade, entered the village of Ku-li along with the unit driving out the enemy remnants.

Raising a hoarse cry, he rushed about with the soldiers in pursuit of the enemy, who were fleeing from alley to alley. The enemy did not know the village layout. Chinese towns and villages were shot through with alleys, many leading nowhere. When driven into a dead end, the enemy soldiers would throw away their weapons, dash into a house, tear off their uniforms, and change into civilian clothes. But they lacked the time to dispose of the discarded uniforms.

"You!" shouted the army priest in a thick voice and swung the spade sideways. Though the blade was not sharp, it bit deeply into a man's head, sending up a spray of blood as he collapsed.

"You! . . . You!"

The priest dealt one lethal swipe after another, the rosary at his wrist dryly rattling. With the sleeve of his military uniform he mopped the sweat pouring from his cheeks to his beard and slowly left the alley, supporting himself on the spade, which dripped blood.

Black plumes of smoke rose into the sky from ten or so burning houses. These had been set on fire to end the resistance of the enemy soldiers holed up within.

As he boiled his rice over the evening campfire, Genchō

could think over the day's carnage not only without the slightest pangs of conscience, but even with exhilaration. Every unit had its priest, but none killed the foe as valorously as he.

"They'll have to give the Order of the Golden Kite to Mr. Katayama when he gets home," said the interpreter, chuckling over the priest's bravery. Armed with neither pistol or sword, the priest used whatever lay at hand for a weapon. At the North China front he had killed no fewer than twenty men.

While they were in North China, Regimental Commander Nishizawa had once spoken with him about it. "The army priest kills the enemy quite courageously."

"I kill them, sir. Yes, sir," replied the priest, straightening up like a soldier.

"I see. I suppose you do pray over the enemy dead, don't you?"

"No, sir. There are army priests who do, but I myself do not."

"The living we must kill, but there's nothing wrong with praying for the soldiers who died in battle, is there?"

"That's right, sir, but somehow I can't bring myself to do it. When I think of them as my comrades' enemies, I hate them."

The adjutant, an affable man, smiled and said, "That's human feeling for you."

"I guess it is," nodded Colonel Nishizawa. "But what does that make of your religion?"

Genchō fell into a perplexed silence for a while but finally raised his head and replied hoarsely, "A mess."

Both the commander and the adjutant laughed. The commander scratched his stubbly chin and said, as if to himself, "So religion doesn't cross frontiers, does it."

Those were disheartened words. The colonel felt a loss of

hope in religion and its devotees. Perhaps he was suffering from moral anguish over his role as a leader in a great massacre. Not that this surfaced in his consciousness or in any way affected his conduct as an officer. War was the undertaking of a nation, and the spiritual contentment of a single man held no claim to consideration. Of course he knew that. But while Colonel Nishizawa felt parental love toward his own subordinates, love for the enemy was not unfamiliar to him either. Though he would not hesitate to kill untold thousands of captives, yet the deed filled him with a certain sad emptiness. It was this emptiness that he thought religion could console. As an officer he possessed neither the leisure nor the freedom to mourn the enemy dead but expected that an army priest would do it in his stead. When he heard that this priest, although willing to pray for his comrades, refused to join his hands for the sake of the enemy dead, he felt darkly disappointed. The one remaining dream of peace embraced in the warlike wilderness by an instinctively peace-loving man, crumbled. Colonel Nishizawa had hoped that a religion existed that was mighty and great-hearted enough to transcend national boundaries.

The army priest himself, while peacefully conducting services at his temple, had believed that his faith rose beyond borders. That the same religion was professed in the same way in India, China, and Japan seemed to him to prove it. His had been a simple belief. When he left the temple after volunteering for the army, he had planned to hold funeral services for the Chinese soldiers as well as his own. But after coming onto the field of battle, his resolve to do so vanished.

The battlefield appeared to possess an astonishing power to transform all combatants into men of identical characters, identical thoughts, and identical needs. It stripped bachelor of medicine Kondō of his intelligence as it did Katayama Genchō of his faith. All it left the priest were the knowledge of scriptures and funerals. The moment he removed his clerical robes to put on a military uniform, he lost the heart of a priest and acquired that of a soldier.

But army priest Katayama was not necessarily to blame for this. In peacetime his faith had been sufficiently broad to cross national frontiers. That it could no longer do so in wartime was not so much because religion had grown powerless but rather because those frontiers had grown insurmountably high.

An INCIDENT occurred the next morning before departure.

Several pillboxes lined the village outskirts. The area had been cleared and sentries posted the previous night. After sunrise, a soldier from the Kitajima Company, thinking of relieving himself in the privacy of an abandoned pillbox before the march, walked up to one, paper in hand, and peered in. Instantly felled by a pistol shot, he was dragged in through the dark opening and disappeared.

When he heard about this, Corporal Kasahara's jaw dropped —for him, an expression of ultimate fury. "Right. Get me a machine gun!" He grabbed his sword and broke into a run.

The circular pillbox rose above a low embankment in the middle of the fields; five or six Chinese corpses lay scattered nearby. Some of them seemed to have been ravaged by famished dogs during the night; their thighbones protruded from the half-devoured flesh of the buttocks. Two soldiers lay prone in the field, rifles at the ready.

Kasahara ran up and stopped short. Damn! There was no way of getting at the pillbox. Four or five soldiers crawled up with machine guns, but firing them had no effect.

"Hey!" Kasahara turned to his subordinates. "Get me smoke grenades. Three or four. Quick!"

Bending low, two soldiers raced back over the vegetable field, kicking up clods of dirt. Kasahara ground his teeth and growled curses as he waited for them to return.

At last the smoke grenades were tossed in. Thick billows surged out from the openings on either side of the pillbox. Kasahara pushed aside a soldier, stretched himself out flat in the mud of the ridge, and fitted the machine gun butt to his shoulder.

Before long a Chinese army regular, thickly clad in blue, jumped out of the fumes; holding his head with both hands, he began to run. He simply ran in a straight line, heedless of direction. *Ta-ta-ta-ta*—the machine gun burst shook the ground.

"One dog down!" shouted Kasahara.

Two more men jumped out in the same way.

"Two dogs; three dogs down!"

The machine gun stuttered on, spitting fire as Kasahara counted. After eleven he stood up and strode forward.

Reaching the still-smoking entrance, he whipped out his sword, bent down, and crawled in. Three soldiers followed him.

Presently he emerged, and then behind him came the soldiers carrying their dead comrade. The body had been hacked to pieces by the eleven enemy regulars. The men quietly laid it to rest in the furrowed field.

"Attention!" shouted Kasahara. The soldiers brought their heels together where they stood. "Salute!"

Kasahara's voice was choked and husky. He brought up the

sword in front of his face, then lowered it to his right side. His eyes brimmed with tears. The men, who had no rifles, raised their hands in salute and remained motionless.

"Take him and let's go."

With a sniffle, the corporal started off. A dead Chinese soldier, dog number eight, lay at his feet. Kasahara vehemently kicked him in the jaw.

TO CORPORAL KASAHARA, killing enemy soldiers was no different than killing carp. The carnage he perpetrated did not affect his emotions in the least. The one emotion that did move him mightily was a virtually instinctive love for his comrades. He was truly a splendid soldier, the very epitome of a soldier. If he lacked Colonel Nishizawa's exalted military spirit, he was equally free of the unstable romanticism of First Class Private Hirao, bachelor of medicine Kondō's disoriented intelligence, and the delicate sentiments hindering the actions of Lieutenant Kurata. The magnificent steadiness of his mind persisted unshaken amid severest combat and the most bestial slaughter. In short, he was unburdened by either oversensitivity or the intellectual's habit of self-criticism, neither of any use on the battlefield. It was precisely his type of courageous, loyal fighting man that the army wanted. During lengthy exposure to the battlefield, men like Hirao and Kondō would gradually grow to be like him, they could not do otherwise. Corporal Kasahara, before ever coming to the front, had been a youth cut out for war.

His one flaw was that acting on his own authority, he was apt to become unpredictably violent. Violence was the other aspect of his bravery. By contrast, Lieutenant Kurata's bravery, though identical to his own, was backed by a kindly sentimentality.

First Class Private Hirao differed from both. His bravery was somewhat desperate and tinged with sadism, a courage verging on derangement. Behind it echoed a raging shriek that marked the disintegration of his romanticism. But even that shriek would subside if Hirao's life on the battlefield continued for long. He was bound to locate some point of compromise soon, something to stabilize his state of mind.

5

O n the highway leading from Ku-li to Ch'ang-shu, the Nishizawa Regiment met up with the front-line units pursuing the enemy from Mount K'u. Preparations for the siege of Ch'ang-shu began.

A large force followed a stream running north of Ch'ang-shu and occupied the heights of Mount Yu to the west. Units approaching from the south crossed Lake K'u-ch'eng and landed at Mo-ch'eng-chen. The Nishizawa Regiment was entrusted with making a frontal attack.

A driving rain mixed with sleet was falling. The previous day's warmth gave way to severe cold. The city of Ch'ang-shu was a misty blur on the other side of the ramparts; it seemed inconceivable that anyone lived there.

In the afternoon a furious fight began, a wretched battle carried on without respite in the midst of rain and intensifying cold. Caked with mud, the soldiers ran and fought in grim silence.

Enemy trenches had been dug in three, sometimes four parallel lines. Seizing the foremost trench, the men found it a river of mud. Steeped in the muck to their ankles and higher, they were forced to endure an unbroken barrage of hand grenades and mortar shells. Irritation mounted. Both officers and men grew eager for a quick charge and a quick end to the fight. The morale was none too high; an aura of sullen pain lay heavily over the entire battlefield. The persistent boom of cannon and rattle of machine guns sounded unusually heavy and dull under a lofty sky pouring streaks of rain.

When war came to this, Company Commander Kitajima was the first to lose his temper. The tippling captain kept wiping his mustache, now soaked by the raindrops coursing down his cheeks, and repeating, "Ah, it's a mess." It was clear to anyone that they could stay here shooting at each other forever. If this were not settled, the soldiers would be forced to spend the night on their feet in this bog of a trench. Not only would that be painful, but it would cripple their fighting capacity the next day as well.

"We'll have to charge," Kitajima muttered. "If we don't charge, it's a mess." He lowered his head and surveyed the condition of his men. Their numerical strength did not seem much diminished.

He decided on a charge. Directly in front, hand grenades were exploding in rapid succession. It was less than a hundred yards to the enemy trench. "All right!" he shouted, thrusting his hands into the mud to scramble out of the trench. Flourishing his long sword, he issued the order and lunged forward.

The charge was a fiasco. When the soldiers were in good spirits and working in concert, they and their commander would rush forward in a straight line and swoop onto the enemy like a net. But this time, though the men wished to advance and end the fight quickly, a leaden depression weighed them down and threw their coordination into disarray. The company commander had abruptly shouted the order and sprinted ahead. The soldiers flanking him sprang forward with a great cry and followed him without delay. But the right and left wings lagged behind, making the assault line resemble two sides of an obtuse triangle, with Captain Kitajima forming the apex. As might be expected, the enemy machine-gun fire concentrated on the company commander.

Captain Kitajima was a glorious sight as he led the charge. A scarf of pure white rabbit fur flying from his neck, gripping a pistol with his left hand and holding aloft the sword with his right, he ran at full tilt in long strides, kicking up the hem of his greatcoat. His breathtakingly heroic charge was sure to overwhelm the enemy. He leaped over a row of three small grave mounds, pitched forward, and fell flat into a muddy rice field, not to rise again.

The company stormed ahead and took the enemy trench but suffered a great many killed and wounded in the center of the attack, closest to the commander. First Lieutenant Furuya immediately assumed command of the company.

After the trench had been fully secured, Second Lieutenant Kurata took along two men and went back to collect the commander's body.

Rifle and bayonet at the ready, a soldier lay in the mud tightly against the captain's body; but seeing the Lieutenant approach, he rose, presented arms, and crisply announced, "The company commander has fallen, sir."

Without a reply, Lieutenant Kurata knelt beside Captain Kitajima, turned the prone body onto its back, and laid it across his knees. Half a dozen machine gun bullets had struck the captain's neck, chest, and stomach. The spotlessly white rabbit fur wrapped around his neck was stickily drenched with blood and mud. Pouring sleet washed the mud from his cheeks. His head was large and aged, framed by a sparse growth of beard. With the sleeve of his own coat, the lieutenant carefully wiped the mud from the captain's lips. In the meantime, the two soldiers found a pair of bamboo poles used by local farmers for transporting straw, then took a tent out of a knapsack and made an improvised stretcher.

Another war cry rang out over the front as First Lieutenant Furuya set off in hot pursuit of the enemy. A sergeant would be taking charge of the Kurata Platoon.

Lieutenant Kurata raised his face to look at the distant attack, then at the soldiers lying dead or howling with pain in the rice fields. Japanese artillery shells flew whining overhead. Fresh units could be seen advancing from the rear. Horses and gun carriages appeared a hazy gray in the rain.

"You two take the company commander to the rear," said the lieutenant.

Two soldiers picked up Captain Kitajima and lowered him onto the stretcher. The lieutenant wiped the captain's sword clean and sheathed it, then lifted the pistol from the mud and replaced it in the holster. It suddenly occurred to him that there might still be *sake* in the company commander's canteen. For the first time he felt his eyes grow moist.

The soldiers raised the stretcher to their shoulders and set off.

"Tell the medical corpsmen to come right away. There are many wounded," Lieutenant Kurata said. He turned to yet another soldier and ordered him to stay and care for the wounded. Then snapping to attention and saluting the departing remains of the company commander, he ran splashing off toward the front along a muddy path.

IN THE COURSE of the night, Japanese troops broke through the gates on three sides of Ch'ang-shu and poured into the city. Rising Sun flags atop the gates flapped wetly in the rain. Mopping-up operations began at early dawn and lasted until noon, by which time the occupation seemed complete.

The soldiers lit fires throughout the city to dry their clothes and slept near the flames.

Following a short rest, all the surviving soldiers of the company lined up and bade farewell to Captain Kitajima's mortal remains. First Lieutenant Furuya lit the funeral pyre. Later, with the chopsticks he had made of wood and bamboo, he picked up the bones and placed them into an unvarnished wooden box, wrapped it with white cotton cloth, and hung it from his neck so that it rested on his chest. The soldiers did the same with the bones of their friends. In the evening the bones were put alongside each other on a shelf over the dirt floor of a house now used as a barracks. Some of the men managed to find rapeseed oil and offer consecrated lights; those who could not lit cigarettes and stood them before the bones in lieu of incense sticks.

Second Lieutenant Kurata, unable to write his diary the night before, brought it up to date this evening: "November 20, 21. Rain. From noon 20 to noon 21, full-scale attack on Ch'ang-shu, 24 hours of severe engagement. Company commander has fallen. Infinite sadness."

He was feeling a vast change within himself. His grating anxiety seemed already abated along with the confused urge to die. In a sense, what had until now been fueling his unease, impatience, and courage was the instinctive terror of a life in peril. But having seen the company commander die before his eyes, that terror had passed into a separate dimension. His emotions soared— or plunged. Perhaps this was a sort of numbing of the sensibility, instinctively activated to avert a disintegration of the self. He grew lighthearted and began to sense a brightness inherent in this life. A feeling did remain that if he probed deeply into that brightness he would uncover a darkness at its nadir, but he was no longer in the least inclined to inflict such probing on himself. He began to feel a great breadth of spirit, a sensation of freedom surpassing all morals. He was already starting to cultivate a character that would enable him to participate calmly in the most gruesome slaughter. That is to say, he was catching up with Corporal Kasahara.

This evening the corporal was seated by the fire in the same barracks as the lieutenant and was sniffling as usual like a child. He had a chubby, round face, and his cheeks, lips, and tip of the nose glowed with the ruddiness of a mischievous boy. Taking off his shoes, he thrust his feet out rudely toward the fire and swore.

"The damned skin of these feet is waterlogged. It looks like I went into that blasted trench to scoop out carp!"

He wore a silver ring on his plump little finger. Lieutenant Kurata noticed it. "What have you got there, Corporal?"

"What, this? This is one of those, sir," he grinningly replied, then gripped the hand of the soldier next to him. "He's got one, too, sir!"

"Where did you get it?"

"A *ku-niang* gave it to me, Lieutenant, sir!"

The soldier roared with laughter.

"In exchange for a pistol bullet, right, Kasahara?"

"That's right!" rejoined the corporal. "I turned it down, saying I don't need it, but she begged, 'Oh please, Mr. Kasahara, I so much want you to have it,' so I just had to take it, sir."

Chinese women used silver for their wedding rings, and every woman wore one. Some were finely engraved and many had names carved into them.

"I'd love one for a souvenir myself," said the lieutenant, laughing. Kasahara grew even more high-spirited.

"You'll have to get it yourself, Platoon Commander, sir," he gleefully shouted. "When we get to Wu-hsi or someplace, find a *ku-niang* right away and she'll give you one. It's already too late for Ch'ang-shu. Not a female in sight. Something happened to them all. Ah, hahahaha!"

A UNIT that had entered Ch'ang-shu from the south was proceeding west in pursuit of the routed enemy, and the Nishizawa Regiment was marching in its rear. It was still raining, and the mile-long unbroken line of infantry, pack horses, tanks, military cars, signal corps, regimental colors, and supply wagons meandered over the muddy road. Interspersed within it were thirty Chinese porters brought along all the way from Chih-t'ang-chen. It also included fifteen water buffaloes and fifty Chinese horses and donkeys.

Recently officers had changed their minds about the way to train military horses. Japanese horses were pitifully weak. At the barracks they had been punctually drilled and fed at set times. Had such life continued, the horses' condition would have remained excellent; but in the heat of battle, with neither regular feeding nor rest possible, they deteriorated into near paralysis.

The Chinese horses, on the other hand, being accustomed to abuse, proved of real worth on the battlefield. Short and stocky, their legs thickly coated with hair, they appeared ungainly and stupid but were immensely helpful. The soldiers, however, seemed incapable of feeling any affection for the horses of an enemy nation. They mistreated them mercilessly and when they collapsed, abandoned them without a backward glance. During the night the discarded horses were set upon by wild dogs and their hinds and viscera torn apart.

All the enemy forces, having relinquished Su-chou and Ch'ang-shu, fled westward to the stronghold of Wu-hsi. A walled city of two hundred thousand inhabitants, Wu-hsi was a trading center for farm produce and raw silkworm cocoons. It was strategically located on the Great Canal and the Nanking-Shanghai railway and was therefore of vital importance to the defense of Nanking. On the twentieth of November, a Japanese naval air unit passed overhead to carry out an intense bombardment of the enemy encampment at Wu-hsi.

Attack by the ground troops commenced on the twenty-first. The units giving chase after the fall of Su-chou made a long march from Wang-t'ing along the Nanking-Shanghai railway, while the Nishizawa Regiment and others, advancing from Ch'ang-shu, crossed a number of small rivers and closed in from the east. The enemy was consolidating defenses by constructing concrete pillboxes and bunkers.

Furuya Company entered the fight in the afternoon and seized a forward trench but was still firing rifles and machine guns from it when dusk enveloped the front. Faced by a strongly fortified enemy, the company could not move into a position to charge. As it began to grow dark, the gunfire grew sporadic on both sides and then temporarily ceased.

Rice had been reaped and the fields stretched bare and flat, interrupted only occasionally by the low roof of a farmhouse. Behind each house was a canal bringing in water from a stream. At twilight the water shone with the color of lead, and the thin ice, clinging since morning to the roots of dry grasses at water's edge, glowed a faint white. The low walls of Wu-hsi were strung out in the distance, topped by the blue sky of a Hiroshige print. To the rear, moving figures of medical corpsmen ministering to the wounded floated over the fields in shades of a monochrome ink painting; distinct from them, the thickset form of army priest Katayama sought out the dead, lingering by each body to join hands and pray for otherworldly happiness.

A modest farmhouse stood near a trench in which Lieutenant Kurata, First Class Privates Hirao and Kondō, and Corporal Kasahara of the machine gun squad sat smoking side by side, wearing steel helmets. An artillery shell had blown a hole through the farmhouse roof, the door had been knocked to the dirt floor, and the vegetable garden trampled. The deepening darkness seemed more impenetrable in the vicinity of the house. A woman's weeping emanated from within. With the gunfire silenced, it suddenly reached the men's ears.

"If it isn't a crying woman!" exclaimed the lovesick Corporal Kasahara. "A *ku-niang!*"

"What's she doing here?" Lieutenant Kurata muttered to himself.

Overhearing this from a few feet away, First Class Private Hirao offered to investigate. He jumped to the top of the trench and trotted off toward the house.

"It's dangerous, be careful!" warned Lieutenant Kurata over his shoulder.

"I'll keep him company!" Corporal Kasahara climbed out of the trench, glanced back, and smiled.

As the soldiers watched intently, the two men strode past the smashed door and disappeared into the darkness. The crying stopped. The soldiers tensed up. Deprived of contact with young women, they could think of nothing else.

Before long, Kasahara and Hirao slowly emerged. They jumped back into the trench, and Hirao explained.

"Her mother's been killed by a bullet. *Ku-niang*'s seventeen or eighteen. Poor girl."

"Is she good-looking?" asked a soldier.

"Yes, she's good-looking," replied Hirao in an oddly angry voice.

Intermittently, almost as an afterthought, enemy bullets whined by with a sharp, faint sound, striking the nearby mud. The very faintness of their passage spoke eloquently of their cruel capacity to maim and kill.

Resting their cheeks against gunstocks, some soldiers napped; others slowly munched frozen rice, waiting for each mouthful to melt before biting into it. The enemy's fitful firing stopped altogether as the night wore on, and a hush settled over both sides. Clear and unobstructed, the nocturnal sky stretched overhead in a vast, starry dome. The number of stars here seemed many times greater than in Japan. The soldiers could spot the familiar shapes of the Big Dipper and Orion and were vividly reminded of home. With these stars visible, they felt, this could not truly be China. A gossamer sentimentality settled over the trench, quieting them.

It was now that they became keenly aware of the woman's cries.

"She's still crying," First Class Private Hirao murmured softly.

He was thinking of the girl he had seen. The household was poor. The mother was not very old; her inert hands and feet stood out whitely against the gloom. The daughter wore cotton-padded trousers resembling the work-trousers Japanese women wore and a jacket with a thick collar. Holding the mother's head to her breast, she rubbed her face against the mother's hair and wept. Hers was not the awkward, monotonous weeping of a Japanese woman; it expressed her sadness directly and intricately.

As the night deepened, the cries grew more intensely sorrowful and shook the darkness of the silenced battlefield. They shifted from unrestrained wailing to stifled sobs, and from disconsolate, animal howling to shrieks.

None of the listening soldiers uttered a word. The woman's grief seeped deeply into them and weighed them down. They felt a burning sympathy that grew steadily stronger until it yielded to irritation.

Second Lieutenant Kurata tightened the chinstrap of his helmet until his cheeks bulged, crouched leaning on the trench wall, and pulled out the diary from his chest pocket. He switched on a flashlight and flipped open the notebook, but the woman's screams put him so on edge that he could not write. Switching off the light, he closed his eyes and listened. The screams raked across his brain. Suddenly he heard a different voice.

"Shut the hell up!"

Turning around, he made out First Class Private Hirao springing out of the trench, his bent back silhouetted against a myriad stars.

"Where to?" asked First Class Private Kondō from inside the trench.

"To kill the bitch!"

Gripping his bayonet and stooping low, he ran off. Five or six soldiers, shoes noisily clattering, followed him over the top.

They burst into the pitch-dark house. Dimly lit by the star-light streaming in through the shell-torn roof, the weeping woman still crouched in the same posture as hours earlier. Hirao grabbed her by the collar and pulled. She clung to her mother's body. A soldier pried her fingers away from the corpse. Her hips and legs trailing along the floor, they dragged her out of the front door into the garden.

"*Ei, ei, ei!*"

Screaming shrilly like a lunatic, Hirao thrust his bayonet three times into the woman's chest. The other soldiers joined in, stabbing her at random. In little over ten seconds, the woman was dead. Flat as a layer of bedding, she lay spent on the dark ground; a warm vapor, thick with the smell of fresh blood, drifted upward into the flushed faces of the frenzied soldiers.

Lieutenant Kurata stood tiptoe in the trench and peered into the darkness; he guessed correctly what had happened but said nothing. As the soldiers breathlessly returned, Corporal Kasahara sat cross-legged at the bottom of the trench and smoked. Merrily he growled, "You men sure know how to waste a good lay!"

His brief remark acted like a balm on Lieutenant Kurata. Biting his lip, he thought, Yes! He gazed at Corporal Kasahara seated in the depth of the trench, lit by the dim glow of his cigarette. Lieutenant Kurata's nerves were incapable of tolerating the kind of atrocity that had just occurred. He could countenance the deed on the grounds of safeguarding troop morale; in that sense the act was justifiable and unavoidable. But such theoretical reasoning did nothing to keep his nerves from being riven by anguish. It was only Corporal Kasahara's supremely brazen utterance that came to his rescue: You men sure know how to waste a good lay!

What marvelous audacity, thought Lieutenant Kurata. He envied it. Filling his lungs with the chilly night air, he drew back his shoulders, and thought afresh, Yes! The battlefield before him seemed to grow conspicuously brighter.

First Class Private Hirao felt none of the brightness. The carnage consummated, he returned to the trench and sank to the ground.

"Quiet at last," he murmured softly.

While forced to listen to the woman's cries, his emotions had been inexorably trapped. Though he well understood what war meant to the nation and why it left no margin for criticism, he could not bear to contemplate the tangible misery that war brought to the individual. Even now, his romanticism smoldered on. He knew, too, that killing her, far from alleviating his pain, was likely to make it much worse. That he was nonetheless the first to plunge the bayonet bespoke both a frenzied effort to flee from the pain in the only way attainable and the lashing out of his romantic brand of sadism. His one source of great joy was that several soldiers had joined him in killing her. Tears of gratitude to his comrades rolled down his cheeks.

The woman was dead and her cries cut off. Night on the battlefield reverted to silence. Now the hushed, starlit stillness began to grow unendurable to Hirao. A desire seized him to scream from the center of his soul. He needed to boast but could not do it here. He pursed his lips and started faintly to whistle.

Listening to the light rhythm of the melody, First Class Private Kondō returned again to his stalemated logic. With human life so easily snuffed out, what place had medicine in this fugitive life? What of life itself? Life on the battlefield was like so much refuse, and medicine like the flies swarming over the refuse. A bitter smile flitted across his face. Nothing made any sense. The death of the woman he had killed had left no traces on him; his nerves were that robust. Or perhaps, like a seashell, he knew how to protect himself and was able to seal off his feelings hermetically. It was a skill he had had to master while conducting medical research.

Medicine seemed to have equipped him with a philosophical attitude. Viewing the battlefield as an external object, he possessed the strength not to succumb to it. Consequently he was more immune than anyone from acquiring Corporal Kasahara's personality. His killing of the female spy differed from Kasahara's killing of the Chinese arsonist and Hirao's killing of the weeping *ku-niang*. Thoroughly reflecting on what he had done, he yet went on to surmount the reflection. His intellect, in short, had reached an understanding with the battlefield.

It was close to noon on the following day.

Furuya Company had advanced less than six hundred yards before coming upon a deep stream. A stone bridge spanning it had been blown up by the retreating enemy. Acting under Lieutenant Kurata's orders, Hirao and Kondō set out in search of a boat.

Flanked by four-foot-high banks, the stream meandered into the distance. A few houses clustered together some six hundred yards downstream. No boats were likely to be found any nearer.

Machine gun fire from both sides continued with hardly a break; from time to time the peculiar howl of a trench mortar shell cleaved the air. Bending low, the two men ran along the foot of the bank, jumping over clumps of dry grass and enemy corpses that lined the water's edge.

Having run about three hundred yards, Kondō turned around and, striving to be heard over the sound of the gunfire, shouted, "Hey, Hirao, there's a *ku-niang!* Look, she's alive!"

He was pointing to the opposite bank. On the slope by a dead willow crouched a woman bending close to the ground. The stream was just a dozen yards across, and she was clearly visible. Raising her white face, she watched them. She was a young farm woman.

"She's holding a child!" yelled Hirao, appalled. Under her breast she was embracing an infant as if to conceal him.

Lacking time to pause, the two ran on.

"What the hell is she doing around here?" Hirao was out of breath, but the matter seemed to weigh on his mind.

At last they reached the houses. Not a boat was in sight. They ran two hundred yards farther and finally found one.

Clambering aboard, they poled the boat upstream as rapidly as they could. As they neared the spot where the farm woman had sought shelter, the baby's furious crying reached their ears. The woman had rolled to the water's edge and lay on her back, her arms and legs flung out. Not far from her breast, the baby, too young even to crawl, lay face down in the dry grass, screaming with all his might. A thin line of blood flowed threadlike from the woman's temple, gathering blackly in the hollow of her ear.

Standing stock-still at the prow and gripping the pole, Hirao kept his eyes fixed on the two figures. Kondō, poling diligently at the stern, gave vent to a sarcastic chuckle.

"Hirao," he called, "you'd better kill that child, too. Just like yesterday. It's the merciful thing to do. If you leave it as it is, by tonight or so, dogs will devour it alive."

Hirao's eyes never strayed from the mother and child as they gradually faded away into the distance. His cheeks were trembling; he bit his lip and sobbed. This time his romanticism had plunged him into a delirium of despair.

6

The defense of Wu-hsi was as unyielding as expected, with none of the city gates breached even on the second day of fighting. On this day the Nishizawa Regiment lost its standard-bearer. A single bullet having pierced his left chest, he breathed his last even before being lifted onto a stretcher.

"Tell the regimental commander I'm sorry," were his final words.

The regimental commander and the adjutant were on their way to inspect the firing line less than four hundred yards ahead when a regimental standard escort ran up with the news. The commander faced the stretcher as it was carried past a grove far to the rear and quietly saluted. Then he silently went on, stepping around the shell craters in his way.

"Sir, the standard-bearer said, 'Tell the regimental commander I'm sorry,'" reported the soldier.

The colonel turned sharply and looked at the soldier's face.

"Did he say anything else?"

"No, sir, he soon passed away."

The soldier was looking downward, his lower lip clamped between his teeth. The colonel turned away and spoke softly.

"Tell the army priest to conduct a memorial service with all due ceremony."

The fight raged on throughout the night; on the following morning, the twenty-sixth, Wu-hsi at last fell to the attacking troops. Exhausted by prolonged combat, soldiers took possession of the city houses, crept into the citizens' beds, and slept.

At nightfall, the regimental commander ordered that the fallen standard-bearer's bones be brought to him. A soldier presented them in a box of unvarnished wood; then the colonel stood before it in silent prayer, placed it on a shelf at his bedside, and slept under it.

WHILE MOST of the troops drove on toward Ch'ang-chou in pursuit of the vanquished enemy, the Nishizawa Regiment stopped in Wu-hsi for three days of rest. It was at times like these the surviving soldiers most desired women. With bold strides they roamed the city streets, searching for women like dogs chasing rabbits. Such unbridled conduct was strictly controlled at the North China front, but here it was difficult to restrain the men.

Each of them felt as triumphant and willful as a king, a despot. When they could not achieve their aim within the city limits, they ventured to the farmhouses beyond. Enemy stragglers were still hiding in the area and many of the inhabitants had arms, but this did not make the soldiers hesitate in the least. They felt themselves the mightiest creatures alive. Needless to say, in the face of such conviction, all morality, law, reflection, and humanity were powerless. The soldiers returned from their expeditions sporting silver rings on the small fingers of their left hands.

"Where'd you get this?" their comrades asked; and each man laughingly replied, "It's a memento of my late wife!"

THE REGIMENTAL SUPPLIES had not yet landed at Shanghai and were only now approaching its harbor. This meant that the front units could not rely on being replenished by the transport corps to their rear but were forced to improvise, requisitioning on the spot whatever they needed.

Rice and vegetables were relatively abundant, but spices extremely hard to find. The shortage was at its most acute during their stay in Wu-hsi.

The soldier in charge of cooking at the regimental headquarters was jealously hoarding a bowl of leftover refined sugar.

"Listen up! This is for the regimental commander, so nobody lays a finger on it!" Lance Corporal Takei wrapped it in paper and put it on a shelf. He used it only when cooking for the colonel, and then sparingly, but even so, the amount dwindled to a mere cupful. "There must be sugar somewhere."

Whenever free from kitchen duty, he scoured the city for sugar but found none. That evening, planning finally to use the last of the sugar in preparing the colonel's supper, Takei reached for it, only to discover it gone.

Vegetables were boiling in the pot; table legs and broken boxes blazed steadily underneath. Takei stood gaping in front of the stove.

"Hey! Where's the sugar I kept here?"

Soldiers on duty chorused that they did not know. Some said it was there at lunchtime, some speculated that the wind might have blown it off the shelf. In the end the suspicion arose that the Chinese kitchen workers were most likely to have stolen it. Five Chinese, brought all the way from Chih-t'ang-chen, worked in the kitchen.

The lance corporal's face flushed with rage. Unable to speak to them, he slapped the Chinese nearest him, a youth of about seventeen. This one seemed to him to have done it. He ordered a subordinate to call the headquarters interpreter.

"Ah, what a lovely fragrance!" Interpreter Nakahashi sauntered in, a cigarette dangling from his lips.

Takei quickly explained the situation and asked that he interrogate the boy.

The Chinese, industrious and obedient, had been doing kitchen work ever since Chih-t'ang-chen. Nakahashi did not think him guilty but went through the motions of interrogating him. The boy said he did not know, perhaps a soldier had taken it.

"A soldier would never take it!" thundered Lance Corporal Takei, eyes flashing with rage. They decided to search the boy.

Deep in his pocket they found a crumpled piece of paper, clearly what the sugar had been wrapped in. Not a speck was left; the paper had been licked clean.

Lance Corporal Takei was sputtering with fury. He grabbed the boy and hauled him off to the edge of a reservoir sixty yards away. On the opposite bank First Class Private Kondō was washing rice in his mess tin, preparing to cook his evening meal.

Takei drew his knife and without a moment's hesitation stabbed the boy through the chest. With a groan the boy toppled into the reservoir, sending waves rippling thirty feet across to the bank where Kondō was rinsing rice. Kondō sprang up in alarm.

"What did he do?"

"That son of a bitch stole the sugar I'd slaved to get for the regimental commander, and licked it up!"

"I see." Limply holding the mess tin, Kondō stared at the boy's back as it floated in the water.

The lance corporal stormed off. With a sense of regret Kondō realized he would not be able to wash rice in this pond anymore. A human life could be taken for taking a lump of sugar. Once again, what was human life? Suddenly he recalled the words of Christ: "Though a sparrow be worth less than a penny, yet the Lord has made the sparrow beautiful."* A sparrow's life was no different from a human's. Though their lives be worth less than a lump of sugar, yet the Lord has made the Chinese boys beautiful. . . . Kondō clamped down tightly on his sensibility and resumed his understanding with the battlefield. Dangling the dripping mess tin from his right hand and humming, he strolled back to the campfire.

When Lance Corporal Takei returned to the kitchen, the four remaining Chinese glanced up at him with anxious, searching eyes and began frantically to cook. Takei roughly washed his hands, marched up to the pot filled with boiling vegetables, and stirred them about. Nakahashi was still standing there.

"You killed him?" he asked.

"Yes, I killed him," Takei answered.

"What did you have to do that for? He was a good, hardworking fellow. Learn to control your temper."

"Try imagining how I feel!" Takei burst out and averted his face. Nakahashi started: The man was crying! Being robbed of sugar for the regimental commander's supper had triggered this much sadness. The interpreter silently left his side.

Presently Takei heaped the cooked food onto a plate and took it to Colonel Nishizawa's room. He had only one dish to serve him.

---

* A somewhat garbled Biblical reference (to Matthew 10:29–31).

The colonel was seated at a soiled table, intently studying the list of men killed.

"Tonight we lost our sugar, sir, so the dishes are tasteless," said Takei, bowing his head. "Tomorrow I'll be sure to look for some."

"That's fine," replied the colonel without looking up.

"I'm sorry, sir."

He bowed once again and returned to the kitchen. Squatting before the stove, he stared into the swirling flames.

"Takei, aren't you going to eat?" called out a soldier.

"Later," replied Takei, not budging.

ON THE MORNING of departure from Wu-hsi, the soldiers set fire to the houses in which they had been lodging. Many simply left without extinguishing the cooking fires, confident they would eventually engulf the buildings.

They did this not only to demonstrate to themselves their resolve never to retreat, but also to deny refuge to their scattered enemies. Moreover, they felt that burning this city to the ground was the surest way of consolidating its occupation.

The line of march drew away from the city walls to advance across the vast, sweeping plains, while behind it boiling clouds of black smoke darkened the sky over Wu-hsi, concealing the sunlight. The shooting flames were audible from afar; they howled like a windstorm. In this city of two hundred thousand, there was hardly an inhabitant left, except for a handful of guards. The fires blazed from intersection to intersection and from street to street, subsiding in the end of their own accord.

This day the regiment marched parallel to the railroad and

spent the night in Heng-lin-chen. There it was learned that Ch'ang-chou had been swiftly seized by friendly forces.

To Nanking, to Nanking!

Nanking was the enemy capital. That made the soldiers happy. Nanking differed from cities like Ch'ang-chou and Wu-hsi: The capture of Nanking would signify definitive victory. The excitement was palpable.

The number of Japanese horses in the marching column had sharply decreased, while Chinese horses and buffalo were more numerous. Chinese porters rose in number as well. It was a strange sight: Chinese were helping attack their own capital. Barefoot, wearing baggy black cotton-padded trousers, they walked briskly, pulling the buffalo along by the muzzles. With rifles slung over their right shoulders, the soldiers marched beside them, smoking and prodding them with their elbows.

"*Nii!* Nanking *hao ku-niang to-to yu?*"

Making sense of the mangled words, the Chinese let forlorn smiles faintly crease their dusty cheeks and answered briefly.

"*Yu . . .*"

Thus assured there were many fine girls in Nanking, the soldiers broke into broad grins and nodded. "All right!" they shouted, but realizing the word was not Chinese, they felt chagrined not to know its equivalent. They wished to learn as many Chinese words as possible and imagined impatiently how enjoyable it would be if only they could speak fluently. A great serenity was to be found in these broken conversations with the Chinese. And yet, even during such peaceful moments, they could not quite overcome their contempt for the Chinese, so stubbornly and deeply was it rooted in their hearts.

A number of soldiers marched carrying the bones of their

dead comrades. None of the bones had been sent to the rear since the landing at Pai-mao River; all continued to advance in their comrades' embrace. As the front moved forward, the dead multiplied, while the units' numerical strength correspondingly diminished. The proportion of soldiers carrying the bones doubled and kept growing. It was truly a march of survivors. At the conclusion of each battle, those still present felt thoroughly amazed to be alive. The awareness of being among the living was especially poignant when waking at dawn in villages where they were billeted.

In the early morning of the thirtieth of November, Nishizawa Regiment assembled prior to leaving Heng-lin-chen for Ch'ang-chou. Daybreak mist crept whitely over the place of assembly outside the village. Walking toward it, Lance Corporal Takei chatted noisily with a group of kitchen-duty soldiers. He hoisted onto his back a friend's bones that he had been carrying in hand, and while fastening the bundle's knot, he began loudly to sing. It was a popular song to whose tune he had fitted his own fragmentary verses.

> "We swore we'd die together,
> And yet, and yet,
> My heart beats on without yours;
> Cruel fate I've met."

"Your lyrics are good," a soldier commented.

Takei kept his friend's bones in a length of bamboo plugged up with cotton. At first he had carried them in a plain wooden box slung across his chest, but the wood's whiteness had attracted enemy bullets from the outset of every fight. Some of the soldiers put the bones into empty cans they had washed, and then carried them in their knapsacks. Far from feeling toward the bones any of the dread or repugnance such objects ordinarily evoked, they actually felt profoundly close to them. It was as if the bones were still alive for them, or rather their own aliveness was but a temporary condition that might transform them, even in the course of this day, into bones just like these. Perhaps they themselves were nothing but living bones.

In this way, the dead soldiers together with the living continued to press toward Nanking.

7

The bulk of the Nishizawa Regiment arrived before noon at the recently occupied Ch'ang-chou, found quarters throughout the city, and ate lunch. Destruction outside the walls was so great that there was not a roof left on a single house. A Rising Sun flag fluttered atop the desolate walls, and the figures of two sentries with fixed bayonets stood small against the clear sky.

After a march unmarred by fighting, the soldiers rested, feeling quite tranquil. They were even having fun, as if on a group tour to see the sights. The fine weather, mild and springlike after three days of cold, added to the happy mood. Waves of sasanqua blossomed in the gardens of ruined homes, and famished dogs lay languidly in the sun beside the wreckage of sandbagged emplacements.

Some soldiers got hold of donkeys from the nearby countryside and took turns riding them through the deserted avenues; others returned leading pigs by ropes tied around their necks. The pigs, of course, would become the day's supper.

The soldiers in charge of preparing the meal produced a large, old-fashioned Mauser seized from a Chinese. To test it out, they fastened a pig to a tree and fired at it from twenty yards away. The shots struck the animal's torso, failing to kill it. The watching soldiers, worried lest too many bullet holes reduce the amount of edible meat, put a stop to the firing practice and dispatched the pig with a single shot between the ears. Before the flesh could even cool off, it was cut up into chops and tossed into the pot.

As night fell, the men gathered around campfires to trade idle talk and to sleep. What were the newspapers writing about them? Why had they not received any letters or packages from home since Dairen; where were they being held up? The rear units were getting their packages but not the front units doing the fighting. There was not even a plan for getting the mail through. That made the packages nothing but luxury goods, did it not? Having exhausted these topics amid the heavy white smoke that irritated their noses and throats, the soldiers, removing neither gaiters nor shoes, pulled their greatcoats over their heads, yawned, and were asleep before they knew it.

On the same night, in the emergency hospital set up within the city walls, there was a horrendous sight.

The hospital building—a wooden, two-story structure painted blue—appeared to have housed a government office. In the middle of a large room measuring some eighty square yards stood a small table; on it a solitary candle burned with a tall, flickering flame. The candle being the sole source of light, almost nothing was distinctly visible. On the floor of this room lay seventy-six wounded men. Those with lighter injuries such as leg or shoulder wounds sat leaning against the walls to give more space to the badly injured. The air was thick with the stifling smell of blood and feverish breath. The only sounds were the quiet, low moans of the severely wounded and the footsteps of the army doctor and nurses who tended them, struggling to push past the bodies that covered the plank floor. One doctor and three male nurses could not attend to them all. In such darkness it was difficult even to distinguish clotted blood from wounds.

The army doctor finished treating one man and moved to the next. The soldier raised an unsteady left arm, clumsily bandaged by himself, and pointed to his neighbor.

"Sir, please take a look at this man. I think he may have just died."

Mutely complying, the doctor pushed open the man's eyelids, bringing his forehead close to peer at the pupils. He unbuttoned the tunic and felt the chest with his hand. Then he returned to the previous soldier.

"Dead, sir?"

Without a reply, the doctor set about ministering to his wounds. Bearing up under the painful probing, the soldier turned his face toward the man beside him and looked closely at the dead face. He knew neither his company nor his name, nor had he ever spoken to him. But he was now determined to remember this soldier's face well. Still young and attractive, it was framed by a sparse beard; the weariness of interminable fighting had etched the white brow with deep shadows.

Another soldier's hip joint had been shattered by a shell fragment. Turning to the doctor who was cleaning the wound, he asked, "How long before I can fight again, sir?"

The doctor's reply was harsh in words but gentle in tone. "Don't be an idiot. Look at this mess."

"Will it make me a cripple?"

"Sure."

The soldier's spirits fell. With a weak smile, he tried to imagine his upcoming return to Japan, dressed in hospital white, and the reactions of people at home. But it did not yet occur to him to think of the dozens of years of life as an invalid that awaited him.

It was true indeed, as First Class Private Kondō often suspected, that a man in battle, while scorning his enemy's life as so much refuse, scorned his own life no less. It was not that a soldier deliberately forced himself to consider life as being light as the proverbial feather; it was rather that in despising the enemy he came unawares to despise himself as well. Losing sight of their lives as individuals, the men lost the capacity to deem their lives and bodies precious. The symptoms resembled a form of nervous breakdown, but so long as the men were not injured, they fought on as if sleepwalking through the war, oblivious to the loss of countless comrades. Only when a bullet tore a hole in their own flesh did they come to with a start, to discover themselves alive and confronting death.

First Class Private Hirao experienced just such a curious awakening the following day while taking part in a mopping-up operation outside Ch'ang-chou.

A broad expanse of fields adjoined the city. The skirmishing line was deployed in these fields, whose level surface provided no cover at all. Hirao lay flat in a furrow, firing his rifle continuously. With the furrow less than six inches deep, his body was almost entirely exposed.

The enemy bullet whipped past his steel helmet and along the length of his back, perforating the heel of his shoe and sending a powerful jolt up his right leg as far as the thigh.

"I'm hit!"

He felt gooseflesh ripple across his entire body and his scalp grow numb. The battlefield that spread before his eyes suddenly seemed a mysterious terrain, as if he had hurtled out of a tunnel into a heretofore unseen landscape. Artillery explosions registered in his ears with unprecedented crispness; each rifle shot and machine gun burst acquired a clarity that set it apart from all the others. He had the impression the guns had just now commenced to fire, intruding their pandemonium into the soundless environment he had been inhabiting. Unexpectedly finding himself sprawled in the middle of a field, he suddenly grew conscious of the innumerable dangers surrounding him and trembled.

Hugging the soil as closely as he could, he drew in his leg for a look. The shoe heel had been pierced diagonally; he could see his soiled sock but realized he was quite unhurt. He heaved a deep sigh and lay his throbbing head on the ground. Had the heel been only an inch higher, his leg might have been crippled for life. Had he raised his head an inch, he would now be an insensate corpse lying in this field.

Cold sweat poured from his forehead and armpits. Seized with nameless terror, he could not move an inch. He had known such terror often when, after landing at Ta-ku and advancing out of Tientsin, his unit had run into its first battles along Tzu-ya River, but it had ceased to affect him after that. Now for the first time, the terror had revived with a stunning swiftness and intensity.

ON THE FIRST of December, the Nishizawa Regiment, marching in the wake of friendly units that had fought their way into Penniu, entered the city and spent the night in the vicinity of the railway station. The following morning, the regiment advanced to Lu-ch'eng and stayed overnight. On the third, it marched into the already occupied city of Tan-yang. Simultaneously, sizable friendly forces overpowered the battery at Chen-chiang to the north, raising the Rising Sun flag over its fort, while the units to the south, having crossed Lake T'ai and taken I-hsing, Li-yang, and Chin-t'an, continued to push westward. Every day the troops drew closer to taking up their positions for the great siege of Nanking.

Nanking's next! Warming their thighs by the evening bonfires, the soldiers echoed each other's thought: Must not die before Nanking!

While Corporal Kasahara had been billeting in a home in Dairen, he fell under the spell of a movie actress whose portrait had appeared in a magazine. He wrote her a letter asking for a signed photograph and was impatiently awaiting its arrival.

"At a time like this, I have to take good care of my valuable self. I'll go to Nanking and rest. The letter will come. It'll be addressed to Mr. Kasahara Shōzō. I'll melt with love. In the back it'll say 'from Takakusu Sayuri.' I'll open it up. My hands will be trembling. A photo will come out. It will be signed! I'll take her into my arms and go beddy-bye. Ah, haha!"

Nanking. The city was on everyone's mind. To enter it alive or dead, but by all means to live until the start of the Nanking offensive. If a man escaped death long enough to march into Nanking, he could wash off the dust of the last month's battles and recuperate at leisure. If the fall of the capital brought an end to the war, he might even see the great day when he and his comrades marched home in victory.

It was around noon on the fourth of December, the second day of their stay in Tan-yang, that an incident occurred which sent a shudder through the soldiers just as they had begun to entertain those hopes and dreams.

Second Lieutenant Kaname of the Third Battalion was killed

while returning from guard inspection. He was walking past a girl of eleven or twelve standing absentmindedly in the sunlight at an alley corner. The girl was staring up at his face, but he passed by, taking no notice of her. Before he had taken three steps, he was shot in the back with a handgun; he crumpled to the pavement and died on the spot.

The girl dashed into a house, but the soldiers who had heard the shots ran up, encircled the house, and crashed through the door. They found her crouched, staring at the floor, next to a Chinese-style bed carved with arabesques, and promptly felled her with a hail of rifle fire. There was an old man in the same house, and he, too, was summarily shot.

It was not in the least surprising that a soldier should be fired upon in an occupied city, but the fact that the assailant was indisputably a noncombatant, and eleven years old at that, infuriated the soldiers who heard of the incident.

"Fine! If that's what the Chinese have in mind, we'll kill them all. We'd be idiots not to wipe them out!"

With such sentiments prevailing, it became impossible to estimate the number of Chinese that were killed for arousing the most trivial suspicions or committing the vaguest offenses. Tragic incidents were difficult to avoid when combatants could not be clearly distinguished from noncombatants. There were more than a few cases similar to that of the young girl, but what particularly exasperated the soldiers was the Chinese regulars' unfailing practice of throwing away their uniforms when cornered, then mingling with the populace. Even many of the so-called peaceful citizens wearing their Rising Sun armbands were most likely Chinese army runaways. It was obvious, moreover, that the closer Nanking came, the more widespread grew anti-

Japanese sentiment, further intensifying the soldiers' distrust of the population.

An order was handed down by the military high command immediately following the Lieutenant Kaname incident: "Because from this point westward, anti-Japanese thought is known to be strong even among ordinary individuals, extreme caution is to be exercised even when dealing with women and children. You are permitted to shoot anyone who resists, civilians included."

FOR THE ENEMY ARMY, which had lost Ch'ang-shu, Wu-hsi, and Ch'ang-chou, there was nothing to do but strengthen the capital's defenses by reinforcing the surrounding hills, Mount Tzu-chin, and the powerful city walls themselves. Consequently, after abandoning Ch'ang-chou and Tan-yang, the Chinese army wavered and then surged toward Nanking, so that even the front-line Japanese units met with no major battles as they began to advance into the increasingly mountainous country west of Tan-yang.

The First Battalion of the Nishizawa Regiment took the lead in attacking K'o-jung. The town contained an infantry school, an artillery school, a military airport, and a number of enemy soldiers who fought back with all the tactics at their disposal. Land mines exploded one after another. Striking a mine, a small tank would have a hole blown through its belly armor and flip over two or three times, its crew dying horribly. The enemy units were not large, but their resistance grew predictably desperate as the fighting approached Nanking.

By the time K'o-jung had been taken and the headquarters of the Takashima Division set up in the artillery school, even the divisional commander's horse could not advance without stepping over corpses.

All units engaged in pursuit battles faced the problem of what to do with prisoners. Soldiers about to take part in heavy fighting could hardly afford to guard and shepherd them long. The simplest method of disposal was to kill them. But even killing was difficult once the hordes of prisoners had been brought in. The explicit order to kill captives on the spot was not actually given out, but it was the general course of action indicated by the top command.

Corporal Kasahara excelled in carrying out such tasks. On one occasion he briskly cut down thirteen men tied together in a row. They wore army uniforms but were barefoot. On their backs, over blue padded-cotton coats, they carried long, narrow bags filled with roasted rice. Two of the men, seemingly noncommissioned officers, were somewhat more neatly attired and wore shoes.

The thirteen were brought to the bank of a brook at the edge of the airport and made to line up. No sooner did Kasahara draw his sword, so nicked that it could hardly cut, than he slashed deeply into the base of the first man's neck. Seeing this, the other twelve dropped to their knees and began all at once to wail, drool, and plead for mercy. The two who seemed to be noncommissioned officers were especially pathetic in their terror. But Kasahara, wasting no time, cut down the second man and the third.

Then he saw something strange. The crying abruptly stopped. Those still alive sat flat on the ground, put both hands on their knees, closed their eyes, and slackened their jaws. They were pale with loss of hope, and silent. Their bearing was magnificent.

Kasahara felt the strength ebb away from his arm. Summoning up his will, he cut down one more but then turned to his comrades.

"Somebody else chop the rest."

Not surprisingly, no one stepped forward to behead them. The soldiers drew back about twenty paces, aimed their rifles, and finally disposed of their troublesome prisoners.

FIRST CLASS Privates Kondō and Hirao were quartered in a residential street next to a large, quiet mansion surrounded by trees.

"What a pompous house. It's impudent. Let's pay it a little visit. Kondō, come on."

Kondō, who had been about to doze off, stood up, yawning. "If there's a *ku-niang* in there, she's mine."

"You ass, we'll toss for her."

Not bothering to take his rifle, Hirao set off first, a piece of bamboo for a cane.

The old-fashioned gate had been broken in, giving way to a garden beginning to bloom with allspice flowers. A flagstone path curving among a thick growth of plants led to a western-style entrance. Its door, too, was open.

Swinging his bamboo stick, Hirao strode into the parqueted vestibule.

"Hello. Anybody home?"

Naturally, no one answered. The retreating Chinese troops seemed to have plundered the house. Curtains and dishes lay strewn along the corridors. The rooms had been mercilessly ransacked; drawers of the large rosewood wardrobes fitted with mirrors lay scattered across the floor. The tub in the western-style bathroom was filled with dirty water, and the tile floor was littered with excrement.

They walked everywhere but found no traces of *ku-niang* nor anything else likely to excite their interest. Finally, Hirao entered a spacious room on the second floor, apparently used for receiving guests. He turned toward Kondō, who was lagging behind, and folded both arms in front to greet him in the Chinese manner.

"Welcome, noble sir. So happy to see you, my dear Kondō of Kondō and Company. It has been a while since I've had the pleasure."

The tranquil sumptuousness of the room inspired him to sudden levity. Kondō promptly responded.

"Ah, Hirao of Hirao and Company! Forgive me for interrupting you at such a busy time."

"Well, do have a seat. Indulge in a moment of repose, please."

As befitted men of stature, the two ensconced themselves in the large, comfortable armchairs and looked about. Made of delicately carved rosewood, the chairs resembled those of the priests in the main hall of a temple. A broad vermilion-lacquered table, a fireplace overlaid with marble, mirrors mounted atop shelves, an antique chandelier—signs of an opulent lifestyle abounded. A number of lightly colored landscape scrolls hung from the walls; two more lay spread out on the floor. Just outside the window a profusion of bamboo rustled in the wind, casting ceaselessly swaying shadows over the room.

"Now then, my dear Kondō, the world seems to be in quite an uproar these days. What do you think will come of it?"

"Indeed, even our old boy Chiang Kai-shek has been making a nuisance of himself.* I finally went to see him again the other day and urged him to put a stop to his rowdyism, but I can't be sure he will listen to me."

"Oh, it is high time that fellow quit politics."

Great man Hirao suddenly rose and walked over to the fireplace to discover a curious object on top of the stone mantelpiece. He took it in his hands. Two inches by five, made from wood, it had a round, flat surface inscribed with the twelve horary signs, and the four cardinal directions of the compass.

"It's a sundial!" he exclaimed with a grave face. "Look, Kondō, a sundial."

Although the sundial did not seem very old, the compass needle was coated with rust. Nevertheless it still tremblingly pointed north.

Slanting rays of the evening sun bathed the room with a pale red glow. Hirao pulled up the vermilion-lacquered table and leaned over it. Using the compass to align the sundial properly, he flipped up the rusty vertical pin. Its shadow formed a slender, distinct line between the signs of Monkey and Bird. Hirao folded his arms and gazed at the sundial.

"This is a great find," said Kondō, but Hirao remained speechless until asked about his silence. Then he broke into a histrionic murmur.

---

* Chiang Kai-shek (1887–1975) was a Chinese nationalist leader. Initially allied with communists, he ordered their liquidation in 1927. Defeated by the communists in 1949, he fled to Taiwan, where the U.S. helped him establish a government.

"Ah, the eternal China, in the present but not of the present. China is dreaming of its ancient culture; breathing the air of its ancient culture. Just think: Though surrounded by this much luxury, what the master of this house delighted in was sipping tea, folding his arms, and gazing at this sundial."

Hirao's romanticism was awake once more. At moments like this his grandiloquence burst forth without warning. He threw himself back in the chair, spread out his legs, and gesticulated with his arms.

"The four hundred million people of China are as serene and ancient as the Yangtze River. China hasn't changed a bit since Huang-ti, Wen, Wu, T'ai-tsung, and Yang Kuei-fei lived and died.* China will never perish. Chiang Kai-shek and his friends have had their try with the New Life Movement and the rest, but changing people like these is absolutely impossible. We, too, can do our damnedest to occupy China's entire territory, but any notion of converting the Chinese to Japanese ways is a dream within a dream within a dream. China is what she is and will everlastingly be. It boggles the mind. Ah, it boggles the mind!"

Kondō grew bored and stood up. "What are you moaning about? Let's go back."

---

* Huang-ti (twenty-seventh century B.C.), the semimythical "Yellow Emperor," is credited with many cultural accomplishments. Wen (the "Cultured Emperor," 204–157 B.C.) and Wu (the "Martial Emperor," 140–87 B.C.) were prominent sovereigns of the western Han dynasty (202 B.C.– A.D. 8). T'ai-tsung (600–649) founded the T'ang dynasty (618–907), during which China produced some of its most brilliant literary and artistic works and powerfully influenced the development of Japanese culture. Yang Kuei-fei (719–756) was a celebrated beauty whose love affair with an emperor ended tragically when he was forced by his own royal guards to have her killed.

Reverently holding the sundial, Hirao rose and placed it gingerly into the inner pocket of his tunic. He felt as though he had managed for the first time to fathom this country named China. Century after century the masses of China had continued to lead lives free of any ties to politics. It did not interest them in the least whether they were governed by the Ch'ing dynasty or Sun Yat-sen.* He began to feel a boundless love for these Chinese people and their millennia-old spirit. Japan was fighting Chiang Kai-shek, but the masses, remote from the Chiang regime, were neither anti-Japanese nor pro-Soviet nor anti-British nor pro-Communist. Hirao's voice was like a wistful sigh as he followed Kondō down the staircase.

"It is genuine anarchism the Chinese are living, each practicing it in his very own way."

Such simple-minded admiration was distasteful to Kondō. "There are many kinds of anarchism, you know. If that's anarchism, then beasts are all anarchists. Consider the pig, for instance: There's a consummate anarchist for you."

"Idiot, you've got no sensibility."

"And you're theorizing like a blind Indian groping to describe an elephant."

"Say whatever you like."

In theoretical dispute, Hirao was no match for Kondō. Gripping his bamboo stick, he leapt out the front door, shouting, "Farewell! Many thanks for the gift!"

---

* Sun Yat-sen (1866–1925) was a Chinese revolutionary leader revered by many as the founder of republican China.

8

On the eighth of December, the First Battalion of the Nishizawa Regiment launched a vehement attack against the enemy
entrenched in the heights of Mount T'ang. By evening it had succeeded in occupying the surrounding highland, but the enemy,
having constructed a series of sturdy pillboxes with mined
approaches, prevented any further advance. The battle raged
with spectacular ferocity.

In the meantime, the other units marched along a road and
entered the village of T'ang-shui-chen, a hot-spring resort emp-
tied of inhabitants. In the inns, bubbling hot water overflowed
from pools laid with white tile, sending up wreaths of steam.

The regiment set up its headquarters in one of the inns,
enabling Commander Nishizawa to wash off the dirt accumu-
lated during more than a month's campaigning. The soldiers
were overjoyed. Dragging out great vats and tubs, they filled
them with hot water and stripped in the open air.

"What a blessing! This is why I like China."

Joking, they scrubbed their rough skins discolored by blood
and grime. Lance Corporal Takei was among those who emerged
from the tub only to exclaim, "Why, I'm still filthy!" and plunge
back in. He took five baths that day.

"This was your fifth time in the tub, was it not?"

When asked that by the company commander, he replied with a serious face, "Yes, sir, and I'm finally clean. Now no matter when I die, I won't have to be washed for burial."

But some of the soldiers held firm against bathing, lest a fleeting return to the world of cleanliness only make them more miserable later on.

Already Nanking was less than a day's march away. T'ang-shui-chen was the last place they could sleep at leisure. Beyond it, there was no telling when they would rest under a roof again. Understandably nervous, the soldiers felt a renewed awareness of being on a battleground and wondered what tomorrow held in store for their lives.

That evening the soldiers put their knapsacks in order and packed them with rice and sweet potatoes. They inserted 120 cartridges into the ammunition pouches lining their belts. Each man slipped a final letter into his wallet or between the pages of a notebook kept in an inner pocket.

"December 8. This may be the final entry. Dying is nothing to be sorry about." Second Lieutenant Kurata wrote in his diary, snapped the pencil in two, and tossed it into the bonfire. He was calm and highly alert. He wiped the blade of his sword, tested his pistol, and cleaned the rifle barrel. After filling his canteen with hot water, he carefully wrapped a box of matches with oilpaper and tucked it into the knapsack. "Well, tomorrow it finally begins," he said to himself, all preparations complete. Then, to be well rested, he went to sleep early.

"Well, tomorrow it finally begins!" shouted Corporal Kasahara to no one in particular. But he neither wiped his sword blade nor so much as peered into his canteen, and it never would have occurred to him to pack a box of matches.

NEXT DAY, the Nishizawa Regiment reached the Ch'i-lin Gate. Mount Tzu-chin rose in sharp outline a mere five miles away. This was the outpost line of the great Nanking offensive. In the afternoon, the opposing troops started to exchange intermittent gunfire, but at nightfall the enemy began a rapid withdrawal. With their rear already threatened, it served no purpose to stay and fight. In their wake they left mines that blew apart several horses.

By now Nanking was under siege. The units advancing from Mo-ling Kuan in the south approached the main enemy position at Mount Niu-shou and commenced to fight their way up its heights, while the enemy troops kept on retreating in the direction of Yu-hua-t'ai outside the Nanking city walls. Other units, driving westward after breaking through the enemy defenses at So-yeh-chen, seized Ch'un-hua and continued in swift pursuit. The northern units reduced the artillery stronghold overlooking the riverbanks at Mount Wu-lung and proceeded upstream to confront the battery at Mount Mu-fu. The Takashima Division and additional units followed the Nanking Highway from the Ch'i-lin Gate toward the Chung-shan Gate. Along the way, the Nishizawa Regiment separated from the rest of the division with the order to attack Mount Tzu-chin.

At noon a Japanese army airplane flew over the city of Nanking, dropping a letter urging surrender, addressed by the commander in chief of the Shanghai Expeditionary Force to the Nanking garrison commander, T'ang Sheng-chih. The reply deadline was noon the next day, the tenth of December; the place of delivery, the sentry line along the Chung-shan Road and K'o-jung Highway. If there was no reply, the attack on the city would commence. According to the letter's preamble, the advice to capitulate was prompted by a just and merciful reluctance to destroy a center of East Asian culture.

The fighting outside the city raged on throughout the day, with the encirclement growing tighter by the moment. The soldiers watched at close range the long, brownish-black undulations of the Nanking city walls, and waited.

Noon of the following day came but brought no reply. At one in the afternoon the order to open the all-out offensive against Nanking was passed down the length of the line.

The Nishizawa Regiment attack on Mount Tzu-chin had started in the morning of the tenth. Some of its units skirted the base of the mountain to advance north along a railroad line. Pushing beyond the T'ai-p'ing and He-p'ing Gates, they divided forces to attack the Hsia-kuan train station and occupy the quays. Other units began to climb the mild eastern slopes of Mount Tzu-chin.

Its highest summit rose more than five hundred yards above sea level. Segmented into three peaks, the mountain appeared gently beautiful viewed from Sun Yat-sen's tomb at its southern base, but the opposite northern slope was a mass of jagged rocks, so steep that men could not climb it without clutching trees for support. Troops advancing along the highway from Mount T'ang toward the Chung-shan Gate were given the task of attacking the Chung-shan Mausoleum at the mountain's southern foot, while two battalions of the Nishizawa Regiment received the order to assault the precipitous northern slope.

The mountaintop was fortified with rows of solid pillboxes and firing trenches dug in long multiple lines. Gun muzzles glared down the slope, machine guns already firing. This was a foremost stronghold in the defense of Nanking, and so long as the mountain held out, the success of the Nanking offensive was in jeopardy. Realizing this, Division Commander Takashima entrusted the attack specifically to the two battalions of the Nishizawa Regiment, the most dependable troops under his command.

The men of the Furuya Company spread out and started the ascent, pulling themselves up among rocks and young pines. The leading units were already engaged in sharp fighting. Topographically, their position could not have been worse. While the enemy fired from trenches and pillboxes, showing nothing but their heads or machine gun muzzles, the friendly forces had to struggle upward, their entire bodies exposed. Fully aware of the predicament, the regimental commander, together with the standard-bearer and the adjutant, moved up to the forefront of the battle, coming repeatedly under fire.

In a fight like this, the enemy's most effective weapons were hand grenades and machine guns. Pelted from overhead by grenades, the attackers found it virtually impossible to advance.

Like a black stone, a grenade hurtled from a trench. Trailing a plume of white smoke, it struck a rock, rolled hissing toward a climbing man, and burst in a blossom of sound and smoke. A cloud of dust and sodium nitrate fumes cleared above a blood-drenched, groaning soldier. "Long live the Emperor!"

With that voice ringing in his ears, the man's comrade tensed and spun around. "Hey! Kusama, hey!" But the friend did not answer.

The soldier fell silent, pressed the gunstock against his cheek, and squeezed the trigger over and over again. The cartridges grew fewer by the moment, and the ammunition belt lighter. And yet he could not advance a step. With the cartridges all spent, he grabbed the rifle and ran stumbling downhill past rocks and pines. Wounded comrades lay everywhere, some applying their own field dressing as they sheltered behind rocks, others sprawled under pine branches, staring emptily at the sky. He ran among them until he reached the supply soldiers just outside the firing zone, then toppled onto his side, shouting "Hey! Give me ammunition! Ammunition!"

Katayama Genchō, having found a Chinese broadsword somewhere, wore it slung diagonally across his back. By now he had hacked to death dozens of Chinese soldiers and felt at peace. Venturing almost up to the firing line, he nursed the wounded or stood before the killed, pressing his hands together in prayer. Stray shots whizzed over his shoulders. The priest wore a steel helmet.

It was nearly noon and the sunlight blazed down over the mountain ridge into the faces of attacking soldiers. Dazzled, they could not see the enemy. Sudden streaks of white smoke sped across the clear blue sky. Whining eerily, trench mortar shells streamed overhead, jolting the earth as they exploded among the soldiers. The men struggled to hurl grenades at the summit, but these never reached the enemy trenches. Instead, spewing smoke, they rolled back toward the soldiers who had thrown them.

Heavy field guns, hauled into position by tractors, stood arrayed below Mount Tzu-chin. The large shells glistened as they were loaded. The guns discharged with a strangely dull, broad sound, and the shriek of the shells rent the sky. The shells flew over the ridge of Mount Tzu-chin, for the artillerymen were not firing at the summit but were bombarding the environs of the Hsia-kuan train station far away.

Rapid-fire cannons were drawn up at the base of the mountain, near the row of heavy field artillery. They were now the infantry's greatest hope. What precision! Penetrating the narrow loophole of an enemy pillbox, a rapid-fire cannon poured in not one, but eight shells out of ten. The loophole belched white smoke as the interior exploded.

Did it! thought the soldiers. But their faces showed no emotion and they mutely continued to shoot. The enemy was subjecting them to a steady hail of machine gun fire. Striking the rocks, the bullets shattered them into fragments. The branches of a young pine shook continuously; soon it tilted and crashed to the ground. The sheared-off trunk overflowed with resin glistening moistly in the sun.

Sword unsheathed, Second Lieutenant Kurata crept up from rock to rock, followed by the surviving soldiers of his platoon. Reaching one rock, a soldier fired some ten shots and started to crawl toward the base of the next. From rock to rock: At present, rocks were their only strongholds. The soldiers advanced by inches. A hand grenade came rolling toward them; with a gasp, they ducked their heads. The explosion reverberated deep in their bodies. Covered with sand, they crept on.

Lieutenant Kurata's sword could not reach the enemy trench. He collected five grenades from his men and climbed ahead. Supporting himself against a rock with his left hand, he raised his body slightly, yanked out the safety pin with his teeth, and struck the fuse. Instantly the grenade began to hiss and emit smoke. He counted to four and swung his arm. Trailing white smoke, the black missile flew into the trench. Good! He lay flat. Then he gripped his sword again and moved on in search of another rock.

In the midst of the battle, Commander Nishizawa paced leisurely about. He noticed a wounded soldier being carried down the incline on the back of a comrade. The soldier's complexion had already deteriorated and his lips were black. His head rested on his shoulder and his arms hung limply. Eyes vacantly opened, he spoke in snatches.

"Put me down . . . Please put me down. I'm hit in the stomach. It's hopeless. I can still shoot. Let me shoot some more. Hey, please, put me down."

Amid the deafening noise the colonel heard his words. Gazing wide-eyed after the two descending men, he spoke to the soldier beside him, his voice husky as if with anger.

"Who is that soldier? Find out his name!"

The soldier ran off. Never until that moment had the colonel so intensely felt the august virtue of His Majesty the Emperor and the sterling worth of the soldiers.

"That is an extraordinary soldier!" he said to the adjutant, his lip quivering.

The Japanese continued to sacrifice their lives at a steady rate, but the desperately energetic enemy defense prevented them from advancing a step. Such a conventional assault was much too costly.

An unexpected way was found to break the impasse: The uphill attack could be turned to advantage by setting fire to the mountain. The pines and weeds would burn well. The matches Second Lieutenant Kurata had brought along proved admirably useful.

Fires were set all along the attacking line. The young pine needles blazed up, spreading the flames along the grass from branch to branch. The individual fires gradually converged into a fiery sea that surged toward the summit, incinerating the Chinese corpses in its path. Thick yellow smoke enveloped the front as the flames, invisible under the noon sun, swallowed one tree after another. Following the fire, the troops drove swiftly forward.

It was thanks to this ingenious stratagem that the second highest peak of Tzu-chin Shan was seized with the sun still high. The pillboxes and machine gun nests crumbled feebly before the sudden fire attack, leaving the enemy no choice but to retreat along the ridge to the highest peak.

There was a break in the fighting while the troops occupied the height. Shells fired from the enemy-held summit still came flying across the shallow interjacent valley. Utterly fatigued, the soldiers stretched out their legs in the pillboxes and trenches that the enemy had constructed, and shut their eyes. Hundreds of Chinese soldiers lay sprawled about; all had bags of roasted rice on their backs. The soldiers took the rice from the corpses and quietly chewed on it. Oilcans filled with water stood about by the hundreds, each covered with a thin coat of ice. They had been brought up the mountain, for there was not a drop of water on Mount Tzu-chin. The soldiers greedily drank the water the enemy had drawn.

About this time, the Kobayashi unit, having advanced up the Nanking Highway, occupied the Chung-shan Mausoleum at the mountain's southern base. The granite-paved paths and the stairs had all been painted blue-gray or otherwise camouflaged. The tower gate, the main shrine, and other structures were concealed by scaffolding of quartered bamboo and looked as though crates had been placed over them. Such were the air-raid counter-measures.

Hundreds of students of the Central Officers School had entrenched themselves here and put up a stout resistance. Sun Yat-sen was their idol, and to protect their idol they died. Were there more tragedies among the victors or the losers? The soldiers of the victorious Kobayashi unit ran up the broad approach to the shrine, jumped onto the backs of the two huge stone lions, and planted the Rising Sun flags. On the stone pillars of the tower gate, using blood for paint, they wrote in large letters, "Occupied by the Kobayashi unit on December 10!"

Then they launched an attack against the enemy remnants at the Ming-hsiao Mausoleum. The great stone statues lining the front approach to the shrine looked on mutely with grave faces as strings of mines exploded all around their massive pedestals.

From atop the second peak, heavy fighting could be seen raging in front of the Chung-shan Gate. The gate was enfolded in powder smoke but could not easily be breached. From the main peak of Mount Tzu-chin, enemy field-guns and howitzers fired volleys at the besieging army.

Soon night fell and the gunfire quieted down. To prepare for the eventuality of a night attack, one unit remained skirmishing at the front line; the rest of the soldiers, embracing each other against the cold that covered the mountaintop with frost, slept soundly. They lay alongside their dead comrades, guarding their bodies as they slept. A single overcoat served to cover two men. There were neither living nor dead. A live soldier was identical to his dead comrade; nothing set them apart. The stony ground they slept on made their heads ache, so some men pulled up Chinese corpses and used their stomachs for pillows. "Ah, what comfort!" they remarked.

In the depths of the night, the city of Nanking blazed in a welter of flames. Some of the fires were the result of bombardment, but many were deliberately set. Inside the city, the Chinese soldiers were already looting savagely.

ON THE FOLLOWING DAY—the eleventh—an attack was launched against the summit, but the enemy troops, having already been cut off from the rear, fought with the ferocity of cornered animals, making an easy breakthrough impossible. Engineers of the Nishizawa Regiment, crawling under the sparse pines and hiding behind rocks, inched forward toward the enemy advance line, carrying steel shears to cut through the barbed-wire entanglements. A splendid new concrete trench, constructed in the shape of a horseshoe and backed by a cluster of pillboxes, jutted out from the summit, enabling the enemy machine guns to lay down a withering curtain of fire. In addition, the enemy unrelentingly shelled the crowds of Japanese troops closing in on the city gates, of which Chung-shan, T'ai-p'ing, Hsuan-wu, and He-p'ing could be seen from the summit. With the last of the capital's defenders fighting so resolutely, it was not surprising that little headway could be made throughout the day's combat. The stalemate continued into the night.

Lying behind rocks, rifles steadily pointed at the enemy, the soldiers spent an uneasy night attacking, repelling counterattacks, and intermittently dozing as they awaited the dawn of the twelfth.

The Chung-hua Gate had already been occupied and flew the Rising Sun flag. But even with this gate in their hands, the troops could not set foot into the city. The entire attacking force was waiting for Mount Tzu-chin to fall.

Day broke. The worn-out soldiers opened their eyes and raised their heads to see the enemy trenches less than ten paces away. Even the facial expressions of the enemy soldiers were clearly visible.

The war of hand grenades and machine guns started up again. Around noon, the Furuya Company was finally able to take the first line of enemy trenches. Company Commander Furuya, however, was wounded and taken to the rear, whereupon Second Lieutenant Kurata instantly took command of the company. First Class Privates Hirao and Kondō, Lance Corporal Takei, and Corporal Kasahara of the machine gun squad wore such blurred expressions that they looked like imbeciles but were nonetheless still alive.

Deprived of their first trench, the enemy instantly counter-attacked. Raising a tremendous cry, they came flying across the rocks, brandishing broadswords, bayonets at the ready. Machine guns rattled away. The assault was repelled as the Japanese attacked in turn. But no sooner did they clear the edge of the rocks than they toppled in droves, and the attack ground to a halt. Once more, the enemy counterattacked.

Corporal Kasahara crouched inside the trench, manning a light machine gun. Voices of the charging enemy rang out, coming closer each second. Yet he did not fire.

"Hey, aren't you going to shoot?!" shouted a soldier beside him. Kasahara's grimy face broke into a grin.

"It's all right. Be quiet and pray."

Two rocks lay in front of him, nearly five feet apart. Pressing his head against one of them, he took aim but did not pull the trigger. The enemy voices sounded almost overhead, and the running footsteps sent vibrations up the elbows of the aiming soldiers. When the leading attacker's foot landed atop the nearest rock, Kasahara's machine gun sprang to life. His marksmanship was excellent. Dozens of enemy soldiers fell, one upon another, within his arm's reach.

Kasahara sniffled like a child. "Eh, hehe! That's the way to kill them! Not a shot wasted."

Although the attack was beaten back, the Japanese troops lacked the strength for an attack of their own. Noon passed.

It was then that a stern order from the divisional headquarters was delivered to the Nishizawa Regiment: "Mount Tzu-chin is to be completely occupied by six o'clock this afternoon."

The regimental commander had in fact expected to accomplish that task the next day. It could be done without costing too many lives, he had thought. And yet, considering the severe losses a day's delay would inflict upon the mass of troops pressing in on the city walls, he conceded that a more intensive assault might be unavoidable. Faced with the new order, the colonel had to resign himself to an extraordinarily large number of sacrifices among his subordinates.

Another order was soon transmitted to the units: "Occupy the summit by six in the afternoon. Attack in full force."

The regimental commander simultaneously issued an additional order: "Reserve units forward. Colors to the fore!"

Already the battle was taking a distressing number of lives.

Now a full-force attack was launched. This was when Lance Corporal Takei was killed.

A machine gun bullet struck him in the shoulder. But because he was lying flat, the bullet tore lengthwise through his entire torso, exiting below his hip. Takei flipped over onto his back, clenching his rifle in agony. Hirao dragged him behind the shelter of a rock.

"Son of a bitch, son of a bitch! I'll die when I get to Nanking, not before Nanking . . ."

Even as he spoke, his complexion altered and his lips began to tremble. Blood welled up around his tongue and overflowed his throat, so that he could moan only intermittently, though he writhed with pain. Just then the regimental flag came into view, weaving forward among the smoke-enshrouded branches of young pines.

"Hey, it's the regimental flag. The regimental flag is here!" shouted Hirao into Takei's ear.

Then this nearly dead man opened his eyes wide and rolled over by himself. The regimental flag was about twenty paces away, advancing toward the line of fire. Could his eyes still see it? Lying prone, he raised his left hand in front of his face and brought his blood-stained right palm tightly against it.

"Please. *Please!*"

What he meant by this was unclear. It was simply a word that surfaced into his consciousness just before dying. Perhaps it was a request, directed at the regimental standard, to be sure and win although he himself could no longer fight. He died with his hands clasped together.

Soon after that, the regimental standard-bearer was killed, shot through the abdomen. It was common knowledge among soldiers that abdominal wounds were beyond help. The standard-bearer knew it, too. One merely suffered a long time and then died.

He quickly turned to the guard.

"Please call the regimental commander. I must return the colors intact."

Gentle and brave, the standard-bearer was a good soldier. One of the regimental commander's best-loved subordinates, he was also the superior the soldiers loved and respected the most. He breathed his last while being carried to the rear. Looking at the face of the soldier carrying the stretcher, he asked, "Soldier, do you have a wife?" The soldier replied that he did. The standard-bearer faintly smiled and said he had hoped to die after entering Nanking. Then he expired.

At five-thirty in the afternoon, only twenty-five minutes before the decreed deadline, the summit of Mount Tzu-chin was completely occupied. The first to breach the enemy defenses was a replacement soldier from a farm village, a simple man who ordinarily attracted little notice.

He crept up to the base of a large rock in the center of the projecting, horseshoe-shaped enemy trench. Because the enemy hand grenades, hurled from atop the rock, flew over his head to land at the rear, he was actually in a safe spot. Lying there, he surveyed the situation. The enemy were under attack on the right and were concentrating all their attention in that direction. He crawled to the left of the rock and suddenly leapt into the trench. An enemy soldier sprang upon him, but he shot him twice through the chest. The trench was narrow, enabling him to attack one man at a time. The enemy commenced to flee single file, and he pursued them, firing; one of those who fell was definitely an officer. Then all at once other Japanese soldiers poured in.

As soon as the mountaintop shelling of Chung-shan and other gates had ceased, the units pressing against them launched a spirited assault, throwing them all wide open by nightfall. The tank corps burst into the city. The corpses of the enemy soldiers were run over and crushed under the caterpillar treads.

A quiet night settled over the summit, the cold and the north wind freezing the site of the recent battle. The soldiers crunched on the roasted rice they had taken from Chinese corpses and shivered in the cold wind; then they slept. Corporal Kasahara piled up three enemy corpses, positioned one more to serve as a pillow, and addressed Second Lieutenant Kurata.

"Company Commander, sir, if you'd like to sleep here, there's no wind and it's comfortable. This one's freshly killed, so he's still warm."

"Well, thank you," replied the lieutenant, laughing. Not a trace of his former sentimentality remained. Kasahara began stacking up three more corpses to make his own bed.

Below, the city of Nanking was a vortex of flames. Smoke reflected the fires, lighting the night sky crimson.

On the thirteenth of December, units of the Nishizawa Regiment advanced along the ridge past an astronomical observatory and descended the mountain. Taking a detour around the city, they marched past the Hsia-kuan train station and arrived at the quays, where after more than a month they saw again the waters of the Yangtze River.

On this day, the mopping-up operations within the city reached their desolate climax. During the previous day the commander of the Nanking garrison, T'ang Sheng-chih, had gathered his soldiers and fled via I-chiang Gate to Hsia-kuan.

About two thousand Cantonese soldiers were guarding the I-chiang Gate. Their orders were to defend this gate and not permit the Chinese army to retreat so much as a step outside the city. T'ang Sheng-chih and his subordinates mounted machine guns onto trucks, crashed through the gate, and escaped to Hsia-kuan.

The Japanese army did not attack the I-chiang Gate until the very end. The enemy soldiers trapped within the city rushed through this single gate and surged toward the quays of Hsia-kuan. Here the river confronted them. There were no boats; the land escape routes were cut off. They threw themselves into the water, clinging to tables, logs, wooden doors—anything that would float—and struggled to cross the great Yangtze's current toward P'u-k'ou on the opposite shore.

About fifty thousand men made the attempt, inching across the river's surface in a black, teeming mass. Those who succeeded found that the Japanese army had already arrived and was waiting for them. The machine guns opened fire. As if chopped by a rainstorm, the water erupted into fine slivers of spray. The men tried to turn back, but by now the Hsia-kuan quays also bristled with Japanese machine guns. Gunfire from naval destroyers struck the finishing blows against the floundering enemy soldiers.

Mopping-up operations within the city continued on the fourteenth. Shopping districts were littered with discarded army uniforms, their owners all having put on civilian clothes and mingled with the refugees. Sun-in-blue-sky flags lay strewn about restaurant kitchens; Chinese broadswords and gaiters cluttered the floors of china shops. It had become increasingly difficult to dispose of genuine soldiers without harming civilians.

The fifteenth and sixteenth of December were spent in mopping-up operations outside the city. At noon of the seventeenth, the Nishizawa Regiment assembled along with the other units outside the Chung-shan Gate to take part in the triumphal entry into Nanking. While dozens of airplanes streaked overhead, casting shadows onto clouds, rows of regimental banners, cavalry, infantry, artillery, and tanks passed through the arched gate and advanced in a straight line into the deserted heart of the city.

The Nishizawa Regiment took over the Nanking municipal government building for its headquarters, and the Takashima Division set up its headquarters in the stone-built Central Hotel. Division Commander Takashima and his staff commandeered the private residence of Chiang Kai-shek and Sung Mei-ling, which was connected by a garden to the Officers School.* The home was a simple, small, two-story structure surrounded by frost-withered grass and red sasanqua blossoms.

---

* Born 1897, Sung Mei-ling was the second wife of Chiang Kai-shek. As of this writing, Ms. Sung resides in New York City.

9

Having crossed the river, some of the units continued to advance north from P'u-k'ou; others left Nanking to head some fifteen miles south in pursuit of the routed enemy. But for the soldiers who remained stationed in Nanking, tranquil days had at long last arrived.

There was not a single work of art in the Nanking Art Museum, but it did contain mountains of South Asian rice. For the present, rice was in ample supply. Vegetables could be had in abundance by going to the fields adjoining the city. Water buffalo and pigs provided the meat. Hand grenades thrown away by the fleeing Chinese soldiers lay about all over Hsia-kuan. By tossing them into the Yangtze River or a city pond, hundreds of carp could be caught at once.

"These carp sure are fat. Must have gobbled up lots of Chinese soldiers." The soldiers laughed as they cooked the fish.

Accompanied by shouts, a cart was trundled in from the side gate of the Nanking municipal government building; it carried a water buffalo with its legs trussed up. The men skinned the animal beneath the two-story municipal gate, which was said to be a representative piece of Chinese architecture. Soldiers riding donkeys about in the sunshine called out happily, "So that's what we're having for dinner tonight!"

Supply unit soldiers, arriving in the wake of the main force, brought great earthenware jars from somewhere and had Chinese laborers fill them with hot water. Japanese *sake* abruptly materialized. The men bathed and drank, and soon the city resounded with popular songs and ballads.

Interpreter Nakahashi and army priest Katayama shared a room next to some signal corpsmen. They quickly equipped it with a stove and sufficient coal. Then the interpreter brought along a young Chinese from the refugee zone. Originally a restaurant cook, he was a good-natured boy named Chang. The interpreter, who called him by the pet name Lao Chang, asked, "Make us some noodles tonight, would you?"

Chang mixed the flour in a washbasin, brought a cut of buffalo meat from the army kitchen, and made the noodles. Kasahara and Hirao came to the feast. Army priest Katayama, soup trickling into his beard, said he wanted to offer a bowl to the regimental commander.

"Hey, *nii,* bring us some *ku-niang!*" said Kasahara with a horsey laugh. He was depressed, for the photograph of his favorite film actress had not arrived. Although the Shanghai-Nanking railroad had been reopened by the army and the transport along it resumed, soldiers of the Nishizawa Regiment had not yet received a single letter.

Supply unit soldiers brought in a kerosene-powered generator they had found in a factory; they also had kerosene. Soldiers with industrial school backgrounds started the engine. One evening the lights suddenly came on throughout the municipal building, greeted by happy cheers. But since a strict blackout was in effect, the men had to drape the windows with black cloth.

Dozens of airplanes that had arrived at the two city airports rose daily into the sky and flew about. The enemy airplanes staged repeated night attacks but were invariably repulsed.

A canteen was opened at the corner of Chung-shan Road. It sold canned goods, cigarettes, *sake,* and sweet bean jelly. Garrison soldiers from Hsia-kuan, five miles away, drove up in a truck to do their shopping. They bought fifty half-gallon bottles of *sake* and a hundred packages of sweet bean jelly.

Garrison troops outside the city were in charge of digging up land mines. They used Chinese laborers for the task. Trembling with fear, the Chinese dug into the earth. The soldiers watched, laughing, a safe distance away.

Nanking's remaining inhabitants had all been herded into the refugee zone. They were said to number two hundred thousand, but a thousand or so army regulars seemed to be hiding among them. In the other parts of the city, there were hardly any Chinese in sight; only the Japanese soldiers strolled about, shopping at the canteen or foraging for goods.

Corporal Kasahara often went requisitioning with interpreter Nakahashi. The objects they sought to acquire were such luxury items as down quilts to help them sleep during the cold nights, slippers to wear inside the barracks, or fine photographs of *ku-niang.* Every shop along the main streets of the large city had been savagely looted and was either empty of all goods, littered with their remnants, or reduced by fire to a heap of tile and brick.

Walking around the devastated city, Second Lieutenant

Kurata keenly felt its misery. In the evening, while drinking *sake* with several platoon leaders, he posed a question.

"The wealth Nanking has lost must amount to billions. Regardless of the war's outcome, I'm grateful with all my heart that this war didn't take place in Japan. A nation's treasure is lost, its people have neither food nor clothes, its women are brutalized—if this were Japan, what would you think about it?"

One of the platoon leaders responded.

"I myself don't think Nanking can ever recover. Well, two thirds of it are burned down. There's nothing that can be done with those scorched ruins. Those who lose a war suffer real misery, and there's no help for that. So I think a country must not be rash about getting into a war, but if it does fight, it ought to do its damnedest to win. Even if it means saddling its children's children with debt, it had better win."

With a knock at the door a soldier entered, paused to salute, and asked to see the company commander. Lieutenant Kurata promptly rose and straightened himself.

"Report number one: Infantry First Class Private Fukamauchi Saburō was today ordered discharged from the hospital," the soldier announced.

"Good."

"Report number two: Infantry First Class Private Fukamauchi Saburō was ordered promoted to Lance Corporal, effective December twenty-second. End of report."

"Well, congratulations, Lance Corporal!" Lieutenant Kurata's face showed joy for the first time. "Has your wound healed?"

The soldier tried bending his right elbow.

"I can't move it enough yet, but the doctor says if I keep doing it, it'll get better and better."

"Well, that is very good. You used to carry the grenade launcher, right?"

"That's right, sir."

"You'd better not carry anything heavy for a while. Have a comrade carry it for you."

"Yes, sir."

"How about a drink to celebrate?"

Lieutenant Kurata personally handed him the glass and poured the *sake*. Still standing, the soldier received the cup, then suddenly relaxed and launched into an anecdote.

He had been wounded at the battle around the Ch'i-lin Gate. When Nanking fell, all the sick and wounded soldiers were taken to a large hospital next to the Officers School.

That day he had a fever and was groaning with pain from the wound, but when he heard a hospital orderly say that some fifty enemy stragglers had been captured and were marching past the gate, he leapt up, shouting, "I'll kill them!" and rushed downstairs and out to the gate. The captives came trooping by in their blue uniforms. He had no weapon, so he asked a soldier guarding the gate for his sword, but the man refused. He then grabbed a Chinese soldier with his left hand, slapped him across the face, kicked him in the shin, and turned back.

"But I couldn't climb up to the second floor anymore. Somebody helped me and I finally made it on all fours." The soldier laughed, straightened up, saluted, and left.

Second Lieutenant Kurata had obtained a new pencil and now began once more to write the diary he had recently neglected. First Lieutenant Furuya, who had once teasingly asked him if he thought he would be opening the diary again, had been wounded; a great many men had been killed; and he could not help marveling that he had lived long enough to sit calmly in the room of the municipal government building and write in his diary. He was no longer impatient to die, nor were his emotions upset beyond endurance. He felt serene and benevolent, his mind expansive and poised. In the end he had managed to gain confidence in his own actions. He had acquired an untrammeled state of mind suitable for carrying out his demanding duties as a military man and citizen of a nation.

Unlike First Class Private Kondō's compromise with the battlefield, his was a wholehearted affirmation of it. It gave rise to a sense of equilibrium. Gone was the impatience to die caused by an instinctive fear of death, gone the clinging to the life he had been living until now. It was not that he had arrived at a clearly thought-out philosophical view of life and death, but rather that scorning the enemy's life, he had unawares attained the extremely intuitive, spontaneous mental state of scorning his own. At any rate, a transformation of this magnitude turned him into a distinguished military officer and lent him, even as acting company commander, an authority worthy of the soldiers' confidence and respect.

By contrast, First Class Private Kondō, having objectified the battlefield and compromised with it, experienced neither the intense anguish Lieutenant Kurata had known nor a major transformation. But the battlefield he had externalized lost its immediacy for him, and his intelligence grew blunted in the war's confusion, resulting in a debased form of adjustment and an indolent soldier who lacked seriousness in all he did. Interested only in the worst aspects of soldierly behavior and ready to follow others in self-degradation, he was like a serious student enjoying the process of becoming a delinquent, proud that he, too, could hunt for *ku-niang,* deliberately step on a Chinese soldier's corpse, or set fire to a house. On his way back from the canteen, even if he had purchased only a single can of food, he would grab a passing Chinese and order him to carry it. Reaching the barracks, he would slap his face and thrust him away, snarling, "Get lost!" This was the way things were done in wartime, he proudly announced.

Corporal Kasahara, on the other hand, possessed an inherent diligence and goodness that impelled him—when he was not committing outrages and delighting in the freedoms accorded to victors—to busy himself by foraging for coal to heat the rooms and flour to make noodles, or going to distant ponds to catch carp with grenades and so enliven his subordinates' meals. His astonishingly strong character seemed impervious to war. A day after a battle he was already back to normal; violence and simplicity appeared to coexist within him.

With the arrival of peace to Nanking, First Class Private Hirao began to feel intoxicated with his own frame of mind. Assuming he had reverted to his ordinary self, it might be said that for him war was nothing more than rich nourishment for his romanticism. It was surprising, in a man as highly emotional and sensitive as he, that external events never penetrated the inner structure of his being. His emotional sensitivity served to absorb the incoming shocks.

He placed the sundial on the windowsill and absentmindedly gazed at it. With the help of this sundial he intended to savor the mental framework of the Chinese gentleman, serenely disengaged from politics and culture. This was the true, practical anarchism, with its primeval freedom of living and dying with nature, its peace and satisfaction. Having vaulted this high, he was content. It became his habit, when going out into the street, to offer a cigarette to a Chinese and enjoy a broken conversation. He drank *sake* and held grandiosely forth, sympathizing with Chiang Kai-shek in his last days.

Arriving in Nanking, Katayama Genchō suddenly turned greedy. Using as a pretext the matter of repatriating the bones of the dead, he went to see Division Commander Takashima and had him inscribe a roll of silk he had found somewhere, showing it off later to interpreter Nakahashi:

> *Imperial Army presses open the Chung-shan Gate;*
> *Nanking's fires of war dye the night crimson.*
> *A brimming cup in my fist, my thoughts turn homeward*
> *As the crescent moon sinks over the government building's*
> *tower.*

He next began to go through abandoned antique shops and temples, looking for treasure. Carrying away a small statue of Buddha, so ancient the gold leaf had all peeled off, he tilted his head to the side and scrutinized it, gratified that it appeared centuries old.

JAPANESE TRADERS from Shanghai were arriving one after another, having obtained permission from the military to open canteens in Nanking. They were allowed the use of Chinese shops along the corners of Chung-shan Road, and there they set up business selling popular Japanese dishes. The soldiers appeared in droves, walking two or three miles for a bowl of sweet bean soup with rice cake. In the entire city of Nanking there was not a single store run by Chinese. Canteens offered the only meals to be had outside the barracks. Fully aware of this, the traders served up atrocious fare. Many soldiers flung away their chopsticks halfway through a ten-sen bowl of sweet bean soup.

The Chinese in the refugee zone, lacking essential goods, received passes and began emerging from the zone in increasing numbers to make purchases. Taking out their banknotes, they asked the traders to sell, but the traders would not hear of it and waved them impatiently away. Unable to buy anything, crowds of bewildered Chinese lingered in front of canteens. Dressed in felt hats and cloaks with trailing sleeves, they stared vacantly at the soldiers eating sweet bean jelly and drinking soda pop. The misery of belonging to a defeated nation was glaringly evident.

The soldiers took an interest in acquiring the large Chinese silver dollars as souvenirs. They offered fifty sen for each, and the Chinese promptly accepted. With the fifty sen the Chinese bought ten packs of Golden Bat cigarettes at five sen a pack, bowed their heads, and returned to the refugee zone. There they went into business selling the cigarettes for twelve sen a pack, thus making a seventy sen profit. In the refugee zone, where people had money but hardly anything else, all manner of articles were for sale and at high prices. Men stood on the crossroads hawking a single drinking glass for twenty sen. Although no one in the zone was short of cash, the scene resembled a beggars' market.

The area was put under international control, and sentries were posted at its boundaries. The refugees were supplied with passes and Rising Sun armbands and set free. After a brief walk through the city, they discovered they had neither a place to live nor anything to eat. In the evening they headed back to the refugee zone, shaking their heads in the forlorn realization that they had better stay there.

The true objective of the Japanese traders was not to operate canteens but to accumulate Chinese bank notes. The purses of the Chinese were filled with them, and even the Japanese soldiers collected some to take home. The traders told the soldiers that the notes were as good as wastepaper now that the Nationalist government had been crushed, and both the Chinese and the soldiers tended to agree. The traders bought ten-dollar notes for as low as a fifth of their nominal value; then they returned to Shanghai, where the worth of one dollar even now was one yen, ten sen. They were adroit buyers. Why did a dollar cost more than a yen although the Nationalist government had collapsed? It was a quirk of international economics; the Chinese economy continued to thrive. The crafty traders became wealthy overnight. An armed struggle was transforming into an economic one. Before long the military police began to enforce strict control over such practices.

For the benefit of the Japanese soldiers, two brothels were opened within the city of Nanking. The men's natural fleshly desires, exacerbated by tedium, needed to be relieved.

Corporal Kasahara and First Class Private Kondō left the municipal government building together. The city had grown so calm that it was no longer necessary to carry a rifle when walking the streets. From time to time, a Chinese regular or two, streaked with dirt and stupefied, was found in the recesses of a ruined house and hauled off, but otherwise the depopulated city was almost free of danger, empty except for the strolling soldiers.

Humming a tune, they walked along a sunlit pavement. The

so-called law-abiding citizens released from the refugee zone could be seen entering the houses in the commercial district and carrying off such things as tableware, clothing, oil, and bean paste. They were plundering each other. Shouldering thick poles of split bamboo heavy with stolen clothes, old women hurried by unsteadily on their small, bound feet.

Loudly challenged—"Hey, you stole that, didn't you?!"—they muttered in reply, "Oh, oh," then left the goods by the side of the road and fled.

Amazingly, a young woman crossed the street. Kasahara called out, "Hey, *ku-niang!*" The girl broke into a run, trotting off on her tiny feet like a donkey.

"Ah, hahaha, she escaped!" laughed Kasahara like an indulgent despot.

Corpses were still lying about, even along the main streets. As the days passed, they blackened and shriveled. Eaten away at night by cats and dogs, there was less of them left each morning. One body was already a veritable skeleton, but the head was still covered with hair, and the gaiters remained coiled about the shinbones. When they got to be this old, even dead bodies looked like nothing more than garbage.

"Hey, Kondō," Kasahara remarked. "This one's got his shoes on. Still thinking of running away. Ah, hahaha!"

They passed by a tobacco shop across whose entrance lay a corpse partly covered with a straw mat and surrounded by five cats with glittering eyes. The cats warily watched the street, their noses dyed a deep red.

And yet both dogs and cats were starving. Corpses of cats knocked down and flattened by cars were a frequent sight. Dizzy with hunger, the cats lacked the strength to dodge the cars that came speeding down the deserted streets.

The men stopped at a canteen and drank beer, then headed for the brothel in the southern part of the city. Roughly a hundred soldiers stood about, forming two lines and laughing boisterously. The entrance to the alley was barred by a grating manned by three Chinese. Tickets were sold through a small window in the grating where hours and prices were posted:

1. Hours: noon to six, Japanese time
2. Price: cherry blossom access one yen, fifty sen, military currency only
3. Procedure: proceed to house of choice, hand over ticket, await instructions

They bought their tickets at the window, joined the long line, and waited. As one man came out past the grating, another was let in. Fastening his belt, the man who had emerged grinned at the line and walked away, swinging his shoulders. He was the personification of tension relieved.

Half a dozen small houses lined both sides of the alley, with a woman in each. The women were Chinese *ku-niang*. Their hair bobbed and cheeks rouged, they did not neglect to apply makeup even now. Then, for thirty minutes each, they entertained enemy soldiers whose language and identities they did not know. To ensure the women's bodily safety, military policemen with fixed bayonets stood by the grated entrance.

The two men walked back in unexpectedly low spirits.

"How was it?" asked Corporal Kasahara, ripping a placard from a corner as he passed. The placards spelled out such messages as "If you have money, give money; if you have strength, give strength," "Kill traitors!" and "Young students, if you will not rise now, when will you rise?!"

"Dull," replied Kondō with a mirthless laugh.

"Why's that?"

"There's just no passion."

"Idiot! What the hell do you expect?"

Kasahara jumped over a corpse that had almost caused him to stumble, and laughed loudly.

First Class Private Hirao frequented the brothels daily. Returning, he explained to his comrades, "I do not go in order to buy women. Haven't you heard? 'Harlots do not know a ruined nation's rancor, but sing "Courtyard Blossoms" still, far from home rivers.' I go in order to comfort the women of a ruined nation."

THE FIRES did not cease day or night. Soldiers were explicitly forbidden to set them at random, and yet a climb to the top of a crumbling city gate never failed to reveal five or six burning somewhere in the city. They blazed up unchecked and subsided after consuming everything combustible. Even if onlookers were present, none tried to extinguish the flames, leaving them instead to rise in tranquil splendor. In the end the spectators departed and the fires raged on throughout the night along the lifeless back streets, all the more ghastly for being ignored.

The rumor spread that they were the work of enemy soldiers disguised as civilians, who set them to help their airplanes locate bombing targets. Come to think of it, there were quite a few fires in the vicinity of the occupiers' barracks. Air raids took place almost every other night just before dawn, but the sleeping soldiers paid them not the slightest attention. Awakened by the noise, one man quietly swore and groped for the slippers under his creaking bed; then he shuffled into the courtyard of the municipal government building to urinate by the edge of a pond spanned by a stone bridge. The moon was nearing the horizon of the starry sky as several airplanes with lit wings roared out of the darkness at a dazzling speed. Unable to distinguish the enemy craft from his own, the soldier glanced up admiringly and shuffled off back to bed.

10

The year drew to an end and New Year's Day arrived. It was a New Year with hardly any gate pines or rice cakes. Only *sake* was copiously available.

Free of duty, the soldiers lay about in bed, drinking, chatting, and singing. After twenty days of rest they were bored, and many were beginning to think of home. The rough chatter of the signal corpsmen easily penetrated the single wall separating their room from that shared by interpreter Nakahashi, army priest Katayama, and the boy Chang.

"Ah, I want to go home."

"I want to go home, too. I wonder how my old lady is doing."

"Don't you worry, stupid, she's got herself a boyfriend."

"Shut your trap. My old lady lives waiting morning and evening for me to get back."

"Jackass, blockhead, imbecile! By now she's got you locked away in the corner inside the family altar. Hahahahaha! And look at the proof: You haven't had one letter from her."

Such was the New Year. With too much time on their hands, the soldiers grew peevish. They were receiving no letters, newspapers, or packages—nothing at all. Various rumors began to circulate.

According to one, a powerful earthquake had struck Osaka on the morning of the second, starting a conflagration that was still raging. It was a plausible report, said to have been radioed to the warships at Hsia-kuan. Since no one knew whether it was true or not, the rumor spread far, but there was no way of verifying it, and it gradually died down. The next rumor had it that the units were soon to move on. To return home in triumph, possibly. No, to go to Hang-chou. To Canton. War with Britain seemed in the making, so Hong Kong was the likely destination. It was back to North China, a newspaperman said. At any rate, it was certain they were to move on. The proof of it, all agreed, was that the hospitalized soldiers, even those lightly wounded and soon to be released, were steadily being sent to the rear.

A rapid evacuation of the sick and wounded soldiers was indeed under way. Khaki-colored trucks lined up daily in front of the hospital next to the Central Officers School. The wounded, bundled in white cotton-padded robes and hats, climbed aboard. In columns of four or five, the trucks drove toward the quays at Hsia-kuan. As the wounded men enviously watched soldiers lounging in front of canteens and peered curiously at the Nanking streets they were seeing for the first time, the trucks passed I-chiang Gate and left the city. At the quays, a hospital ship was waiting to take them aboard and sail down the Yangtze.

Convinced that a move was imminent, the troops were eager to get mail from home before departure. Acceding to their wishes, the authorities decided to send someone to Shanghai to look into the matter. It so happened that army priest Katayama had been given the task of accompanying the bones of 183 soldiers to Shanghai's Nishi Honganji branch temple before traveling briefly to Japan to repatriate them. He was about to set out with two escorts when permission was given them to search for the letters.

First Class Privates Kondō and Hirao received the order on the morning of the fourth of January. Together with the bones, they left the barracks on the morning of the fifth.

At the quays of Hsia-kuan, the garrison troops were using 150 Chinese porters to unload ships. The darkly tanned porters were given the soldiers' leftovers every morning and evening and were paid fifty sen and a pack of Golden Bats every five days. They chattered boisterously while shouldering the loads. The hospital ship, its cabins tightly packed on two decks, was a light vessel of some thirty tons, painted a cheerful yellow. The bones were placed in cabins draped with white cloth, and incense and flowers were properly offered them for the first time.

That day at dusk, swept by the cold river wind, the ship began to sail down the Yangtze. Turbid waters slopped over the banks, along which every building had been destroyed by fire, reducing the harbor to a ghastly evening landscape. Minesweepers were at work clearing the river; navigation was not yet safe. A bright string of lights shone over the darkening water as the hospital ship steamed quietly downriver. The wounded soldiers slept peacefully in the immaculately white beds.

The following morning they reached Chen-chiang. Nearly forty more wounded soldiers boarded; then the ship sailed on. It arrived in Shanghai in the evening on the eighth of January.

THE JAPANESE settlement of Hung-k'ou looked almost like a pleasure resort. True, blackout was in effect and marines nightly stood guard at the crossroads while trucks full of armed soldiers patrolled the streets. But by day the Japanese-run shops lining the length of Wu-sung Road milled with thousands of shopping soldiers; and in the evening the cafes, teahouses, movie theaters, bars, and restaurants jostling for space in Cha-p'u Road just to the rear thronged with reveling officers and men. All had finished their battles and returned from the front to rest.

As the night wore on, military cars drew up before the dark gates of posh restaurants that had been turned into officers' brothels. Even if the enlisted men got drunk enough to try to gain entrance, they could not, for the houses were filled to capacity. The nearby Garden Bridge, divided into two defense zones— Japanese on this side, British on the other—was guarded by the sentries of both countries, ostentatiously standing shoulder to shoulder halfway across. At its opposite end, homeless and hungry refugees, expelled from Hung-k'ou in midwinter, loitered barefoot along the pavements or clustered, shivering, beside the road. The heads of the Green and Red gangs had left for Hong Kong, and their leaderless followers were rumored to have turned terrorist, given frequently to throwing hand grenades.*

The three days it took the army priest to attend to the bones at the Nishi Honganji branch temple provided Hirao and Kondō with an opportunity to amuse themselves.

Having come this far, Kondō began to feel severely disoriented. Arriving at the inn, he was able to immerse himself in hot, clear water, stretch out full length across the straw mats, and eat and drink over a red-lacquered table. A young Japanese woman waited on him. In the pubs along Cha-p'u Road, he could feast

---

* Organized crime, which included the Green and Red gangs, controlled gambling, prostitution, and the drug trade in 1930s Shanghai. Gangsters were also utilized to maintain order in the city's international zone.

on Chinese delicacies while sipping fragrant whiskeys. Life, which he had long since grown to despise, began to seem valuable again. He went to movie houses packed with soldiers watching Russian women perform coarse dances, the men whooping in unison and applauding the vulgarity.

The vigorous revival of sexual interest was easily assuaged. A bar girl sat on his lap, put her arm around his neck, and sang. He rose and danced with her to the accompaniment of a record, his army shoes clumping against the floor. Such longed-for city pleasures flourished throughout the sector.

The debris of burned-out buildings still lay in grim stillness along the Bund riverfront and around Yang-shu Bay, but here in Hung-k'ou, all traces of war had vanished. Life was respected here. Law, ethics, religion, and conscience safeguarded the lives of others as they safeguarded one's own. Medicine, too, came to seem worthy of respect again.

"Ah, I'm alive! It's a wonder. What a blessing to have lived through it!" Kondō drank, leaning his head against the barroom wall, while two lance corporals heatedly quarreled off in a corner. Paying them no more attention than he would a distant thunderstorm, he felt deeply thankful to have survived. But what about those who had been killed?

They had lightly thrown away their lives in battle. That had been unavoidable. In return, their brethren venerated their fallen lives, did they not?

True enough. But the dead could no longer drink *sake* and dine over red-lacquered tables laid out on straw mats, nor could they enjoy nights in the pleasure quarters. The joy of their individual lives had been terminated. What about that?

They had flung away such personal lives for the sake of the

nation. This was why the nation and its citizens enshrined their extinguished lives with undying gratitude.

With his environment changed from battlefront to pleasure resort, his compromise with the battlefield became unnecessary, and First Class Private Kondō appeared to regain the intelligence of bachelor of medicine Kondō. He was inclined to pursue his questioning further, but he already knew the answer. It was a problem without an absolute solution; every society in every age strove to solve it by adopting a course suited to its own conditions, choosing the path of individualism, socialism, or fascism.

He bent his head and closed his eyes. The immensity of the tempest he had passed through revealed itself fully before him, sending tremors of blinding terror coursing up his spine. At the same instant he felt a fierce attachment to life reviving hotly in his chest and grew even more afraid.

Taking steady gulps from his glass, Hirao listened to the conversation of three civilian customers seated at the next table. One was a consular official, the other two were merchants just arrived by passenger ship from Nagasaki. Having obtained from a friend a letter of introduction to the consular official, they had brought along a large quantity of gifts and were here to make a fortune. Tonight they were enlisting the official's cooperation by treating him to a lavish dinner at the pub.

The Chinese inhabitants of Hung-k'ou had all moved out, leaving behind vacant houses. Japanese merchants were given permission from the consulate to turn the vacant houses of this occupied zone into their own shops. These two came with the same intention. There were many more like them: Merchants from every place west of Osaka continued to pour into Shanghai by the shipful. The Japanese-operated stores in Hung-k'ou grew more numerous by the day, flooding the sector with all sorts of Japanese commodities.

The armed conflict over Shanghai had ended. The essential purpose of armed conflicts was to break deadlocks caused by economic conflicts. Without even waiting for the war's conclusion, economic warfare had reopened with favorable prospects of victory. These two merchants had spent the afternoon searching the city for a suitable house—a Chinese house, of course, filled with household belongings. Prying open its nailed-up doors, they would transform the place into a store of their own.

The consular official told them an anecdote. A few days ago a Chinese visited a Japanese who had just opened a store and asked him to leave, pointing out that the house and all it contained were his. The Japanese replied, "What are you talking about? This is occupied territory. Every single building in Hungk'ou is under the administration of the Japanese army. Go home!" The Chinese dejectedly left, looking back time and again.

Hearing this, Hirao was suddenly moved to tears by the sorrows afflicting the people of a vanquished land. The woman that had fallen below the bank still holding her child, the weeping woman clinging to her mother's corpse—these scenes in all their tragedy revived vividly in his mind.

He put down his glass, rose, and walked over to the cash counter to tell tall stories to the proprietress.

THE BONES of nearly 20,000 soldiers rested in Nishi Honganji and other temples. Even though they were being loaded 450 per ship, the bones of the Nishizawa Regiment would not be returning to Japan before April.

Unable to wait in Shanghai that long, army priest Katayama decided to return to his unit. Together with Hirao and Kondō, who had located a vast quantity of letters and packages, he boarded a Nanking-bound freight train at the Northern Station in the early morning of the twelfth of January.

The train cars were fully packed with mail and supplies for the units stationed along the railway line. The train crew consisted of railroad workers dispatched by the Osaka Railway Bureau. They had received an eighty percent salary increase and had come to China in a group of three or four hundred. The conductor, who wore gaiters and a sword, unloaded the mail at each station.

Rattling and shaking, the train sped across bleak plains covered with morning mist. Rows of gun carriages lined a university stadium in a Shanghai suburb; magpies flew over the dry, rusty-red fields, spreading their long tails and showing spotlessly white breasts.

A soldier riding in the same carriage said, "I'm from Kyushu and we have those birds at home, too. They say there are many of them in Korea, and when Hideyoshi came back from the Korean expedition the birds came with him and stayed. In Kyushu we call them 'victory crows.'"

When the China Incident ended and the Japanese army returned home, these birds would surely follow the troops once more and spread out all across Japan. At least some of the Chinese culture would make its way to Japan along with the returning units. The war was certain to bring about a sort of merging of the two countries.

The morning sun rose over the wilderness. Ta-ch'ang-chen, Nan-hsiang, An-t'ing-chen—all the towns and villages were devastated beyond recognition, and only the Rising Sun flags flying over the army lodgings hinted that there were people amid the rubble. But the farmers were already working in the fields. Brown water-plants covered the surface of streams; the bodies of Chinese soldiers floated, wedged by thin layers of ice. And yet the local farmers, attaching nets to the tips of long bamboo poles, continued to fish in the proximity of the corpses.

Kondō and Hirao slid the carriage door open a few inches, wrapped themselves in blankets, and gazed at the battleground scenery. While he looked, Hirao sang one song after another.

> "Ten thousand miles of winds blow heavy with fresh
>   blood . . .
> My sword is broken, my horse fallen, autumn wind buries
>   corpses in the native hills . . .
> Treading ice the army marches on through the snow . . .
> We left the country pledging boldly to win and to come
>   back . . ."

No doubt something in each of these songs seemed to express his own emotions as he watched the battleground scenes rush past. The essential truthfulness of the lyrics struck him repeatedly, and he sang them with gusto. And yet his romanticism being as it was, singing the songs weakened the force of sorrow that the battleground sights aroused in him, so that it merely brushed his skin and was gone. By the time he got to Nanking and stepped off the train, he would most likely have forgotten all about it. Even if he did not, it would simply provide a topic for one of his occasional outbursts of boasting.

First Class Private Kondō, who for a time had accommodated ignobly to the battlefield and lapsed into indolence, was now the one trying seriously to look at the facts.

Every hundred yards or so along the railroad tracks, the corpses of Chinese soldiers lay in batches of two or three. Some sprawled, dry and shriveled, on their backs beside the rails, the speeding train showering sand and dust upon their faces. Others had tumbled down the embankment of a stream and been stopped by the roots of willow trees, then torn apart by wild dogs. The fields were pockmarked with shell craters covered whitely with ice, but the sun shone with exhilarating brightness over the view of peaceful, fertile farming villages. A freight train riddled with holes from an air attack lay on its side parallel to the tracks; a blown-up steel bridge rested in the water. In the middle of a cultivated green field, the pale red ribs of a horse, its flesh entirely devoured, stood pointing at the sky like outspread fingers. Their meat supply gone, a pack of some ten emaciated wild dogs lolled about on a sunny hilltop. But the farmers were already tilling the soil, and the railway guards strolling along the tracks in groups of three stepped nonchalantly over the corpses.

The train passed K'un-shan and Su-chou. On board the men ate congealed rice for lunch and drank chilled water from their canteens. They reached Wu-hsi; from here on they would be following the traces of their own battles. The outskirts of Wu-hsi remained fresh in their memory, as did Heng-lin-chen and Ch'ang-chou. The corpses never ended.

Corpses this old were truly no different from trash. Too ancient and withered to be human, they looked more like rotten wood. But Kondō suddenly felt for them something akin to love. It was not in his nature to join hands and pray for the repose of their souls. He simply sensed a certain peacefulness in their decayed forms. In the bitter cold of the night, they froze, as so did their blood; warmed by the morning sun, they thawed, as so did their fat. Yet they remained absolutely still. Was it not because these fallen soldiers had entered a world of ultimate tranquility? Chained while alive by the stern discipline of the Chinese army, rounded up to fight a war it was not in their hearts to fight, running about, gasping, amid a losing battle—had not all these fetters dropped away, freeing them to repose in hushed serenity? Was this tragedy or was it bliss?

Perhaps Kondō was indulging in his own brand of sentimentality, and perhaps he should not have been. But he was feeling keenly alive and beginning to suffer the pain of having survived. While enjoying the women and *sake* in the Shanghai bars, he had been deeply grateful to be alive, but now that he was returning to Nanking to take up his military duties again, life came to be a stifling weight that pressed down on his chest. He was entering the frame of mind that formerly had made Second Lieutenant Kurata yearn for a fierce battle and a quick death. Kondō had never felt that before. Reveling in Shanghai's pleasures had awakened in him an attachment to life; now it impelled him to do his utmost to shield that life in battle. He fully knew that this was out of the question, and yet he could not help being beguiled by the vision of peace he had enjoyed while engrossed in medical study at the university laboratory.

A handful of soldiers of the railway guard who had boarded the train at Pen-niu were carrying on a lively conversation with a civilian passenger.

"What are they saying at home? Do they think the war is about over?"

"Well, I really don't know."

"Have you heard anybody say the reservists are going to be replaced?"

"No, I've no idea."

"Hmm. You see, we're not like soldiers on active service. We're pushing forty, and we have families and work waiting for us, so if the war is going to be over we'd all like to be replaced as quickly as possible."

The civilian was a man approaching fifty who, according to his own account, had recently brought a number of Japanese women to China. He had received a sudden order and in three short days had assembled eighty-six bar hostesses in and around Osaka and Kobe, paid off their debts, and sailed with them from Nagasaki to Shanghai. Dividing them into three groups, he took some to Su-chou, some to Chen-chiang, and the rest to Nanking. The women were under a three-year contract but might, if the circumstances warranted it, be sent home after a year or two. Having undergone a rigorous health examination and been granted good working terms, the women were said to be happy. The man himself seemed a crafty type, well versed in the business of nighttime entertainment. He wore a thin overcoat and shivered as he spoke.

"Just three or four days ago, geisha started working in Nanking. About five of them. They used to be in Hankow. One time they ran away back to Nagasaki, but now they're in Nanking again. Pretty young and good-looking girls."

He talked on in the manner of a man possessing all the inside information, and the soldiers were impressed. The train passed Tan-yang. By the time it reached Chen-chiang, the sun had begun to set.

The men curled up in the back of the carriage and slept. It was completely dark when the train pulled into the Hsia-kuan station. They loaded the mail aboard two trucks and drove the five miles to the municipal government building.

"Ho! The letters are here!"

The guardhouse instantly sprang to life as soldiers ran out to greet them. Hirao and Kondō went into Lieutenant Kurata's office to report. The long-awaited letters and packages from home were distributed the next morning, and the soldiers spent several animated hours gloating over their new towels, waist-cloths, and shirts.

AS WAS TO BE expected on returning to the front, nothing but bloodcurdling stories were making the rounds.

In the afternoon day before last, two soldiers had left the city in search of vegetables, and vanished. Early the following morning, fifty soldiers divided into teams to rummage through every house in the area where the men were thought to have gone.

In the garbage dump of one of the houses they discovered a cigarette case believed to have been owned by one of the soldiers. It was clear they had been brutally murdered and probably thrown into a pond.

The soldiers swiftly rounded up all the Chinese living in the vicinity and threatened to kill every one of them unless they exposed the culprits, who turned out to be five men. Needless to say, they were executed on the spot.

Kasahara explained the procedure. "It was like filling rubber balls with water and whacking them with a stick. You feel the bounce and then the blood just shoots out, all rising with steam!"

The previous afternoon, interpreter Nakahashi had climbed to the second floor of a tailor shop to find himself a muffler. The shop had been thoroughly looted; not a scrap of textile was left within the clutter. Behind a cutting table lay the stark-naked bodies of two young women. With the steel shutter half lowered, their white skins stood out prominently against the dark floor. The breasts of one of the women had been gouged out, eaten by cats. The interpreter covered the bodies with their clothes.

"That woman was pregnant, I tell you. She smelled of milk, and that's why the cats ate her, I'm sure."

He spat on the floor.

At last the units seemed about to move. Field rations were being distributed: crackers, powdered bean-paste soup, packs of uncooked rice. The loading of supply wagons had begun. Now that the move had been decided upon, the soldiers, bored as they were by the long rest, wished they could stay to enjoy Nanking a little longer.

Where they were going next, none of them knew.

11

"Hirao, let's go buy a geisha."

"Geisha? One of those Hankow runaways? Hmm. Know where we can find her?"

"Sure. I asked the old man at the canteen today."

"Where?"

"Not far from the canteen."

"All right . . . Wait, let me borrow a gun."

Kondō was feeling strangely euphoric. In fact he was very tense. As he waited, he kept rapping his head with the knuckles of his right hand. Hirao, to be safe when walking at night, had gone to borrow the interpreter's big, antiquated Mauser, captured from a Chinese.

"Good evening. Lend me your revolver, would you?" Hirao asked.

Interpreter Nakahashi, Corporal Kasahara, and the army priest were noisily discussing the Mount Tzu-chin battle and the regimental standard-bearer's death.

"You're going somewhere this late?" The interpreter was wearing a woman's terry-cloth nightgown with red stripes.

"Yes, we're going to buy a geisha. You're too young, so you can't come."

"Hey, first class private!" thundered Kasahara. "Who gave you permission to go?"

"We don't need permission."

"Fathead! Don't you know the regulation that no one is to go buying geisha unless led by a noncommissioned officer?"

"I don't. There's no such thing."

"There is. As long as it's just you privates, going out is forbidden, but with Corporal Kasahara in the lead, you may go. Ah, hahaha! Well, let's go."

With the priest and the interpreter laughing after them, Kasahara and Hirao left the room and joined Kondō. At such a time as this it was the soldiers' sensible practice to forget differences of rank and enjoy themselves freely. It was nearing dusk when the three stepped out of the gate and started down the street. Very few soldiers walked the streets after supper, and except for the light of several fires burning far and near, the city was almost completely dark.

The canteen was about ten blocks away. Kasahara and Hirao kept up a steady chatter, but Kondō lagged a step behind, taking no part in the conversation. He had a light but jarring headache. It seemed he had caught a cold. He badly wanted to go to Shanghai once more. Most of the houses on both sides of the street were burned down. Zinc sheets dangling from the eaves rattled with each gust of wind, and neon light tubes plummeted, bursting against the pavements. Stars shone brightly in the increasingly icy air.

The front door of the canteen was already shut. They proceeded onto Chung-shan Road and turned left. Armored motorcars sped along the deserted thoroughfare, scattering clouds of sand.

The long brick wall of the Officers School stretched blackly on, covered with a row of large letters glowing white in the twilight, which read: "Ethics is the essential basis for restoring national greatness. Loyalty, filial piety, humaneness, and love of peace are the inherent ethical principles of the Chinese people.— A teaching of our late president. Promoting domestic products and developing the industries are the ways to make the nation prosperous. The New Life Movement is a movement of national regeneration. Citizens, practice New Life in the spirit of 'seeking truth by verifying facts' and 'improving, daily improving.'— A wise saying by Committee Chairman Chiang."

Reaching the end of the wall, Kondō turned left again. This was the neighborhood, and he soon spotted the house. All the buildings on one side of the street lay in ruins, but those opposite remained intact, and one was lit. It was an imposing structure set behind a half-closed gate and a courtyard thick with vegetation. An allspice in full blossom stood out from a circle of surrounding trees.

The men entered the courtyard and heard cheerful voices emanating from the second floor; this surely was the place. They climbed the steps and approached the door. The face of a Japanese woman of about fifty was visible through the glass. She looked very much the mistress of a geisha house. Hearing Kasahara's voice, she took up a candle and came out.

"Welcome!"

"You've got some *sake* for us, right?" asked Kasahara.

"Yes, but the upstairs parlor is all full, so if you wouldn't mind downstairs? You'd have to sit on chairs, though . . ."

"Any good-looking girls around?"

"Oh, yes."

"Then we don't care where we sit. Ah, hahahaha!"

The woman groped about the dark earth floor for her clogs, then led them along the corridor to a western-style room enclosed by windows on three sides and placed the candle on a table, speaking as if to herself.

"It is truly inconvenient not to have electric lights. What an awful place I've come to. There isn't even anything to cook with yet. But we have got a lot of *sake*. Tonight seems cold, doesn't it. I'll bring the fire in just a moment."

Kasahara listened in silence. When she had gone, he nostalgically murmured that he had not heard a Japanese woman's voice since Dairen.

The room was numbingly cold. Thinking that wind was coming in from somewhere, Kondō turned to look. The glass in one of the windows facing the garden was broken, and within the dark hole stood a large white cat, its glittering eyes glaring sharply at Kondō.[*]

"Damned beast!" He reached for the gun at his hip. The cat turned and soundlessly jumped into the garden, leaving behind it an eerily dark square hole.

"That cat's been eating human flesh," he muttered, feeling his neck grow chilled. Some hateful apparition seemed constantly to be floating before his eyes, causing him unbearable strain. It appeared to be that of the female spy he had stabbed to death long ago. The revolver with which he had tried to shoot the cat had been hers; the cartridges in its cylinder had been put in by her.

"I think I have a fever. Must've caught a cold."

---

[*] In Japanese mythology cats may represent vengeful female ghosts.

Kasahara turned to peer at Kondō's white face by the trembling light. "Drink and you'll get well," he said lightly. "If you die, we'll give you a proper burning. We're used to cremations, aren't we, Hirao?"

Kondō felt a sudden hatred for Kasahara. The corporal was a man long accustomed to scorning human life, the Chinese soldiers' as well as his own. Did he mean to apply that to me, too? wondered Kondō. He grew maddeningly confused. The room's darkness made everything worse. The municipal government building shone with electric light, but here the light of a single candle permitted icy shadows to settle over the recesses of the room until something spectral come from the battlefield seemed to pervade the entire room.

There was a clatter of sandals, and a young woman appeared, attired in a brilliantly colored kimono and carrying a charcoal brazier and *sake*. Glimpsing the woman's shape and her white, made-up face in the darkness of the doorway, Kondō clearly thought he had seen a ghost. It was inconceivable such a woman existed in this annihilated city of death. Both Hirao and Kasahara were struck by the same impression. In these circumstances, a gaudily dressed woman possessed a sinister, terrifying quality.

The three of them silently began to drink *sake*. The dimness of the light seemed to cast a pall over the gathering. From the Japanese-style room on the second floor came the sounds of a military song. "*We warriors face death with open eyes,*" the men were singing. The bright, bold tone of the song was incongruous with the surroundings. Bursts of distant machine gun fire—*ta-ta-ta, ta-ta-ta-ta-ta*—drifted in through the song's intermittent silences.

The bottles of *sake* were steadily replenished; Hirao began to get drunk, and Kasahara, too, began to slip deep into his chair. The dishes they were served—dried sardines and cuttlefish, canned octopus, tangerines—had been brought from Shanghai and left unprepared. The woman's wrists were darkly stained with chilblains; as she poured the *sake* for him, Kondō suddenly had an eerie sensation that he was looking at the wrists of a corpse.

"I seem to have a fever," he said. "Somehow I'm feeling terribly tired."

He leaned his head against the back of the deep chair and looked up. As the candlelight flickered, strange shapes moved across the tall, dark ceiling. They uncannily conjured up for him the vision of the female spy's dazzling white flesh, undulating as it did when she writhed in agony, clutching at the knife embedded in her breast. An irresistible urge to kill a woman suddenly blazed up within his chest. Stunned by its intensity, uncertain whether it was symptomatic of nervous collapse or pent-up lust, he gulped down his drink and turned toward Hirao, who was a little drunk and softly singing.

"I feel like killing a woman again," Kondō said, smiling wanly.

Just then the geisha interposed. "I am a woman, too, you know. Don't say such frightening things."

"Shall I kill you?"

Smiling, his face growing unaccountably paler the more he drank, Kondō kept his eyes on the woman as he drew the pistol and placed it menacingly on the table.

"Speaking of killing women, Hirao," said Kasahara, his tongue somewhat tangled, "what you did back there, you know, killing that girl holding on to her dead mother—that was terrible! That was really rotten, still is. She couldn't help crying, the poor thing."

Hirao forced a smile and started to give the geisha a slightly embroidered account of that night. That, too, was a form of bragging.

Kondō felt fresh shivers crawling up his spine. On an impulse, he turned and looked at the window. The cat was there again.

He grabbed the gun and sprang up. But before he could aim, the cat lightly vanished into the night, and the square hole gaped empty as before.

"Damned animal! Where did that cat come from?!"

"She's a stray. She's always wandering around here. There's nothing for her to eat." With this casual explanation, the geisha returned to Hirao's tale of killing a woman.

Kondō lowered his head over the table and continued to drink. It seemed he could not get drunk however much he drank, or perhaps he was sufficiently drunk already. His head ached as if about to burst, adding to his violent irritation. It was the predicament of an impulsive mind that had lost all power to reflect. Drunkenness only aggravated the condition.

With a grave face, Hirao concluded his story of the killing. The woman, surprisingly unmoved, dutifully proclaimed it very sad.

"Ah, I want to kill a woman," said Kondō again. It had become an obsession. He was convinced that the chaotic state of his emotions ever since Shanghai, the destroyed sense of acclimatization to a life of battle, could be restored to its former tranquility by killing someone again. He yearned for the war to flare up so he could stand at the firing line and break through the boundaries of self. His impatience was identical to that which had once tormented Lieutenant Kurata. Only Kondō sought to rid himself of it by killing a woman.

To break the silence, the geisha said, "Killing women is really wicked."

"What's wicked about it?" retorted Kondō swiftly.

"Well, women are noncombatants, are they not? A true Japanese fighting man would never kill a woman."

Under the circumstances, those were very impudent and contemptuous words. Without thinking, Kondō flung his cup at her. It struck her in the breast and fell to the floor. The woman leapt up with shock and screamed, "I won't put up with violence!" But seeing Kondō grab hold of the pistol on the tabletop, she ran for the door, her long sleeves fluttering after her.

Kondō had no idea whether he intended to shoot her or not, but when he saw her start to run, his finger spasmodically squeezed the trigger. Two deafening shots rang out in rapid succession. With a piercing shriek, the woman fled through the door.

Hirao jumped to his feet, pinned Kondō's arm under his own, and wrested away the gun. Kasahara wrapped his arms tightly around Kondō's. Bottles tumbled to the floor; the candle fell onto its side and went out. The room became almost pitch-black.

"This is no good. Let's get out." Still restraining his arms, Kasahara steered Kondō into the corridor. Hirao followed closely behind.

Hirao thought the bullets had missed. He intended to apologize, settle the bill, and leave. A single candle was burning on a small table outside the room. Kasahara passed it, dragging Kondō along, but Hirao, just behind them, noticed the drops of blood glistening blackly at his feet. Jolted by fresh alarm, he drew his face close to Kasahara's back and whispered, "Looks like she's been hit. There's blood on the floor. Let's leave right away."

From the interior of the house, the woman's earsplitting screams continued without pause. There was a clatter of footsteps as the second-floor visitors ran down the stairs. Still holding Kondō by the arms, the two men hurried out into the courtyard.

"What happened? Hey! What happened?"

A man who seemed to be an officer was calling out to them as he thrust his head from the second-floor window. Making no reply, they hastened through the front gate. No one pursued them. They soon emerged onto the dark, quiet sidewalk of Chung-shan Road.

"I'm sorry, Corporal, sir. I've caused you much trouble." Easing his arms out of the grip, Kondō weakly apologized.

"Idiot! What if you get disciplined for this?!" scolded Kasahara in a low, stern voice. "Anyway, just keep your mouth shut and it will be all right."

Turning to Hirao, Kasahara agreed there had definitely been blood but wondered where the bullets had struck. Hirao himself did not know, though he assumed, since she managed to run to the rear of the house and keep on screaming, that she was not seriously injured.

"Hirao, I'm sorry, forgive me," pleaded Kondō tearfully.

They walked silently back along the dark, starlit road. One side of it was lined with new, furiously blazing fires, untended by anyone. Fanned by the intense heat, the soldiers mutely filed past the flames. Under a tree in front of the municipal government building, a sentry stood motionless, merged with the shadows.

"Who goes there?!"

"Corporal Kasahara, two others."

"All right," mumbled the sentry, letting them through the gate. Donkeys brayed nearby, their hollow cries like sounds of broken flutes, but the place they were tied up in remained invisible.

"Well, just get plenty of rest." The corporal's voice was quiet and soothing. "And don't worry too much."

"Yes, sir. I'm sorry for all the trouble."

"Not a word to anyone."

Rattling his sword, Kasahara strode off to his room.

12

Kondō spent a sleepless night. By the time the morning roll call ended, however, his agitation had somewhat subsided. After breakfast he sat sunning himself on the stone steps facing the yard where the horses were tethered. There were deep saddle sores on each animal's back, exposing the red flesh. A veterinarian was applying a white ointment to the wounds and covering them with paper, then pouring a liquid medicine into the horses' mouths. Kondō watched the animals stir, his mind nearly empty of thought, his emotions pervaded by a dispirited tameness.

Hirao brought his sundial and sat next to him. Placing it on the step, he used the compass to align it and flipped up the pin in the center. A distinct, slender shadow fell between the signs of Dragon and Snake. Hirao lit his cigarette and gazed at the sundial. Very calmly he asked, "What was the matter last night?"

"I don't know what it was myself. I really made trouble. My nerves had been terribly on edge ever since the morning."

But thanks to that incident, Kondō was feeling much less perturbed. The realization that he was ready to submit to military duties and army life filled him with a surprising sense of relief. If he were to be punished, he was determined to endure it in silence.

Soon after lunch, Kondō was told to report to Company

Commander Kurata. He promptly rose and left, rushing into Hirao's room only long enough to whisper, "The company commander wants to see me. I think it's about last night."

"Oh?" Hirao stood up to watch him go.

A military police corporal with gentle, handsome features was sitting in Lieutenant Kurata's office. The lieutenant, his face troubled, spoke at once.

"You are under suspicion of having used a handgun to shoot a woman last night. Did you?"

"Yes, sir, I did."

"I see . . . What made you do such a violent thing? Everything you've accomplished on the battlefield is going to be wasted, isn't it? It is really regrettable, what you did."

"Yes, sir, I was wrong." Suddenly overcome with remorse, he could not stop tears from welling up.

"There's been a summons from the military police. You should go with the corporal. Take care of yourself. Another thing . . ." The lieutenant hesitated briefly. Looking even more forlorn, he rose from the chair and stepped up to him.

"This company may be moving out tomorrow morning. You might not be back by that time. Take your rifle and knapsack with you."

Feeling utterly hopeless, Kondō lowered his eyes. He returned to his room, packed the knapsack with his belongings, and picked up his gun. In reply to his startled comrades, all wondering where he was going, he merely smiled sadly and said, "To the military police."

Once more he entered Lieutenant Kurata's office, saluted, and left with the military policeman. First Class Private Hirao was standing outside.

"Corporal, sir, I was drinking *sake* with First Class Private Kondō last night and would like to go along as a witness. May I?"

The military policeman answered that he would be called if necessary and wrote down his name in a notebook. While he was writing, Kondō clasped Hirao's hand and quickly said, "I may not be back before the company moves out, so take good care of yourself. Give my best to everybody."

With no time for a reply, he turned his back, laden with a large knapsack, and walked off. Hirao gazed after them until they passed through the old two-story gate of the municipal government building.

THE MILITARY POLICE headquarters stood quite near the scene of the previous night's incident. Kondō was briefly interrogated as soon as he arrived. He learned then that he had shot the woman through her left arm, hitting neither artery nor bone, and that she would soon recover. The man in charge of questioning him spoke in a casual, somewhat perfunctory manner, arousing hope in Kondō that his offense was being viewed as trivial.

The preliminary investigation over, he was confined in a room; his rifle, bayonet, and everything else that might serve as a weapon were taken away. His knapsack, too, was removed. The room had white walls and no furniture except for a single table and chair. He stood by the barred windows and looked out. Between the two stone pillars of the main entrance he could see a short section of Chung-shan Road. Just half a dozen feet apart, the pillars allowed a view of the brick wall fronting the Officers School across the street. Soldiers, most likely returning from the canteen, passed by, carrying large cardboard boxes. A truck drove past, full of sick and wounded soldiers heading for the quay at Hsia-kuan.

What would happen to him, he wondered. He had been separated from his unit. Imprisoned here, he would probably be sent to Shanghai under escort, or on to Japan. He was not thinking anything particular. He appeared very calm, or bored, but was perhaps the opposite. Standing beside the window, he watched intently as the soldiers passed along the street. He did not especially envy them.

In the evening he was given the food from his mess tin and a single blanket. He ate quickly, trying to think of nothing. When the room grew dark, he wrapped himself in the blanket and lay on the floor. It was too cold for him to sleep. Suddenly an immense surge of longing for Japan, for everything Japanese, made him desperately eager to go home. He hid his face in the blanket and sobbed. He cried for nearly an hour, then slept.

HE AWOKE at dawn feeling at peace, indifferent to the outcome, yet hopeful all would come out right. That his entire war record was ruined did not in the least disturb him. He had totally failed at military service. If he were discharged after punishment, he would return to his laboratory and quietly study medicine. Whether or not medicine made too much of the despicable phenomenon of life, he would direct his own life toward medicine and never regret it. Until then, he must endure. Be silent and wait, he told himself.

The sound of a great many marching feet reached his ears. He stepped up to the window. The units were passing by. The move had begun. Maybe it was his own battalion. It seemed to be. But he thought nothing of it. His emotions, already detached from military men and affairs, were those of the medical student he had been before going to war. A man who surely looked like Lieutenant Kurata marched past the gate at the head of a unit. Walking four abreast, shoes crashing against the asphalt, the column of soldiers filed swiftly by. It had definitely been his own company. And yet he thought nothing, or was trying not to. About to be expelled from the army, he needed to concentrate now on returning to the laboratory. He would have a chance to become a medical doctor and a hospital director. It was as good an aspiration as any.

The long columns of troops were gone, leaving the space in front of the stone entrance empty. The morning was still too early for soldiers to be going to the canteen. He stretched his arms and gave a great yawn.

There was the sound of a key unlocking the door, and the military police corporal entered.

"First Class Private Kondō, this way."

He mutely followed. Winding along the dark, cold corridors, they arrived at the room where he had been questioned the previous day. There he received a kind of sentence.

"You may go back to your unit. You'll eventually be notified of the disposition."

He panicked. His company was already gone. Worse, the military policeman read him a lecture of warning for the future and would not easily let him go. Released at last, he madly fumbled to bind his equipment to the knapsack, flung the canteen over his shoulder, grabbed the rifle, and flew out of the building.

THE UNIT had gone west along Chung-shan Road. That much he knew. His shoes ringing against the pavement, he ran as fast as he could. Soon he reached the intersection of Chung-cheng and Chung-shan Roads in the city center. A traffic circle occupied the middle of the roadway. He hesitated. Any troops moving out from the city would first go to Hsia-kuan. It was the only point of departure for both trains and ships. He turned into Chung-cheng Road and ran up the straight thoroughfare. The troops ahead of him were no longer in view.

A truck came along, and he called out to the driver at the top of his voice. The truck was carrying two huge bottles of soy sauce, held steady by soldiers. It stopped and he hurriedly climbed in the back. Out of breath, his shoulders heaving, he struck at his chest to lessen the pain. The truck was bound straight along Chung-cheng Road and would not be turning toward Hsia-kuan. After six or seven blocks Kondō had them drop him off and was forced to resume running.

The knapsack was heavy; both rifle and canteen got in the way. And yet he ran as if deranged. He had never before felt such solitude. His company was marching on, utterly indifferent to his presence or absence. Severed from it, he seemed bereft of all value and strength. Not a particle of confidence or pride remained within him, only a single-minded desire to catch up with his unit. To advance along with the unit, to go with it to the end of the world—he could think of nothing else.

Running past the Supreme Court building, he finally caught sight of a long line of men off in the distance. Staggering like a starved dog, he managed to rejoin his company just before it reached I-chiang Gate.

He limped up to the head of its column and gaspingly reported to Lieutenant Kurata that he had been allowed to return to the unit.

"Is that so? That is very good. It seems you won't be severely punished. Get in the ranks."

The lieutenant said it happily, without slackening his pace.

Kondō squeezed into position next to Hirao. His face was ashen; even his lips were drained of blood. Hirao wordlessly took the rifle from him and slung it alongside his own. Then he entwined his left arm around Kondō's right.

"Thank you, thank you." Kondō was bent almost double, painfully spitting as he walked.

Atop the I-chiang Gate, a Rising Sun flag fluttered in the morning breeze. The units passed through the gate, emerged from the city, and pressed onward. To the new battlegrounds! Where those new battlegrounds awaited them, nobody knew.

—Empire Day 1938

Note: It has been the author's aim to produce a fairly free literary creation rather than a faithful record of warfare. Consequently, much in this account —including the names of officers, men, and units—is fictitious.

Bibliography

Beasley, William G. *Japanese Imperialism, 1894–1945*. Oxford and New York: Oxford University Press, 1991.

———. *The Modern History of Japan*. Tokyo: Tuttle, 1982.

———. *The Rise of Modern Japan*. New York: St. Martin's Press, 1990.

Bix, Herbert. *Hirohito and the Making of Modern Japan*. New York: Harper Collins, 2000.

Borton, Hugh. *Japan since 1931: Its Political and Social Developments*. New York: Institute of Pacific Relations, 1940.

Bownas, Geoffrey, and Anthony Thwaite. *The Penguin Book of Japanese Verse*. Harmondsworth, England: Penguin Books, 1983.

Boyle, John Hunter. *China and Japan at War, 1937–1945: The Politics of Collaboration*. Stanford: Stanford University Press, 1972.

———. "Sino-Japanese War of 1937–1945." In *Kodansha Encyclopedia of Japan*. Vol. 7. Tokyo: Kodansha, 1983.

Chiba Sen'ichi. "Zettai tankyūsha no seishin no bōken no kiseki—aruiwa, kongenteki na bunmei hihyō to sekai shinpan no bungaku." In *Fugen, Yakeato no Iesu*, Ishikawa Jun. Tokyo: Horupu, 1985.

Chomsky, Noam. *American Power and the New Mandarins*. New York: Pantheon, 1967.

Churchill, Ward. *Fantasies of the Master Race: Literature, Cinema, and the Colonization of American Indians*. Monroe, Me.: Common Courage Press, 1990.

Cipris, Zeljko. "Radiant Carnage: Japanese Writers on the War against China." Ph.D. diss., Columbia University, 1994.

Clubb, Edmund O. *Twentieth Century China*. New York: Columbia University Press, 1978.

Colbert, Evelyn S. *The Left Wing in Japanese Politics*. New York: Institute of Pacific Relations, 1952.

Collcutt, Martin C. "China and Japan." In *Kodansha Encyclopedia of Japan.* Vol. 1. Tokyo: Kodansha, 1983.

Cook, Haruko Taya. "The Many Lives of *Living Soldiers:* Ishikawa Tatsuzō and Japan's War in Asia." In *War, Occupation, and Creativity: Japan and East Asia, 1920–1960,* ed. Marlene J. Mayo, J. Thomas Rimer, and H. Eleanor Kerkham. Honolulu: University of Hawai'i Press, 2001.

Cook, Haruko Taya, and Theodore F. Cook. *Japan at War: An Oral History.* New York: New Press, 1992.

Coox, Alvin D., and Hilary Conroy, eds. *China and Japan: Search for Balance Since World War I.* Santa Barbara: Clio Books, 1978.

Crowley, James B. "Japan's China Policy, 1931–1938." Ph.D. diss., University of Michigan, 1959.

———. *Japan's Quest for Autonomy: National Security and Foreign Policy, 1930–1938.* Princeton: Princeton University Press, 1966.

Daemmrich, Horst S., and Diether Haenicke, eds. *The Challenge of German Literature.* Detroit: Wayne State University Press, 1971.

Dazai Osamu. *Dazai Osamu zenshū.* Vol. 2. Tokyo: Chikuma Shobō, 1975.

de Bary, Brett. *Three Works by Nakano Shigeharu.* Ithaca: Cornell University East Asia Papers, 1979.

Donadoni, Eugenio. *A History of Italian Literature.* Vol. 2. New York: New York University Press, 1969.

Dorn, Frank. *The Sino-Japanese War, 1937–41.* New York: Macmillan, 1974.

Dower, John W. *Japan in War and Peace: Selected Essays.* New York: New Press, 1993.

———. *War without Mercy: Race and Power in the Pacific War.* New York: Pantheon, 1986.

Drinnon, Richard. *Facing West: The Metaphysics of Indian-Hating and Empire-Building.* New York: Schocken Books, 1990.

Duus, Peter. *The Rise of Modern Japan.* Boston: Houghton Mifflin, 1976.

Duus, Peter, ed. *The Twentieth Century.* Vol. 6 of *The Cambridge History of Japan.* Cambridge: Cambridge University Press, 1988.

Duus, Peter, Ramon H. Myers, and Mark R. Peattie, eds. *The Japanese Informal Empire in China, 1895–1937.* Princeton: Princeton University Press, 1989.

Earhart, H. Byron. *Japanese Religion: Unity and Diversity.* Belmont, Ca.: Wadsworth, 1982.

Field, Norma. "Beyond Pearl Harbor." *The Nation,* 23 December 1991.

Fletcher, William Miles III. *The Search for a New Order: Intellectuals and Fascism in Prewar Japan.* Chapel Hill: University of North Carolina Press, 1982.

Fogel, Joshua A. *The Literature of Travel in the Japanese Rediscovery of China, 1862–1945.* Palo Alto: Stanford University Press, 1996.

Fogel, Joshua A., ed. *The Nanjing Massacre in History and Historiography.* Berkeley: University of California Press, 2000.

The Foreign Affairs Association of Japan. *The Sino-Japanese Conflict: A Short Survey.* Tokyo: Kenkyusha, 1937.

Foulkes, A. P. *Literature and Propaganda.* London: Methuen, 1983.

Fussell, Paul. *The Great War and Modern Memory.* New York: Oxford University Press, 1977.

Gessel, Van C., and Tomone Matsumoto, eds. *The Shōwa Anthology: Modern Japanese Short Stories.* Vol. 1 (1929–1961). Tokyo: Kodansha International, 1985.

Glover, Jon, and Jon Silkin, eds. *The Penguin Book of First World War Prose.* London: Penguin Books, 1990.

Gluck, Carol. *Japan's Modern Myths.* Princeton: Princeton University Press, 1985.

Goodman, David G., ed. *Five Plays by Kishida Kunio.* Ithaca: Cornell University East Asia Papers, no. 51, 1989.

Grigoryeva, Tatyana, and V. Logunova. *Yaponskaya Literatura.* Moscow: Nauka, 1964.

Hall, John Whitney. *Japan: From Prehistory to Modern Times.* Tokyo: Tuttle, 1983.

Hamano Kenzaburō. *Hyōden Ishikawa Tatsuzō no sekai.* Tokyo: Bungei Shunjū, 1976.

Hane, Mikiso. *Modern Japan: A Historical Survey.* Boulder: Westview Press, 1992.

———. *Peasants, Rebels, and Outcastes: The Underside of Modern Japan.* New York: Pantheon, 1982.

———. *Reflections on the Way to the Gallows: Rebel Women in Prewar Japan.* Berkeley: University of California Press; New York: Pantheon, 1988.

Harlow, Barbara. *Resistance Literature.* New York: Methuen, 1987.

Hatori, Tetsuya. "Shōwa Literature." *Kodansha Encyclopedia of Japan.* Vol. 7. Tokyo: Kodansha, 1983,

Hayashi Fumiko. "Jūgo fujin no mondai." In *Bungei Jūgo Undō kōen shū,* ed. Kon Hidemi. Tokyo: Bungeika Kyōkai, 1941.

———. *Sensen.* Tokyo: Asahi Shimbunsha, 1938.

———. "Sensō yomimono." *Chūō kōron,* October 1937, 355–356.

Hino Ashihei. *Hana to heitai.* Tokyo: Kaizōsha, 1939.

———. *Kanton shingunshō.* Tokyo: Shinchōsha, 1939.

———. "Mugi to heitai." *Kaizō,* August 1938, 103–212.

———. *Mugi to heitai.* Tokyo: Kaizōsha, 1938.

———. *Tsuchi to heitai.* Tokyo: Kaizōsha, 1938.

Hirabayashi Taiko. *Jidenteki kōyūroku (jikkanteki sakkaron).* Tokyo: Bungei Shunjū Shinsha, 1960.

Hirano Ken. *Shōwa bungakushi.* Tokyo: Chikuma Shobō, 1963.

Hirano Ken, Ōoka Shōhei, Yasuoka Shōtarō, Kaikō Ken, and Etō Jun, eds. *Sensō bungaku zenshū.* Vols. 2 and 7. Tokyo: Mainichi Shimbunsha, 1971–1972,

Hirayama, Yonezo. *Japan Forges Ahead.* New York: Japan Institute, 1940.

Honda, Katsuichi. *The Nanjing Massacre.* Armonk, NY: M. E. Sharpe, 1999.

Hora Tomio. *Nankin daigyakusatsu.* Tokyo: Gendaishi Shuppan Kai, 1975.

Hsiung, James C., and Steven I. Levine, eds. *China's Bitter Victory: The War with Japan, 1937–1945.* Armonk, NY: M. E. Sharpe, 1992.

Hunter, Janet E. *Concise Dictionary of Modern Japanese History.* Berkeley: University of California Press, 1984.

———. *The Emergence of Modern Japan.* London: Longman, 1991.

Ibuse, Masuji. *Waves: Two Short Novels.* Tokyo: Kodansha International, 1986.

Ienaga, Saburo. *The Pacific War: 1931–1945.* New York: Pantheon, 1978.

Inagaki Tatsurō. "Kuroshima Denji no rinkaku." In *Puroretaria bungaku,* ed. Nihon Bungaku Kenkyū Shiryō Kankōkai. Tokyo: Yūseidō, 1971.

Iriye, Akira. *After Imperialism: The Search for a New Order in the Far East, 1921–1931.* New York: Atheneum, 1969.

Ishikawa Jun. "Marusu no uta." *Fugen, Yakeato no Iesu.* Tokyo: Horupu, 1985.

———. *The Legend of Gold and Other Stories.* Trans. William J. Tyler. Honolulu: University of Hawai'i Press, 1998.

Ishikawa, Takuboku. *Romaji Diary and Sad Toys.* Trans. Sanford Goldstein and Seishi Shinoda. Tokyo: Tuttle, 1985.

Ishikawa Tatsuzō. "Ano toki no ikisatsu." *Hon to techō* 46 (August 1965): 577–578.

———. "Atarashiki jiyū." In *Bungei Jūgo Undō kōen shū,* ed. Kon Hidemi. Tokyo: Bungeika Kyōkai, 1941.

———. "Bukan sakusen." *Chūō kōron,* January 1939, 2–148.

———. *Ikite iru heitai.* Tokyo: Kawade Shobō, 1945.

Itō Sei. *Tokuno Gorō no seikatsu to iken.* Tokyo: Kawade Shobō, 1941.

Iwamoto, Yoshio. "The Relationship Between Literature and Politics in Japan, 1931–1945." Ph.D. diss., University of Michigan, 1964.

Jansen, Marius B. *Japan and China: From War to Peace, 1894–1972.* Chicago: Rand McNally, 1975.

———. *Japan and Its World: Two Centuries of Change.* Princeton: Princeton University Press, 1980.

———. *The Making of Modern Japan.* Cambridge: Harvard University Press, 2000.

———, ed. *Changing Japanese Attitudes Toward Modernization.* Tokyo: Tuttle, 1982.

Kaneko, Mitsuharu. *Shijin: Autobiography of the Poet Kaneko Mitsuharu.* Trans. A. R. Davis. Sydney: Wild Peony, 1988.

———. *Kaneko Mitsuharu zenshishū.* Tokyo: Chikuma Shobō, 1967.

———. "Tōdai." *Chūō kōron,* December 1935, 360–363.

Karatani Kōjin. "'Nihon' ni kaiki suru bungaku." *Asahi shinbun,* 3 July 1989.

———. *Origins of Modern Japanese Literature.* Durham: Duke University Press, 1993.

Kasza, Gregory. *The State and the Mass Media in Japan, 1918–1945.* Berkeley: University of California Press, 1988.

Kato, Shuichi. *A History of Japanese Literature.* Vol. 3. Trans. Don Sanderson. Tokyo: Kodansha International, 1983.

Kawabata Yasunari. *Kawabata Yasunari zenshū.* Vol. 27. Tokyo: Shinchōsha, 1982.

Kawai, Tatsuo. *The Goal of Japanese Expansion.* Tokyo: Hokuseidō Press, 1938. Reprint, Westport: Greenwood Press, 1973.

Kawakami, Karl Kiyoshi. *Japan in China: Her Motives and Aims.* London: John Murray, 1938.

Keene, Donald. *Anthology of Japanese Literature: Earliest Era to Mid-Nineteenth Century.* Tokyo: Tuttle, 1982.

———. *Appreciations of Japanese Culture.* Tokyo: Kodansha International, 1981.

———. *Dawn to the West: Japanese Literature of the Modern Era.* 2 vols. New York: Holt, Rinehart and Winston, 1984.

———. *Japanese Literature.* New York: Grove Press, 1955.

——. *Modern Japanese Literature: From 1868 to Present Day.* Tokyo: Tuttle, 1981.

——. *Travelers of a Hundred Ages.* New York: Henry Holt and Company, 1989.

Kinoshita, Naoe. *Pillar of Fire: Hi no Hashira.* Trans. Kenneth Strong. London: George Allen and Unwin, 1972.

Kitagawa, Joseph M. *Religion in Japanese History.* New York: Columbia University Press, 1966.

Kobayashi Hideo. "Jihen no atarashisa." In *Bungei Jūgo Undō kōen shū,* ed. Kon Hidemi. Tokyo: Bungeika Kyōkai, 1941.

——. *Gendai bungaku taikei 42 Kobayashi Hideo shū.* Tokyo: Chikuma Shobō, 1965.

——. "Sensō ni tsuite." *Kaizō,* November 1937, 218–223.

Kobayashi Shigeo. *Puroretaria bungaku no sakkatachi.* Tokyo: Shin Nihon Shuppansha, 1988.

Kojima Noboru. *Nitchū sensō.* Vol. 4. Tokyo: Bungei Shunjū, 1988.

Kolko, Gabriel. *Main Currents in Modern American History.* New York: Pantheon, 1984.

Komiya Toyotaka. *Natsume Sōseki.* Tokyo: Iwanami Shoten, 1938.

Kon Hidemi, ed. *Bungei Jūgo Undō kōen shū.* Tokyo: Bungeika Kyōkai, 1941.

Kubokawa Tsurujirō. *Gendai bungakuron.* Tokyo: Chūō Kōronsha, 1939.

——. *Shōwa jūnendai bungaku no tachiba.* Tokyo: Kawade Shobō, 1973.

Kubota Masafumi. "Ishikawa Tatsuzō nenpu." In *Nihon kindai bungaku zenshū.* Vol. 86. Tokyo: Kōdansha, 1961.

Kuramoto, Kazuko. *Manchurian Legacy: Memoirs of a Japanese Colonist.* East Lansing: Michigan State University Press, 1999.

Kuroshima Denji. *Kuroshima Denji zenshū.* 3 vols. Tokyo: Chikuma Shobō, 1970.

Lippit, Noriko Mizuta. "War Literature." *Kodansha Encyclopedia of Japan.* Vol. 8. Tokyo: Kodansha, 1983.

Liu Hui-wu, Liu Hsueh-chao, and Yokoyama Hiroaki. *Chūgoku kara mita Nihon kindaishi.* Tokyo: Waseda Daigaku, 1987.

Magdoff, Harry. *Imperialism: From the Colonial Age to the Present.* New York: Monthly Review Press, 1979.

The Man'yōshū. Trans. Nippon Gakujutsu Shinkōkai. New York: Columbia University Press, 1965.

Mason, R. H. P., and J. G. Caiger. *A History of Japan.* Tokyo: Tuttle, 1983.

Mayo, Marlene J., J. Thomas Rimer, and H. Eleanor Kerkham, eds. *War,*

Occupation, and Creativity: Japan and East Asia, 1920–1960. Honolulu: University of Hawai'i Press, 2001.

McClain, James L. *Japan: A Modern History.* New York: W. W. Norton and Company, 2001.

McCoy, Alfred W. *The Politics of Heroin.* New York: Lawrence Hill Books, 1991.

Mellen, Joan. *The Waves at Genji's Door: Japan Through Its Cinema.* New York: Pantheon, 1976.

Miner, Earl. *Japanese Poetic Diaries.* Berkeley: University of California Press, 1976.

Miner, Earl, Odagiri Hiroko, and Robert E. Morrell. *The Princeton Companion to Classical Japanese Literature.* Princeton: Princeton University Press, 1983.

Mitchell, Richard H. *Censorship in Imperial Japan.* Princeton: Princeton University Press, 1983.

———. *Thought Control in Prewar Japan.* Ithaca: Cornell University Press, 1976.

Miyoshi Yukio, ed. *Nihon bungaku zenshi.* Vol. 6. Tokyo: Gakutosha, 1978.

Morley, James W. *Dilemmas of Growth in Prewar Japan.* Princeton: Princeton University Press, 1971.

———, ed. *The China Quagmire.* New York: Columbia University Press, 1983.

Morris, Ivan, ed. *Modern Japanese Stories: An Anthology.* Tokyo: Tuttle, 1962.

Nagano Akira, ed. *Shina jiten.* Tokyo: Kensetsusha, 1940.

Najita, Tetsuo. *Japan: The Intellectual Foundations of Modern Japanese Politics.* Chicago: University of Chicago Press, 1974.

Nakada Masayoshi, ed. *Kōgun shū.* Osaka: Bunkadō, 1939.

Nakagawa, Yoichi. *Nakagawa's Ten no Yūgao.* Trans. Jeremy Ingalls. Boston: Twayne Publishers, 1975.

Neruda, Pablo. *Song of Protest.* Trans. Miguel Algarin. New York: William Morrow and Company, 1976.

Ngugi wa Thiong'o. *Penpoints, Gunpoints, and Dreams: Towards a Critical Theory of the Arts and the State in Africa.* Oxford: Clarendon Press, 1998.

Nihon Koten Bungaku Taikei. *Bashō bunshū.* Tokyo: Iwanami Shoten, 1985.

Niwa Fumio. "Kaeranu chūtai." *Chūō kōron,* December 1938, 63–91; January 1939, 149–298.

Odagiri Hideo. *Watakushi no mita Shōwa no shisō to bungaku no gojū nen.* Tokyo: Shueisha, 1988.

Odagiri Hideo and Kijima Hajime, eds. *Oguma Hideo kenkyū.* Tokyo: Sōjusha, 1980.

Odagiri Susumu, ed. *Nihon kindai bungaku daijiten.* Vol. 2. Tokyo: Kōdansha, 1977.

Oguma, Hideo. *Long, Long Autumn Nights: Selected Poems of Oguma Hideo.* Trans. David G. Goodman. Ann Arbor: Center for Japanese Studies, 1989.

———. *Oguma Hideo zenshishū.* Tokyo: Shichōsha, 1971.

———. *Oguma Hideo zenshū.* Vol. 3. Tokyo: Sōjusha, 1991.

Ōkubo Norio, Takahashi Haruo, Yasumasa Masao, and Yakushiji Shōmei, eds. *Gendai Nihon bungakushi.* Tokyo: Kasama Shoin, 1988.

Ōkubo Tsuneo and Yoshida Hiro, eds. *Gendai sakka jiten.* Tokyo: Tōkyōdō, 1982.

Ozaki Shirō. "Hifū senri." *Chūō kōron,* October 1937, 429–436.

———. "Sensō to kokumin bungaku." In *Bungei Jūgo Undō kōen shū,* ed. Kon Hidemi. Tokyo: Bungeika Kyōkai, 1941.

Parenti, Michael. *Against Empire.* San Francisco: City Lights Books, 1995.

Powell, Irena. *Writers and Society in Modern Japan.* Tokyo: Kodansha International, 1983.

Putzar, Edward. *Japanese Literature.* Tucson: University of Arizona Press, 1973.

Rimer, J. Thomas. *Modern Japanese Fiction and Its Traditions.* Princeton: Princeton University Press, 1978.

Rubin, Jay. *Injurious to Public Morals: Writers and the Meiji State.* Seattle: University of Washington Press, 1984.

Rubinstein, Annette T. *American Literature: Root and Flower.* Beijing: Foreign Language Teaching and Research Press, 1988.

Said, Edward W. *Culture and Imperialism.* New York: Alfred A. Knopf, 1993.

Saigyō. *Mirror for the Moon.* Trans. William R. LaFleur. New York: New Directions, 1978.

Sakakiyama Jun. "Ryūmin." *Nihon hyōron,* November 1937, 450–494.

———. "Senjō." *Nihon hyōron,* August 1937, 393–415.

Sato, Hiroaki, and Burton Watson. *From the Country of Eight Islands: An Anthology of Japanese Poetry.* New York: Columbia University Press, 1986.

Sato, Tadao. *Currents in Japanese Cinema.* Trans. Gregory Barrett. Tokyo: Kodansha International, 1982.

Satomura Kinzō. *Daini no jinsei.* 2 vols. Tokyo: Kawade Shobō, 1940.

Seidensticker, Edward G. *Kafū the Scribbler.* Stanford: Stanford University Press, 1965.

————. *This Country, Japan.* Tokyo: Kodansha International, 1979.

Selden, Mark. "Terrorism Before and After 9–11." *Economic and Political Weekly,* 31 August 2002. Reprint, Znet (zmag.org).

Senuma Shigeki. "Gendai sakka hikka chō." *Shinchō,* September 1956, 33–56.

Shea, George T. *Leftwing Literature in Japan: A Brief History of the Proletarian Literary Movement.* Tokyo: Hōsei University Press, 1964.

Shiga, Naoya. *A Dark Night's Passing.* Trans. Edwin McClellan. Tokyo: Kodansha International, 1981.

Shillony, Ben-Ami. *Politics and Culture in Wartime Japan.* Oxford: Oxford University Press, 1981.

Shimada Akio. "Ishikawa Tatsuzō 'Ikite iru heitai.'" *Kaishaku to kanshō,* August 1973, 104–5.

Shimaki Kensaku. *Shimaki Kensaku zenshū.* Vol. 12. Tokyo: Kokusho Kankōkai, 1979.

Shively, Donald H., ed. *Tradition and Modernization in Japanese Culture.* Princeton: Princeton University Press, 1971.

Stannard, David E. *American Holocaust: Columbus and the Conquest of the New World.* New York: Oxford University Press, 1992.

The Taiheiki. Trans. Helen Craig McCullough. Tokyo: Tuttle, 1981.

Takami Jun. *Shōwa bungaku seisuishi.* Vol. 2. Tokyo: Fukutake Shoten, 1983.

Takasaki Ryūji. *Senjika bungaku no shūhen.* Nagoya: Fūbaisha, 1981.

————. *Sensō bungaku tsūshin.* Nagoya: Fūbaisha, 1975.

————. *Sensō to sensō bungaku to.* Tokyo: Nihon Tosho Sentā, 1986.

The Tale of the Heike. Trans. Hiroshi Kitagawa and Bruce Tsuchida. Tokyo: Tokyo University Press, 1978.

Tanaka, Yuki. *Hidden Horrors: Japanese War Crimes in World War II.* Boulder: Westview Press, 1998.

Tanaka, Yukiko, ed. *To Live and to Write: Selections by Japanese Women Writers, 1913–1938.* Seattle: Seal Press, 1987.

Taneguchi, Masaru. *The Soldier's Log: 10,000 Miles of Battle.* Tokyo: Hokuseidō Press, 1940.

Tanizaki Jun'ichirō. "Genji monogatari jo." *Chūō kōron,* January 1939, 331–334.

Tiedemann, Arthur E., ed. *An Introduction to Japanese Civilization.* New York: Columbia University Press, 1974.

Tsunoda, Ryusaku, Wm. Theodore de Bary, and Donald Keene, eds. *Sources of Japanese Tradition.* New York: Columbia University Press, 1964.

Tsurumi Shunsuke. *Senjiki Nihon no seishinshi, 1931–1945.* Tokyo: Iwanami Shoten, 1982.

Tsuzuki Hisayoshi. *Senjika no bungaku.* Osaka: Izumi Sensho, 1985.

——. *Senji taiseika no bungakusha.* Tokyo: Kasama Sensho, 1976.

Varley, H. Paul. *Japanese Culture.* Honolulu: University of Hawaiʻi Press, 1984.

Waley, Arthur. *The No Plays of Japan.* Tokyo: Tuttle, 1981.

Wilkinson, James D. *The Intellectual Resistance in Europe.* Cambridge: Harvard University Press, 1981.

Williams, William Appleman. *The Contours of American History.* New York: Norton, 1988.

Wilson, Dick. *When Tigers Fight: The Story of the Sino-Japanese War, 1937–1945.* New York: Penguin Books, 1982.

Wilson, Edmund. *Patriotic Gore: Studies in the Literature of the American Civil War.* New York: Oxford University Press, 1962.

Wilson, George M. *Crisis Politics in Prewar Japan: Institutional and Ideological Problems of the 1930s.* Tokyo: Sophia University, 1970.

Wray, Harry, and Hilary Conroy, eds. *Japan Examined: Perspectives on Modern Japanese History.* Honolulu: University of Hawaiʻi Press, 1983.

Yasuda Takeshi. *Sensō bungakuron.* Tokyo: Daisan Bunmeisha, 1977.

Yasuda Takeshi and Ariyama Daigo, eds. *Kindai sensō bungaku.* Tokyo: Kokusho Kankōkai, 1981.

Yoshida Hiro. "Sensō bungaku no shisō." *Kokubungaku,* July 1975, 156–161.

Yoshida, Kenkō. *Essays in Idleness: Tsurezuregusa of Kenkō.* Trans. Donald Keene. Tokyo: Tuttle, 1981.

Yoshikawa, Eiji. *Musashi.* Trans. Charles S. Terry. New York: Harper and Row/Kodansha International, 1981.

Young, Louise. *Japan's Total Empire: Manchuria and the Culture of Wartime Imperialism.* Berkeley: University of California Press, 1999.

Zinn, Howard. *A People's History of the United States.* New York: Harper Perennial, 2001.

About the Translator

ZELJKO (JAKE) CIPRIS obtained his doctorate from Columbia University and is currently an assistant professor of Japanese at the University of the Pacific in Stockton, California. He is the coauthor with Shoko Hamano of *Making Sense of Japanese Grammar: A Clear Guide through Common Problems* (University of Hawai'i Press, 2002) and is completing a book manuscript entitled *A Flock of Swirling Crows: Proletarian Writings of Kuroshima Denji*.

Production Notes for Ishikawa, *Soldiers Alive*

Cover and interior designed by Diane Gleba Hall
Text in Sabon, with display type in Franklin Gothic
Composition by Josie Herr
Printing and binding by The Maple-Vail Book Manufacturing Group
Printed on 50 lb. Glatfelter Hi Opaque, 440ppi